NEXT TIME
It will be Perfect

by

Anne E. Randell

Grosvenor House
Publishing Limited

This book is published by
Grosvenor House Publishing Ltd
28-30 High Street, Guildford, Surrey, GU1 3EL.
www.grosvenorhousepublishing.co.uk

A CIP record for this book
is available from the British Library

ISBN 978-1-78148-691-7

About the Author

Anne Randell is a retired teacher. She grew up in Manchester and still lives in the North West of England with her husband. She has two grown up children, both teachers. Having enjoyed writing Literacy texts and plays for her students she wanted to continue this activity once she left the classroom. Having travelled extensively, Anne has had travel articles published. *Next Time It Will Be Perfect* is her first novel.

Dedication

To my husband Peter without whose unfailing
support, editing and encouragement this book
would not have been written.

Prologue

Murder: Dictionary definition: To kill a human being.
Murder: Religious Education: Exodus Chapter 20, The
Ten Commandments, number six: Thou Shalt Not Kill.

Murder is my speciality. I am rather proud of the fact that having executed (pardon the pun) so many individuals I must surely qualify as a serial killer. My one aim in life is to commit the perfect murder. For it to be afforded that accolade it must be planned meticulously, accomplished without error, must not incriminate me in any way and perhaps most essentially provide me with the overwhelming sense of joy I feel when I kill someone. But enough - the entertainment is beginning.

'Ladies and gentlemen, the case you are about to hear is a particularly distressing one which many of you will find very upsetting. I would ask you to disregard the media interest there has been in this case, and to ignore the articles that will be written during the course of the trial. You must put anything you have read or heard which was not presented in this courtroom out of your minds and concentrate only on the evidence put before you.'

And so the trial is set in motion by the eminent judge, Sir Cecil Montgomery, Q.C.

You may be wondering who I am. The first part is easy. My name is Benjamin Doyle. The mundane facts about me are that I am forty three years of age, six foot two inches tall, have dark hair and have been described as handsome. I am single, enjoy running, watching football and live on my own on the outskirts of Preston in the beautiful county of Lancashire. If those were the only facts about me there would be no story but they don't tell a fraction of the tale. Of far more interest is the reasoning behind my rather unusual ambition of committing the perfect murder. Why have I performed so many illegal acts, which I realise are, to most people, abhorrent? Why do I wish to make killing into an art form and perfect the process? It will take time to answer these and some other questions you may have: time that I been afforded by the weeks I will spend in this court room.

Sitting in the impressive Crown Court, in the centre of Manchester, surrounded by bewigged lawyers and gazed upon by one of the country's top judges, I know I will have the opportunity to look back on my life, on the murders I have already committed and perhaps if I am not totally satisfied to plan the next, the ultimate, the perfect one.

This trial is for my latest murder, the only one to come anywhere near a courtroom. The process is set to last for several weeks which will give me ample time to write. I was surprised when I learnt that it would take so long as I know the outcome; I know beyond the permitted allowance of reasonable doubt that the verdict will be "guilty" and that the sentence imposed will be the only one possible in the circumstances: life.

My writing will not be grand enough to be called an autobiography or even sufficiently erudite to be classed as a memoire. A better description may prove to be selected recollections and carefully chosen explanations of the aspects of my life that I am willing to share. It will never be an apology.

Over the past months the newspapers have been full of a great variety of wonderfully lurid details about this case: the disappearance of a child; the discovery of the body; the gathering of evidence - all have been headline news. Eventually the Crown Prosecution Service, the organisation responsible for prosecuting criminal cases investigated by the police in England and Wales, gave instructions for the trial to begin. The murder of a child is always front-page news and one as unpleasant and executed with such callousness as this one was bound to create a frenzy of media interest. Although I say it myself it was one of my best, giving me the inordinate pleasure I crave when I rid the world of a creature whose future would be undesirable, both for him and the rest of humanity. Let my writing begin.

Chapter 1

Daily Gazette

Toddler, Jamie Richardson, Found in Disused Garage.

The body of the missing toddler, Jamie Richardson, aged two, has been found in an abandoned garage on the Streatham Estate. He had been missing for eight days after being snatched from outside the local general store when his mother went in to buy cigarettes. The owner of the set of garages, where the toddler's body was discovered, spent time in police custody but was subsequently released on police bail. He has not been named and is not believed to be a suspect in this brutal murder.

Jamie's family, a close knit unit in this friendly community, were said to be devastated by the discovery of his body. "We prayed that the little soul would be found alive," his grandmother, Emily Richardson, aged forty-one, told our reporter, "he was the light of our lives, such a cheerful little boy, always smiling and laughing. I don't know how we will cope without him." Neighbours spoke of his "cheeky smile" and "never-ending energy".

His mother, Sharon Richardson, aged twenty, was too distressed to speak to the press but is believed to be overcome with guilt at leaving him outside the shop.

Her older sister, Tammy, aged twenty three, said that it was really unlike her to do this as she was such a good mother.

Many of you will remember Sharon giving a televised interview the day after her son was taken and her heart-breaking plea for him to be returned to the family safe and sound. Her evident distress and love of the little boy touched the nation.

It is believed that the toddler's body was kept some-where else before being moved to the garage as the entire area, including the set of garages, had been searched by the police just hours after Jamie was snatched.

The police are not giving out any further information. The Gazette would like to extend its sincere condolences to the Richardson family at this sad time.

You "good" people may be wondering what made me into what I am. No child is born inherently bad, or so the experts would have us believe, so why have I been driven, by a force beyond my control, to end lives? I am sure that, to you, the acts will seem repugnant. Until the age of eleven, I was a very ordinary individual (well with one exception). My parents didn't mistreat me physically and my two older sisters, Talia and Helen, coped with me as much older siblings tend to do with a mixture of teasing, indulgence and the occasional outburst of annoyance, usually justified. Until then I was, I believe, a reasonably well-adjusted child.

I was a bright pupil at my local Church of England Primary School; a quiet, well-behaved boy, the kind who goes unnoticed in a busy school classroom. There were thirty in my class and most of the teachers tended to concentrate on the very able, those to whom learning came easily and who would go far. The clever clogs were the ones who always had the correct, and often the most impressive answers.

'Copper is a better conductor of electricity than lead,' Roger is now a doctor.

'There were ten plagues, the final one being the slaughter of the first-born, before the Pharaoh allowed the Hebrews to leave Egypt,' Richard became a lawyer.

'In his theorem Pythagoras states that the square on the hypotenuse of a right-angled triangle is equal to the sum of the squares on the two adjacent sides,' and Edward is a financial adviser in New York.

It wasn't until the final year at primary school that I allowed myself to become one of them, though by that time I was so anonymous I continued to go unnoticed. I have absolutely no idea what the clever girls, Amy, Rosie, Petra and Susie are doing, as neither at that age nor now do females really enter my stratosphere, though I have thoroughly enjoyed ending several female lives. My main memory of these class mates is that they always revelled in their supposed superiority, displayed with irritating arrogance, when they were able to boast the top scores in spelling and mental arithmetic tests. That did not bother me then and is certainly of no consequence now.

The quartet in that gruesome coven, were most unpleasant individuals. They were forever gossiping behind each other's backs. Had I been born a girl (heaven forbid) I would have been loath to leave the room for fear of what was being said about me. Each one had also developed and refined "the look": of contempt, disregard, pity and even hatred; the look that kills across the classroom. It has to be admitted that particular skill would have been a most useful weapon in my armoury!

At the other end of the "oh so obvious" intelligence spectrum were the dum-dums, the thickies, the no-hopers. Those poor specimens were the responsibility of the Teaching Assistants, the classroom helpers who seemed to me to have the patience of saints. They would sit hour after hour, day after day trying to get something, anything, some crumb of knowledge, into the unreceptive skulls of their charges. Not a chance, they might as well have been talking to the wall! I had no interaction with them. For most of my seven years at primary school I was happy to be somewhere in the middle, doing what was asked but no more. Then, as now, I preferred to remain anonymous, to blend in with the crowd.

It would surprise them all to know that I would achieve great things academically and that in my twenties I would become a member of Mensa. It would also shock them to learn of my other activities, but more, much more, of both those preoccupations later.

What, you may be wondering, set me on this path of destruction? I think I need to tell you about the event that altered my life and changed me for ever - it may help you to understand. It was a tragic incident that forced me to begin the killings or at least the ones I am willing to admit to and to write about. The very first may take a little longer to commit to paper, but be patient it will come.

The long summer between primary and secondary schooling was, as is so often the case, a dull and rather dreary time. I was bored and the weather was British. There were days of seemingly endless dull skies with drizzle interspersed with heavy downpours. I had few friends and had been away for just one excruciating week in the Yorkshire seaside town of Scarborough, not exactly the centre of the universe, so I was ready to return to the structure that term-time provided. I was sure that the all-boys Grammar school would suit me better than the primary one had.

However the day in question was glorious, how summer days should be. The sky was a deep uninterrupted blue that would not have been out of place in the Med and by mid-day the temperature was in the low eighties. The evening news reported it as the hottest day of the year. As usual I took my dog, a beautiful brown and white spaniel, for a walk through the fields near our house when she ran off. I chased her for about half a mile. The sun was blazing down, and sweat was pouring off me as I searched in vain for her. She had done this before, but had never been gone so long. It was then that I heard it: a single gun-shot and I knew that the bastard had carried out his threat, that if Polly ever got in with his sheep again he would shoot her.

I found Polly's body. The poor bitch was lying at the edge of the field with a hole in the side of her head. I didn't weep, that came later, but, young as I was, I vowed to get my revenge. That was the moment when my first meticulously planned, and in many ways most satisfying, murder was an embryonic idea. At that moment I became Dorian Grey and the picture was in place in the attic. I cannot imagine how many adverse alterations it must have undergone in the intervening years.

At the time we lived in the Trough of Bowland, an area of outstanding beauty in the North West of England. The Trough forms part of the Pennines and is a jig-saw of dry stone walls and sheep and beef farms which straggle across the landscape. The whole region is sparsely populated though many dairy farms continue to flourish in the wooded valleys.

I adored the wild, deserted countryside and walked every day whatever the weather. I always took Polly with me. Polly was older than me by fourteen months and had always been a vital part of my life. I was the one who fed her, took her for long walks down the country lanes and out in the fields. I loved her. She was an obedient dog. My dog! Only once had she failed to return when I called her. Mr Williams had gone berserk when he found her in with his precious sheep though as far as I could tell she had done no harm, being a docile, well behaved dog but his reaction was extreme,

'If I ever catch your bloody dog in with my sheep again I'll shoot her. Do you hear me?'

'She wouldn't do any harm,' I replied, 'she's a good dog, never hurt anybody.'

'Mark my words young man, I mean it, she'll be a gonner if she comes anywhere near my sheep again. I don't spend every God-given hour raising this flock for the likes of you and your mutt to disturb them.'

He had carried out his threat. Mr Williams stood, shotgun still in hand, and watched for my reaction though any response was, at that moment, totally beyond me. Nothing else was said and without a backward glance I picked Polly up and carried her home. She was heavy and the journey took me ages. The day grew hotter with every step. A black hatred filled every part of me, a feeling I had only experienced once before. How dare he kill Polly? Death must have death: the Old Testament Lex Talionis with the command of "an eye for an eye" must be reinstated, to my mind it remains the ideal form of punishment.

'What the devil has happened?' my mother yelled as I arrived at home. My mother never took any change to her

6

mundane routine calmly. Anything out of the ordinary was an event of massive proportions. Life for her was a battle fought with sleeping pills and tranquilisers. She suffered long periods of severely debilitating depression when she would stay in bed for weeks at a time and would end up being hospitalised, a relief for the rest of us.

Photographs of her younger self showed a very different person, smiling and happy. My sisters recalled her telling jokes and giggling like a schoolgirl but that ended abruptly when I was five. Mea culpa. Yes I may have contributed to her sadness and you may eventually judge me and think that, young as I was, I contributed to her depression but my childhood was undoubtedly blighted by her inability to be a loving, caring mother and I remain certain that I suffered a great deal more than she did.

I was told that she had been a beautiful young woman with blond, curly hair, bright hazel eyes and a grin that had made my father fall in love with her at their first meeting at the local Young Conservatives' Club. Once married, they were happy for several years and my two sisters were born. Perhaps it is just as well that my father had no idea how cruel the later years would be and how his laughing girl would change.

My mother became one of the people who are unable to enjoy the good times, always aware, as is undoubtedly the case that it cannot last, that disaster in some unforeseen guise will strike. Father was keen to assure me that my mother was not always thus, but that was her fate during my formative years and it is how I always think of her.

My father, Edward and always to me Father, never dad, lived with his wife's increasingly prolonged periods of depression with an equanimity and stoicism that was impressive. He filled the rest of his life with his demanding job and tried to relax at his twice-weekly Bridge evenings - with a group of friends who never included my mother. He was a tall, good looking man who often attracted admiring glances from women of all ages. Whether he ever sought solace elsewhere I do not know, though I doubt it as he had a strong moral code and was a regular attender at our local church, his God giving him the strength he needed to deal with his difficult life at home.

'That bastard, Williams, he shot her, he shot my Polly,' I sobbed, as I stumbled into the kitchen, the tears now streaming uncontrollably down my face.

'Why on earth did he do that?' mother asked helping me to lay the dog in her rumpled bed in the corner of the kitchen. I explained about his threat and how Polly had run off and not returned and about the shot and the whole sorry story. I was almost incoherent with grief, anger and hatred but mother listened quietly and said we had to wait until my father got home, her answer to each and every problem.

If only my parents had followed up the killing, if they had at least tackled Mr Williams, but no, that did not happen. Not to worry: it would be down to me and I would deal with the situation.

'You see son, if Polly was bothering his sheep, he's allowed, by law, to shoot her. There's nothing we can do,' father muttered when he returned from work. He must have known he was wrong, that he was being a coward. Did he feel guilty because he was refusing to take the matter further? He was a decent human being but he was not a man of action. By this time he was well in his fifties and his once dark hair had turned grey. He had originally been over six feet but was becoming more stooped and was starting to look old. I remember being told that he was dynamic at work where he was a primary school head teacher, full of plans and new ideas but at home his main purpose seemed to be to maintain the status quo, hardly surprising as he was the one who had to cope when mother slumped into one of her depressions. He was a mild-mannered man and I never heard him argue or even disagree with my mother, not wishing to upset her, the consequences being too dire.

The one activity that I remember enjoying with my father was hunting rabbits. His father, Pops, had given him a war-time rifle which he had smuggled back to England in 1945. I have it still and it is a magnificent weapon. A Lee Enfield No.4 Mk 1, in use as the British Army's standard rifle from 1895 to 1957 and still in use with the Canadian Rangers Arctic Reserve Unit. Its nick-name was the "303" as that was the size of its cartridges. I was taught to load it, a thrill for a young boy, and I soon became adept at inserting either one cartridge or the five it was able to fire by means of a five-round charger (but more of this weapon later).

My father and I were almost invariably successful and returned home with at least one rabbit each time we went out. My mother's one attribute, as far as I was concerned, was that, when she was well, she was an exceptional cook and the rabbit stews she produced were memorable. Such food seems to have gone out of fashion though I did see a couple of large bunnies hanging in a butcher's window recently.

Father was in charge of a primary school in one of the less salubrious parts of Preston, thankfully not the school I attended. Many of the children at his school came from deprived backgrounds, single-parent families and those with dads soon lost them to their enforced, but probably deserved, periods in prison. Some of the pupils were also known to the police from a surprisingly early age.

'I feel more like a social worker than a teacher,' was one of his frequent comments. I would listen fascinated by a view of a different world as he stood by the sink after dinner talking to mother as they washed and dried the dishes. 'Young Kyle's in trouble again, he's upped his activities from stealing the odd chocolate bar to running drugs on the estate, and they expect the school to sort him out!' Little did I know that one day my working life would be spent dealing with the Kyles of this world and that in my spare time I would indulge in far more serious pastimes than dealing in drugs.

Despite his protestations of frustration at his job I was told that father went the extra mile to care for his charges. They were, as he often said, "More sinned against than sinning." I think that his devotion to the teaching profession and the harrowing task of looking after his wife left him little time or energy to cope with further youngsters at home. I was born many years after my sisters and it may be that he had done all his parenting long before I arrived. No, whatever the reasons, I do not feel that my father was much of a dad to me and on this occasion he let me down: badly.

I decided that if my father wouldn't do anything about Mr Williams then it was up to me. I might be ten years old (almost eleven) but I would avenge Polly's death. Only another death would suffice.

Chapter 2

Daily Gazette

Murder Trial Begins

Amidst scenes of great emotion the trial for the murder of two year old Jamie Richardson began yesterday at Manchester Crown Court. The Gazette was heavily involved earlier this year highlighting the nation-wide search for the toddler who was snatched from outside the Bayside Newsagents in Timperley, near Preston. His body was found just over a week later in a dilapidated garage a few hundred metres from where he lived in the Streatham Tower block of flats with his mother, Sharon, a single mother, aged twenty. The toddler had been smothered and numerous photos of his naked body, which we believe had been mutilated post mortem, had been left at the scene.

The jury was sworn in and was warned by the Judge, Sir Cecil Montgomery Q.C. that much of the evidence they were going to hear was of an unsavoury nature. They were asked to do their best to ignore the stories that had appeared in the press. Judge Montgomery then advised them to listen most carefully to the evidence presented in court. Only this could be used when the time came to reach a verdict.

The court room was packed, as it is expected to be, for the duration of the proceedings.

Notes made by Sir Cecil Montgomery.

Day one of the trial. Jamie Richardson's murder has been headline news for months and I must follow my own advice and not be influenced by the publicity and media attention this case has attracted. Whilst it was flattering to be selected to preside over such a high profile case I know that for the duration of the trial my life will not be my own. It will fill every waking, and no doubt sleeping, moment. There will be times I will wonder at the depths to which a human being can descend. Dear Jane knows that I will not be quite myself during this appalling case.

The imposing court room is indeed full. Many people are here, quite legitimately, to fulfil their function as lawyers, ushers or stenographers whilst others crowd in like blood-thirsty first century Romans at the Colosseum to witness a spectacle. The room feels overheated though that might be, at least in part, due to the mass of bodies. So many people in a confined space can make one claustrophobic though for some that might be an appropriate preview to the small incarcerated space where they will spend the next portion of their lives. There is a sense of mustiness although I expect the room is cleaned regularly. Perhaps the stories it has heard have become impregnated in the walls: the assaults, rapes, murders and every other kind of human depravity having left their imprint on every surface. Numerous bright lights do little to make the place cheerful, though that is certainly not their main aim. Dark wood dominates and gives the area an added gravitas.

The judge sits in a god-like elevation, looking down on the proceedings ready to deliver his earthly judgement, time enough for the divine variety. Sir Cecil has been involved in several high-profile cases and is known to be a stickler for protocol and a man who does not shirk from pronouncing the toughest sentence within his power.

At first glance, the jury are a motley crew. Twelve assorted citizens here to do their civic duty. They appear to range in age from one young man who doesn't look old enough to shave to an elderly lady who I hope will live long enough to see the end of the trial. Seven men and five women: a fair balance of the sexes. They appear to be stunned into stillness and each one employs a serious expression obviously hoping to create the impression that they are aware of the importance of the public duty they are about to undertake. What are their thoughts about having been selected to play their part in such a notorious case? Do they realise how the next few weeks are about to change their lives and that what they will see and hear will, in all probability, be etched on their memory for ever? What a joy to be the author of such excitement, though I doubt that I will ever receive the credit that is due.

You can have no idea how wonderful it is to have so much time to sit and write. I will be able to describe my life, the events and my innermost thoughts. If I don't write it all down, no one will understand the reasons, and to me the infallible logic, that led to each murder. Whilst the lawyers are droning on I can shut their voices out, after all I, more than anyone else in this room, know what really happened and why. They are calling it "evil" and "inexplicable". I will convince you of its necessity and indeed the need for all the others.

The time has come to record the issue of greatest importance: the moment my life took a new direction without the aid of a Satnav. Maybe everyone can look back and say "that was it; the moment when the course of one's life was determined by a single event. A new life-map was formulated".

There would have been no killing that summer had Pops lived. Pops was my paternal grandfather and the centre of my young universe and he would have dealt with the Polly situation. He wouldn't have let it fester. Pops would have supported me and made sure Mr Williams answered for his actions. He knew William Williams, having brought him into the world, and he often joked that William's parents, after four previous sons, had run out of suitable alternatives when they named him. Pops was the local G.P. for forty years and so knew most of the community, their deepest secrets and untold foibles! A word from him would have quelled Mr Williams and brought, at the very least, an apology.

Pops, at over eighty, was a slim live-wire with bound-less energy and a shock of white hair. He lived with us for four years after grandma died and he became my mentor, guiding light and friend. He had a permanent smile on his face and very little appeared to faze him. His oft quoted opinion that "everything was for the best" was quite amazing in one who had witnessed so many atrocities, both during the Second World War and for a far longer period afterwards as the local G.P. where he had dealt with the unspeakable cruelty of illness on a daily basis. He was a quite remarkable man.

My love of classical music comes from him. As a family we went regularly to concerts in Liverpool and Manchester but it was Pops' daily rendition of operatic arias and songs from the Shows that made me fall in love with music. He didn't sing, indeed he had a poor voice. He whistled, a forgotten art, but one that he had perfected. You could always hear Pops before you saw him and there were times I don't think he knew he was doing it but he could always tell me the name of the tune and the composer. "La donna e mobile" by Verdi, the "Habanera" from Bizet's *Carmen* and the haunting "Summertime" from *Porgy and Bess* by George Gershwin were my favourites and I would plead with him, 'Whistle it again Pops.'

He was a wonderful human being and we had a bond that happens maybe once in a lifetime and that is if one is lucky. We adored each other. When I was six he came to live with us and he read me my bed-time stories, got up in the night when I had nightmares, looked after me during childhood illnesses and taught me to ride a bike and go higher on the garden swing than I thought possible. I, in return, helped him to see that there was a purpose to life after his beloved Amy had gone. I told him everything, sought his opinion and adored his company. My parents relied on each other and although I wasn't an only child my sisters were so much older that I might as well have been. It was they who jokingly told me I was an after-thought, a little surprise, a mistake and so I never felt like an integral part of either my siblings' or my parents' worlds. They say that children of older parents can feel like outsiders, unwelcome, an intrusion and once Pops left me that was how I felt.

Pops died without warning in the early hours of a cold February morning, the year the killings began.

He had been fit and healthy the day before, no warning of his imminent demise. His was what is sometimes called a "good death": sudden, with very little suffering; here one moment and gone the next. As a doctor he must have witnessed every possible kind of death and I'm sure that he would have chosen the sudden, totally unexpected, heart attack as a benevolent way of ending his life. None of us would have wished him a prolonged battle with the grim reaper but I remain certain that he would have wanted to have had the opportunity to say goodbye. It has sometimes occurred to me that as there were no farewells he remains with me, at least in spirit.

My mother came into my room that morning to get me up for school. She stood at the end of my bed and said, 'Ben, I've got something really bad to tell you. Pops died a few hours ago. He didn't suffer. It was all very quick, a massive heart attack. You mustn't be upset, he had a long and very happy life and he would want you to remember him as he was. He wouldn't want you to be sad.' For a few blessed moments I didn't take it in. It wasn't an event that could possibly happen. I had believed with childish certainty that Pops would always be there because we were two souls joined together. We needed each other as surely as Morecambe needed Wise and my world could not exist without him. I stared at her not comprehending a word that she had said. For too short a time I knew what was meant by one's mind going blank. I stood up intending to go for breakfast when my legs gave way and a howl of sheer agony filled the room. I was appalled to realise that I was the one making the unearthly racket.

I was inconsolable. I ranted, I raved. I wept until my eyes were red hollows in my ravaged face. Never had I imagined it was possible to feel such agony. After I had spent a week in bed refusing all food, my parents sent for the doctor who was, I now realise, a slip of a girl, newly qualified and with very little experience of dealing with bereavement and she had certainly had few interactions with children. She sat on my bed and made all the right noises about loss and overcoming it, remembering the good things about him (she called him my grandfather which showed how little she knew) and she uttered that wonderful, overused phrase that "life must go on". No, as anyone who has ever suffered such a loss will tell you, life does not go on, it cannot because the person who was your life is no longer there and you have absolutely no idea how to face it without them. A prisoner kept in solitary confinement has never felt more alone than I did.

Dr. Evans did what was probably her best but she was of no use.

I had been abandoned, left forsaken to face the world.

I was bereft; unable to accept the help that was offered.

I missed his funeral, to this day a source of bitter disappointment. I conducted my own memorial service; silently thanking him for all that he had given me and for the overwhelming love that he had shown. The problem was that I realised that no-one, no-one would ever even begin to replace him. I had been deserted to face the rest of my now unwelcome life alone. After a month I was taken to see a child psychiatrist. God in heaven was he useless, even worse than Doctor Evans had been!

My first visit to see the man epitomises the rest. John Phillipson, the top doctor in his field at the time, saw his patients in the front room of his most impressive house on the outskirts of Bolton. The thinking was that meeting his young clients in a home-like environment might put them at their ease. There were bean bags to sit on and toys and pastimes for every age group. The room was decorated in a mixture of beige and cream no doubt hoping to calm the poor souls who were trapped there for each appointment's endurance test of sixty excruciating minutes.

'Hello Benjamin, how nice to meet you, do come in and choose a seat.' I sat in the wing chair that I suspected was meant for him. He took a chair opposite.

I'm called Doctor John Phillipson, but you can call me John or Mr Phillipson or even doc if you'd rather. What shall I call you?'

A totally ridiculous question. He knew my name for heaven's sake.

'Shall I call you Benjamin or do you prefer Ben?' I didn't even dignify that with a shrug and just gave him a look that I hoped showed that the matter was of absolutely no consequence to me. It really didn't matter what he called me as I had no intention of speaking to him.

He must have been used to his victims remaining silent and was definitely not easily derailed. British Rail have far more trouble with leaves on the line.

'Your mum and dad tell me that you've been very upset at the death of your grandfather. I believe you were good pals.'

What a stupid phrase "good pals". We were far more than that and if he didn't realise it he could be of no assistance whatsoever.

'Would you like to play a little game? It's one of my favourites.' What a sad life he led.

'I'll say a word and you say the next word that comes into your head.' I was no longer looking at him but at the disgusting pattern on the carpet. I got to know that design very well over the next few weeks.

He was determined to play his little game and tried several words including "garden, friend, nonsense", all of which made me think of Pops but I greeted each one with a prolonged silence. I realised that my parents had filled him in on some pertinent, and to me utterly private, details.

His next gambit was to role play with puppets (how old did he think I was?)

'Let's take a puppet each. Do you want to be Pops or would you prefer to stay as Ben?' The carpet became even more alluring. An hour is an extremely long time to remain silent but I succeeded and was duly set free when Dr Phillipson's secretary came into the room with my parents. I left with my father whilst mother spoke to the doctor.

'It would help if you could talk to the doctor,' was mother's advice on the return journey, 'he can make you feel better and believe that life is good.' What a ridiculous thing to say. How could a balding middle aged man who obviously thought that a full beard would make up for a lack of hair and who dressed in tweed suits and smelt of peppermints, possibly understand my agony and be of any assistance? Life was certainly no longer good. Pops and I had been two hands of a clock and with one missing the timepiece was no longer in working order.

'Pops was a doctor and so is Dr Phillipson, you'd have talked to Pops so why not talk to Dr Phillipson?' was her next gambit. How little she knew if she thought there was even a millisecond when the two men could be spoken of in the same breath.

The experience was repeated twice more, my parents growing more desperate with each visit.

I was off school for six weeks by which time I was a scarecrow of a lad, stick thin, sallow skinned and still uncommunicative. The decision was made that the only way for me to return to any kind of normality was to resume a regular timetable, so I was despatched back to school.

I know that most people who suffer bereavement go through its various stages:

Bereavement: The basic five stages in relation to death are (I précis)

- *Denial (Pops can't have died),*
- *Anger (I can't believe he's died and left me),*
- *Bargaining (If only I had been there he might not have died),*
- *Depression (What is the point of carrying on? There is no point!),*
- *Acceptance (I've lost him, the person I loved more than anyone else in the world so how can I move on? I know I can't. This is a totally ridiculous stage).*

They say that time heals. They lie. Time is just time. It cannot be personified and become an aide towards recovery, however infinitesimal. Recovery is not possible as anyone who has loved totally, utterly and completely and been denied the person they adored will testify. We cannot turn time back and enjoy the happiness we knew however much we desire that blissful state. All that remains is to endure an unacceptable existence through the days, months and years. No, they do indeed lie when they say that time has the ability to mend a heart which has been broken irrevocably.

I stayed, and to all intents and purposes continue to stay, somewhere between stages one and two. I will never attain the final stage. Acceptance must mean, despite the advice given, that one has stopped caring. How can I move on? Oh, outwardly, I have done well. I resumed school life and threw all my energy into academia so that I came out with excellent results: the highest A level grades, a First in Jurisprudence from Oxford University and a highly successful career as the lead Legal Adviser in the local Magistrates' Court in Preston. All of infinitely minute consequence, like a single drop of water in a tsunami, compared with losing Pops.

Were Pops still here today he would be in court, supporting me. He would wink, a comical half closing of his right eye, the habitual sign that we were in something together. His love would be, as it always was, truly and totally unconditional. I remember the one day I got into trouble at my primary school. I came home bruised and cut after a fight with Bobby Samuels. I had started it so was in a dilemma: Mrs Jamison, the Deputy Head, had given me the evening to think about the fight and see her in the morning to tell her the truth, in other words to confess. I had spent the afternoon lying my head off and stating, with great conviction, that it was Bobby who had thrown the first punch. His story was, of course, different. Mrs Jamison knew I was fibbing and was giving me a last chance to do the right thing.

'What in the world has happened to you?' Pops asked as he met me outside the school gates.

'Bobby Samuels hit me,' I said, not wanting Pops to get involved.

'Why did he do that?'

'Don't know; he just went for me.'

'No one hits someone else without a reason.'

Pops and I spent the evening talking. I couldn't maintain any deceit with him so he soon learnt the truth that I had started the incident. I have forgotten what led to that long-ago playground altercation but what I do remember is what Pops said, 'Tell the truth Ben, always tell the truth. It may get you into trouble initially but will be much better in the long run. And remember whatever you do I will always love and forgive you.' I may be kidding myself, but I think that, even today, if Pops were here he would continue to love me and find it in his enormous heart to forgive me. It remains doubtful whether many others will.

Chapter 3

Daily Gazette

Defendant Pleads Not Guilty

*The defendant in the trial for the murder of toddler,
Jamie Richardson, has pleaded not guilty at Manchester
Crown Court. His plea brought cries of anguish from the
Richardson family, who sat at the back of court looking
visibly distressed. You, the reader, can only imagine
what they are going through. The loss of a child is truly
shocking and to have to listen to the details of his death
can only be described as unbearable.*

*The Crown Prosecution Service began with an
outline of the case, of the disappearance and subsequent
discovery, several days later, of the body of the two year
old. The impressive barrister, Sir Anthony Pinkerton, in
charge of the prosecution told the jury that it was a very
clear, straightforward, if unpalatable, case - the murder
of an innocent child. The jury was warned that there
were sexual elements to the killing which they would
find abhorrent.*

*He assured them that the verdict would be an
obvious one of first degree murder and that, once they
had heard all the evidence, they would have no difficulty
in convicting the defendant.*

The trial continues and the Gazette, as always, will bring you all the latest details as they emerge. This is a case that epitomises all that is wrong with society today, that life is cheap and sexual gratification is one's right. Some readers may find future revelations unsavoury and even repugnant, but it is our duty as a National newspaper to bring you all the details as they unfold.

Judge's Notes

The defendant must, under English law, remain innocent until proven guilty. However I can hardly look at this man. After so many years I have learnt that one cannot tell the guilty from the innocent merely by appearance. Angelic features can hide the most heinous of crimes and conversely a prison--bound face can be long, somewhat regrettably on occasion, to a blameless character. Unfortunately this defendant is rather good looking which has been known to influence the more gullible members of a jury but he has a sense of superiority and aloofness that I find unsettling. The man has cold staring eyes and an expression devoid of emotion. A "not guilty" plea was expected though many a defendant has changed their plea at the last moment in the hope of a reduced sentence.

Not this chap. He sounded so utterly convincing and I suspect he believes in his own innocence. Having given his plea he appeared to be following my advice to the jurors to make detailed notes. Whilst they will need them when the time comes as *an aide memoire I am not quite sure why he is writing so much. That remains a mystery.*

The article in the Gazette would have made Pops smile. He would have hated the salacious tone and the promise of future titillation. He read the quality papers and even then would argue aloud at some of their more contentious pronouncements. He did, on occasion, read the more popular papers for their sports' sections. As I became more interested we would spend hours discussing the various articles. I was never any good at any sport, except running at which I represented not only my grammar school but also the county and even went for trials for England, being selected as a reserve, though sadly never required. Running, the long distance kind at which I excelled, was a way of escaping from life. I never trained with others, preferring to set off early most mornings to run at least five miles around the country lanes near our house, a wonderful pastime whatever the weather. My runs were never quite as enjoyable once we moved to Preston.

Preston; the home of one of the founding members of the Football League in 1888: Preston North End Football Club, one of my other passions. PNE - The Lilywhites - the Whites - Proud Preston and as will become apparent a not inconsequential influence on this case, but I must not give too much away just yet. They were the first club to win the "Double", the League and Cup in 1889 with the, so far, unrepeated accolades of not losing a single game or conceding a goal in the Cup. They had their glory days about which Pops would wax lyrical with stories about the great Tom Finney.

'I wish you'd seen Finney in action,' he said one day, as we were suffering a game of very poor quality.

Pops was obviously wishing the present team was continuing to benefit from such talent as there was a definite dearth of it that afternoon. 'He was one of the greatest forwards the country has ever seen, watching him race down the wing was poetry in motion personified.'

'Did he play for England?' I asked, thinking that was the ultimate accolade.

'Yes and he scored thirty goals in an England shirt.'

'Did he score many for Preston?' I asked, knowing that Pops, with his encyclopaedic knowledge of football, would know the answer.

'My word, did he score! One hundred and eighty-seven of them in four hundred and thirty-three appearances. Magic!'

'Did you see them all?'

Pops laughed, 'Maybe not every one of them, but most and there were some beauties. Do you know Ben that he earned fourteen pounds a week when he started playing and had to supplement his income as a part-time plumber, working for the family firm, so he had the nickname the "Preston Plumber" and he was so important to the team that some comics called Preston "the plumber and his ten drips." Tom was born in a street just near the ground and was loyal to the club throughout his career. Not many do that these days. I was so pleased when he was named the Footballer of the Year for the 1953 to 54 season, though he could have received it every time.'

My season ticket now places me in the stand that bears his name. More recently the team's fortune has become mixed with the occasional play-off appearances but unfortunately they have not yet risen to the dizzy heights of the Premiership. We have never experienced the wealth of the top clubs but have loyal fans, thousands of us who turn up week after week in all weathers and in all divisions. How many supporters would Chelsea or Man U. claim in the third tier of English football?

PNE play at Deepdale, my home from home and perhaps the place I feel most at ease. It was, of course, Pops who took me to my first match and began my obsession with "the beautiful game". He had been a life-long supporter, as had his father and grandfather. I was four when he took me for the first time. It was a glorious Saturday afternoon, the start of the new season, a three o'clock kick off. We stood at the Shed End with the noisy band and raucous supporters and although I was far too young to understand all that happened I felt as though I had died and gone to heaven. I was transported to a different world with its cacophony of sounds and display of colours. I must have annoyed Pops as I remember that I kept asking questions about what was happening.

'Why can he pick the ball up?'

'What's a free kick?'

'Why is that man shouting so loudly?'

'Who is the man with the whistle? Little did either of us know that many years later a different man with a different whistle would force me into a killing; but a lot more of that at the appropriate time, the story has hardly "kicked-off yet!"

Pops was endlessly patient and explained it all. We (yes, it was we from the start; they were my team and I was a part of the whole glorious spectacle) won by four goals to two and in my enthusiasm I cheered every goal, even those scored by the opposition, our arch enemy, the local and therefore much hated, Blackpool. That was the beginning of the next six years of going to watch football with Pops. It is not the same going on my own but I continue to buy my annual Season Ticket and whenever we score a great goal or the keeper plays a blinder I find myself looking up the sky and saying, 'Did you see that Pops?'

Two years later Pops moved in with us following the death of his beloved Amy to cancer of the liver. Fortunately she wasn't ill for very long but how he must have hated the fact that he could do nothing to save her despite his decades spent practising as a doctor. He must have remembered others whom he had helped and have been distraught that there was nothing to be done for her. At that time, and for a few years to come, he was in excellent health but could not face living alone.

Many years later Father told me the reasons Pops had moved in with us. He recalled his words, 'The house feels like a place of the dead, it's so quiet and I see Amy in every room. I can cope physically, I'm not helpless but so lonely and it will be good to be with the youngsters.' All I can say is that he made life better for us, especially as my mother had, by this time, begun to have her depressive episodes.

My primary school days ended with a year of stultifying boredom and repetitious tedium. How many times does one need to be reminded about capital letters and full stops? Perhaps there are those who would say that they enjoyed their time spent in infant and junior classrooms. Not me. My final twelve months were more wearisome than ever as Mr Jones proved to be an inadequate and predictable teacher more concerned with endless revision and the test results we would achieve at the end of the year. Some of his predecessors had tried, rather unsuccessfully, to inspire me with the business of learning but that final year I did the minimum that was necessary and completed it with ease. Somehow it never seemed important enough to undertake more than the tiniest amount.

Having passed the eleven plus with consummate ease I had no worries when my parents made it look as though they were taking an interest in my education by attending the end of year Parents' Evening.

When they got home that night they were full of enthusiasm and praise for how well I had done. They'd been told that I was one of the best pupils in the class. I should go far and maybe be clever enough to be in the newspapers one day. Then they started to ask me about my interest in murder as Mr Jones had expressed concern as my writing and pictures were so "black!" Fancy old Jonesy noticing that! He'd never said anything to me, though to be honest he generally ignored me and I don't think we'd exchanged many words over the course of the year. He didn't have the best discipline and was more engaged in keeping order, quelling the disruptive elements of the class, than talking to the quieter individuals. I found it pleasing to realise how accurate he was about my interest in the art of murder. That pastime had begun many years before. No need to write about that now, it will keep.

School Report: Year 6 St Agnes' C.E. Primary School

Benjamin is a very quiet member of the class. He has made surprisingly good progress this year despite the fact that he rarely works to capacity. He is far too easily satisfied with output of an average standard. He has a good brain that he seldom uses to capacity. His excellent final results and his award of a place at Preston Grammar

School illustrate his true ability. One feels he has hidden
talents and more potential than he is utilising.

He is unfailingly well behaved but has made little
effort to make friends. It is to be hoped that, with
increasing maturity, his true talents will emerge and that
he enjoys a successful secondary education. I wish him
well at Preston Grammar.
Class teacher: Roger Jones.

"Develop my talents"; "be clever enough to appear in
the newspapers". Could he see into the future? I doubt
Jonesy had murder and a trial in mind when he spoke of
my glowing future.

But I digress. The problem is I have almost too much
time to think about the past. No point listening to the
evidence, I know it all. You want to hear about the
opener, the prelude, the overture to my life as a killer, or
the first I am, at this moment, willing to admit. As I have
indicated there was an ending before that but it is one
that, even now, well over three decades on, I am not
ready to commit to paper. If I were a Catholic I would
have confessed that particular event to a priest long
ago and sought absolution. Should there be divine retri-
bution I will receive punishment. As a confirmed atheist
I doubt whether this will happen but if there is a "Day
of Reckoning" it is to be hoped that God will be lenient
and understand the need for each murder even the unac-
knowledged first. At my Church of England primary
school the teachers always said that God forgives
everything. However should the one in ultimate charge
be the Hindu god Brahman there will, in all likelihood,
be less benevolence and such a quantity of bad karma
will have been accumulated that the inevitable outcome

will be an inferior reincarnation. Please be kind to any slugs you find in your garden!

Polly had been killed. People must take responsibilities for their actions. Mr Williams had to be punished. To be honest I didn't extinguish his life, that would have proved too difficult (and I never want to make life hard for myself) as he was a large, strong man and I was still a child and rather small for my age. I was seventeen before I put on a spurt and attained my present rather impressive height. No I couldn't hope to kill him, so I did the next best thing and rid the world of the person he cared about the most, his mother. William Williams never married and although he didn't live at home he visited his elderly and extremely frail mother every day in her house two doors from ours. I am sure you will agree that someone who could produce a monster like him did not deserve to live.

How to rid the world of such a creature? That was my problem. I spent days, then weeks trying to come up with some way to kill her without endangering myself. I did not want to be caught so her death must look either natural or accidental. How to end her inadequate existence? I was a child and so my imagination roamed through a variety of wonderfully gruesome and bloody methods: stabbing, shooting, strangling and even throwing her downstairs.

Then I had it, the moment of inspiration that I have subsequently found comes if I wait patiently enough and patience has always been one of my virtues.

I had been watching her house for weeks and had become familiar with her routine. Carers went in three times a day to see to her meals and medication. For ease of access her back door was left unlocked until the final evening visit so I would have no difficulty entering her property. I watched her bedroom curtains being drawn every afternoon between two and four so realised that the old girl must have a lie down. Why she needed one as she didn't appear to do anything the rest of the time was totally beyond my comprehension. The more I thought about it the more I realised that I would be doing the world a massive favour by removing her. Someone that old and useless should not be permitted to clog up the limited resources available to the National Health Service and one day you or I might very well need some of that funding.

Then I realised I had the perfect murder weapon........ Monkshood! It is also known as Soldier's Helmet, Friars' Cap or Old Wife's Hood, all due to the shape of the flowers. An old wives' tale has it that witches coated their broomsticks with it to help them fly. The Greek's called it "The Queen of Poisons", one of the deadliest potions known to man and we had it growing in the conservatory. Pops had been an avid gardener and when he came to live with us he had taken over not only our large garden but also the conservatory and greenhouse as well. Our garden was a delight in all seasons so full of colour. He developed an area of roses that could have appeared in a magazine. The smell was wonderful as he loved the old-fashioned varieties with strong scents. He often said that although gardening was a labour of love it was also hard work and it took dedication to keep it looking good. And look good it did. He often told the old joke:

Vicar, leaning over a garden gate, 'My word Tom, you and the Good Lord have made this garden a thing of beauty.'

Tom, 'Ah well vicar, you should have seen it when the Good Lord had it to himself!'

Yes keeping a garden looking as splendid as Pops kept ours took untold hours of hard work. I was allowed to help: sowing seeds, potting the young plants, weeding and my least favourite job, washing the flower pots ready for the following season. Many were the times when I would get home from school and put on my gardening clothes, the ones that were ready to throw out and mum didn't mind me getting dirty, and ask what I could do to assist. Some job was always found whatever the season. On inclement days we would work in the greenhouse but far preferable were the times when we got hours of fresh air outside. To this day I have a garden which, although I say it myself, is one of the best in the area. You may think it strange that someone who has dedicated his life to the pursuit of the perfect murder should enjoy seeing things grow, but I am always near Pops in a garden so that is reason enough for me.

It was mum who warned me about the Monkshood which was kept on a very high shelf. She told me that I should never ever touch it as just to come into contact with it could make me ill and even kill me. I think she was exaggerating so that I wouldn't get hurt but I did know that we had in our possession something that had been used for centuries as a killer.

Pops needed a certificate to allow him to grow it but claimed that this was a small price to pay for the pleasure of looking at such a spectacularly beautiful plant. Some Monkshood can be white, pink or yellow but ours was more traditional, a glorious purple. 'I think it's one of the best plants I've got,' said Pops an hour or so after mum's warning, 'but your mum is right, it is very, very dangerous and you must never touch it. I always put gloves on if I need to deal with it and I always, and I mean always, wash my hands thoroughly afterwards.'

'Which bit is dangerous?' I asked, my young curiosity aroused by the thought that we had something so excitingly hazardous.

'All of it', he replied, 'leaves and roots mostly but best not to touch any part of it. It is said that it was used to kill a famous Roman Emperor, Claudius, by his own doctor.

'Did you use it to kill any of your patients Pops?'

'No not me, I tried to save my patients, but if I had wanted to be so beastly I might have used it as it leaves no trace in the blood and so is undetectable, it just looks as though the victim has died of asphyxia, as though they've choked to death.' Pops amazing ability as an actor then came into play as he pretended to expire, very noisily and dramatically, uttering gruesome sounds as he pretended to strangle himself. I guffawed and snorted until tears were streaming down my face and my sides ached, little thinking that one day the knowledge I had been given would prove to be no laughing matter. No, not funny at all.

This conversation took place a couple of years before I needed such knowledge, the kind that is beloved by small boys, though I think I am correct in surmising that the vast majority will never use such wisdom in order to kill anyone.

Once I knew how I was going to end her days I spent several weeks working on the finer details of the plan. I have always been meticulous, no room for error. I made several trips to the greenhouse, with two layers of gloves on and started to collect various parts of the plant. They remained hidden under my bed until the day I felt I had enough to concoct a potion. That was the tricky part, how to make something that I could slip into a drink. I knew from further reading that it would only require a tiny amount to end a life but how to produce a liquid sufficient to my needs? Then it came to me: mother's liquidiser. You'll be pleased to know that it did receive a very thorough wash after I made the concoction.

The only thing that I held against Matilda Williams was that she had given birth to her fifth son, the bastard who had killed Polly. Aged eighty-four Matilda was an extremely frail and rather pathetic figure. The years had taken their toll, though a visit to Weight Watchers was long overdue. Hair, permed to a thin, frizzy halo, did little to add to her discomforting appearance. Her walking was laboured and she invariably relied on both a brightly patterned walking stick, a Christmas present from my parents, and her carer's arm. She was not the most cheerful old lady and had a weekly moan about the state of the produce in the local shop. How her carers put up with her I could never understand as all I ever heard her do when she was out with them was complain.

'Come on, hurry up with my change, the repeat of East Enders is on soon, I don't want to miss it.'

'Young people, no respect for their elders, it wasn't like that in my day.'

'Don't go so quickly, my legs are killing me.' Thankfully that didn't happen; it would have spoilt my fun.

My, admittedly youthful, view was that she was like many elderly people - totally self-absorbed. There were frequent conversations about her numerous ailments and her experience of life had become very narrow.

Any views she expressed were focussed on the latest vacuous happenings on the TV soaps that she watched from morning to night. Surely even at her advanced age she could have found a more interesting way to pass her days.

The more I thought about it the more I realised that she would not be much of a loss to the world. Apart, of course, to William! What a joyful thought that was.

The rest was surprisingly simple, in fact one of my easiest murders. I happened to be in the local shop one day when Mrs Williams came in with one of her carers to do her weekly shop (how fate lent me a hand, it was as though she was helping me).

'Oh! You and your gin, you do enjoy it,' the carer said in a voice loud enough to accommodate Mrs William's poor hearing.

'It's my one indulgence, a gin and tonic every night before bedtime, works a treat and I sleep like a baby,' she replied picking a large bottle of the spirit off the shelf and looking, for once, reasonably cheerful.

Looking at her size I hardly agreed that it was her one indulgence and her trolley was already amply supplied with bars of chocolate. Nevertheless, I had the vital information that I needed. The rest was literally child's play. I slipped into Mrs William's house one afternoon when I had been left to my own devices.

I had been in the house many times before as my mother saw it as her duty to help the old dear and when I was younger she would often take me with her.

'She loves seeing you, when people get old they need to see young life,' mum would say though she knew I hated the visits and that Mrs W. would not be remotely interested in anything I had to say. 'It's only for a short

time and you can tell her about your day at school.'
As every day at my primary school had been pretty much the same I found any conversation about it as awkward as trying to speak when sitting in the dentist's chair with his hand and a hundred surgical implements in one's mouth, preventing coherent conversation.

'I'll come for a few minutes then I've got homework to finish,' I used to say, knowing that would win the argument as nothing must get in the way of my academic progress.

As I entered the house on that fatal Sunday afternoon, the last day of the summer holiday, I realised, as is usually the case with the homes of the elderly that nothing had changed. The kitchen must have been the same for decades, no spending needless thousands of pounds updating the units, floors or worktops. I crept into the living room, ears alert for any sounds from upstairs, and was delighted to find the "drinks cabinet" where it had always been. I recalled mum and Mrs W. regularly throwing back the sherry and Matilda, as Mum called her, saying that she also indulged in gin as a nightcap. Several bottles of the stuff stood to attention as I opened the sideboard where they were stored, a veritable array of sleeping potions.

The one at the front had been opened and a small amount already consumed and presumably enjoyed. Would the old lady appreciate her next, and I believed her last indulgence?

I had my Monkshood-Mixture in a small bottle in my anorak pocket. As quickly as I was able, needing to be careful not to spill even a single drop, I added a generous helping of what I hoped was the deadly creation to the opened bottle and waited for the fun to begin.

That night I was the one who slept like a baby and it wasn't until the following morning that I allowed myself to hope. Even Pandora could not have appreciated that life-enhancing feeling as much as I did that day. At breakfast time there were two cars outside Mrs William's house, one that I recognised as the carer's and, the heavens be praised, a second one.

'Oh dear that looks like Doctor Evan's new car, I hope there's nothing wrong with Mrs Williams,' mum said, sending my spirits soaring for the first time since Polly's death.

'Maybe it's just a routine visit,' dad suggested, always the optimist.

'It's very early for that, doctors don't usually do home visits so early.'

'Well we'll find out soon enough.'

Not soon enough for me. I had to go to school without knowing, not the best way to begin one's secondary career. If anyone noticed my lack of attention they probably put it down to first day nerves. I sat all day unable to concentrate, my mind totally distracted. Had I done it? Was she dead or alive? When the day at school was finally over I was once again alone in the house. Mum was helping to run the After School Club at the primary school where she worked on a voluntary basis when she was enjoying an "up" period. She arrived home at half past five and I was longing to ask if she had heard anything but didn't want to look as though I was taking too much interest as that might have appeared suspicious; after all I had never shown any curiosity about our neighbours in the past.

Dad arrived home an agonising thirty minutes later.

'Have you heard the news?' mum asked sounding to my keen ears wonderfully sad.

'No, what's happened?' he asked.

'The carer found Mrs Williams dead this morning, sitting in her chair, the television still on, she never made it to bed. They think her heart gave out. She's had problems for years and saw the specialist only last week. At least she died happy, eating her nut chocolate and enjoying her night time drink. Mr Williams told me all about the tragedy when I met him outside as I left for work and he looked totally lost, poor soul. He will really miss her. He said there's no need for a post mortem as the doctor had seen her so regularly for all her various ailments.'

I could contain myself no longer and ran wildly up to my room where I did a dance of sheer joy. I had done it, it had worked. I had taken my revenge on Mr Williams. Now he would know what it was like to lose someone.

My crime went undetected. I had not worried about leaving the incriminating evidence in situ. From conversations that I had overheard my parents having I knew that William Williams had been concerned about his mother's drinking for some time and regularly removed bottles from the house. I was fairly certain that his first action would have been to pour the contents of any opened bottles down the sink. I had touched the deadly one wearing my gloves knowing all about incriminating finger prints. I surmised that even should that particular bottle be left in situ no one would think to check its contents. Why would they?

Chapter 4

Daily Gazette

Prosecution Evidence in Murder Trial.

The Crown Prosecution Service began to outline their case in the horrific and tragic murder of Jamie Richardson. The jury was told that the defendant lived close to the Richardson family and was known to them by sight. His fingerprints and other DNA evidence were found at the murder scene, a disused garage on the Streatham Estate. His DNA was already known to the police as it was on record following his involvement in a fight after a home game at Deepdale between Preston North End and Oldham Athletic.

The defendant had once used the garage, where the toddler's body was found, to house his car before being asked by the owner to remove it. The hushed courtroom was then told that the reasons for this will prove part of the prosecution case and will make for damning evidence when Mr Walters, the garage proprietor, is called as a witness.

The man accused of this most heinous of crimes has lived on the Streatham Estate for many years but was described as "a bit of a loner". Little has been said about his background but he does not appear to have socialised in the area.

Sir Anthony Pinkerton sounded extremely confident as he assured the jury that the right man was in the dock and that the evidence they would hear would prove, irrefutably, that he was indeed the person who had killed Jamie. Sir Anthony went on to repeat the warning given by the Judge Montgomery that much of the evidence would make for most unpleasant listening.

Judge's Notes

The jury looked impressed by Anthony's opening address. However it is early days to be calling evidence "irrefutable" or to ask the twelve to think that the case is already decided. The course of a trial can change in a few minutes and there is a very long way to go in this one. I do not think that the jury realise just how drawn out this case may be. We will almost certainly be here for weeks and there will be many twists and turns along the way.

I had my first official murder under my belt at the age of eleven. Mrs William's death was declared natural, her age and general state of health having taken their toll. As she had seen her doctor recently there was no need for any further investigation. My parents went to the funeral.

'Poor Mr Williams, he was so upset, I did feel sorry for him,' my mother said, her words sounding as good as anything Beethoven ever composed. My father put the kettle on, a cup of tea being his answer to everything, and muttered, 'She was the world to him. I think he's going to be very lonely.' I turned away to hide the smile that I knew was lighting up my face.

At that tender age I little thought that this would be the start of my "career" as a murderer.

Dictionary Definition: Career: chosen pursuit; a profession or occupation.

The general course or progression of one's working life or one's professional achievements.

Yes, the word is most apposite!

If anyone had known about it and asked me I would have said, at the time quite truthfully, that there would be no such events in the future. However I had planned, executed and got away with the demise of Mrs Williams far too easily and it had given me such inordinate pleasure, pleasure such as I never normally derived from everyday life that as surely as ying is counterbalanced by yang more murders must follow. At such a tender age, a mere year into the realms of criminal responsibility, had I been convicted of Mother William's demise I would have spent many years in a secure unit devised to socialise youngsters who have erred. Would this have changed me? Unfortunately there is no way of returning to the past and taking the other path. Life remains full of "what if?" moments.

Once Pops died my life became rather repetitive. From the very first week at Preston Grammar I began to make the outstanding progress that had been forecast. I invariably produced far more homework than was required, often not submitting it all for fear of being noticed. I set myself projects and researched the facts I wanted for hours on end. My interest in crime, especially murders, gradually became an obsession and I would have to hide the material I found in books borrowed from the library from my mother's inquisitive gaze. Unfortunately the delights of the internet with its speedy access to the desired information was some time in the future but has proved a source of constant pleasure in recent years

My sisters had left home by this time and my parents were always busy, with work and their various leisure time activities and my mother was experiencing one of her more positive phases. I was no trouble to them in fact I don't think they noticed I was there a lot of the time. It was during Year 7 that I started running and this was a release and a solace. Other sports on offer at school: football, rugby and hockey were all team games and seemed like hard work. I had never had much time for people of my own age group so I ran alone, for mile after mile through the glorious Lancashire countryside. I can't claim to have been happy but there was some acceptance that this was how my life would be

'Don't overdo the running,' Mr Carlton, the P.E. teacher advised, 'you don't want to burn yourself out. I'll give you a schedule, no more than five miles three times a week with much shorter runs in between.' I pretended that I would stick to his rather limited regime but continued to cover at least twice that distance each week. 'Tommy Lincoln and you would make a good partnership, it's more fun running with someone else and he's almost as good as you.' Saying I would think about the idea got him off my back and I was able to continue my solo excursions. That was my time and no one was going to interfere.

Two years elapsed before I got the urge, the uncontrollable desire, to strike again. Each and every one of my murders has been for a purpose and this was no different. Many people will find this one, to say the very least, distasteful, as it involved a very young baby.

It was the summer my father retired. He had been a Head teacher for almost three decades and managed to carry on beyond the normal retirement age of sixty. Two years later he decided that enough was enough and wanted more time to play golf and have the energy to enjoy additional Bridge evenings. To celebrate his long and successful career, and to spend some of his generous lump sum, he booked a Mediterranean cruise. Our holidays up to that time had tended to be either in England or on French camp sites, so this was to be a really new, exciting experience.

Flying for the first time was amazing. We had an early flight so drove down the motorway and were parked in the long-term car park at Manchester airport just as dawn was breaking. As we stood waiting for the bus to transport us to Terminal Two I knew the holiday was becoming a reality. It had been talked about and planned for so long that I had begun to think it would never occur, rather like a young child being told there were four more sleeps before Santa was due down the chimney, a stretch of time that is both inconceivable and almost unbearable.

We were at the airport. We were going to fly. This was one of the very few times, except when planning a murder, that I have felt almost uncontrollable anticipation. The long wait queuing for our boarding passes was fun. I stood and watched the other holiday makers and wondered where they were going. I realised it could be anywhere in the world. I loved going through the security checks, though father was annoyed when he was asked to remove not only his jacket but also his belt and shoes.

'I'll be lucky if these trousers stay up,' was his loud grumble, 'this pair need a belt.' Fortunately, both for him and us his luck held! I was so pleased when I set the alarm off as I marched through the security scanner, the coins in my pocket alerting the sensor to an un-identified metal. The staff on duty pretended to suspect me of underhand activities and gave me a thorough search much to the amusement of my parents. Pops had been frisked on numerous occasions when going into Deepdale but this was my first experience and I wanted to jump for joy. Was I James Bond in disguise?

Shoes, belts, jackets and cardigans restored we walked through the duty free outlets. Manchester airport suddenly became Aladdin's cave full of exotic and tempting treasures. Even mother, who it must be admitted had been fearful in the days leading up to her first flight, was seduced by the choices available and purchased a small bottle of the kind of expensive perfume that she would only allow herself if it had the dubious accolade of being a special offer. Being without import taxes it was deemed to be a bargain! I was allowed a huge bar of Toblerone the size only seen at airports. The manufacturers must think that this is the ideal outlet for such a mega-size bar and indeed I treat myself to at least one each time I pass through such shops.

Waiting to board the plane was agony; goodness knows whether the bomb ticking inside me would have detonated had we been delayed.

'The flight to Mahon is now ready for boarding,' a song by Schubert could never have sounded sweeter than those words did to me at that moment. Getting everyone, all three hundred of us, seated took an age, then the stewardess had to go over the safety procedures (they were all on the card in the pocket in front of me, couldn't people read?) Taxiing out to the appropriate runway was an endurance test. When would we get going? My patience was being sorely tested.

Take off was worth the wait. Sheer exhilaration. Nothing could have prepared me for such speed. Speed such as mere mortals only experience when a plane accelerates to gain its optimum velocity before soaring like the phantom rising from its ashes into the sky. I was Sterling Moss breaking the land speed record. Not bad James Bond and Sterling Moss in the space of a couple of hours!

The morning was overcast as we took off and I was unprepared for the experience of breaking through the clouds to be welcomed by dazzling sunlight. We appeared to be floating above balls of cotton wool and I was surprised that the speed of the plane was no longer so obvious. Food and drinks appeared and I was one very happy little boy. Mother was calm, apart from one slight panic when we bumped and shook during a brief interlude of turbulence. She grabbed father's hand in a vice-like hold and I could see her swallowing her fear like a child forcing down a Brussels sprout. The journey exceeded expectations and I was optimistic that we were about to have a good two weeks.

We flew to the Menorcan capital of Mahon. It was mid-season and heaving with people who acted like an army of ants dashing at top speed in the same direction, all hell - bent on getting through immigration as quickly as possible. There was little to be gained by being first as the coach transporting us to the ship had to wait for all its passengers.

The summer in England had been dull and somewhat disappointing so to arrive in scorching sunshine put us all in holiday mode. My parents and I had separate cabins, outside ones with full length glass windows affording permanent sea views and with large adjoining balconies with loungers that my parents used each day. The ship was more like a five star floating hotel than the boat I had been expecting.

Walking up the gangway it was hard not to think of pirates clambering aboard for their loot. Excitement remained the order of the day. We walked into the atrium, the gathering spot for the passengers. It was so vast that it reminded me of the Free Trade Hall where, just the week before, my parents had dragged me to endure an evening of Tchaikovsky, still not my favourite composer. A bar, the purser's desk and to my amazement elevators, a grand piano and sweeping staircases completed the picture. There were to be over two thousand people on board but thanks to some excellent organisation we were booked in calmly and efficiently. As I looked around I was rather disappointed to see other children, both older and younger than me. The holiday was not for me a time to socialise, my own age group being deemed boring and vacuous though the presence of children was to work to my advantage.

Anyone who has been on a cruise will know that the ships are a floating delight of entertainment and the aptly named *Gloriana* was true to form: a casino, a night club, shows, several swimming pools, a hot tub and a cinema showing all the latest films with a Children's Choice every afternoon was the impressive list that caught my eye that first day. These amusements were only outshone by the variety of restaurants and cafes that were available. Father had chosen the "Anytime Dining" choice for us so, as the name suggests, we could go to any dining room at any time and wait for the next available table.

Little wonder the average weight gain whilst on board such a vessel is almost two pounds a day!

The ship left the dock, the second deepest in Europe, and we settled quickly into an, even to me, rather pleasant daily routine. I was encouraged to join the Jolly Roger club aimed at my age group and to start with I was surprised to find that I rather enjoyed the pool side activities. The food was mind-blowing and even the evening entertainment was just about bearable to my thirteen year old self.

The one thing that spoilt the entire experience was the couple who were in the cabin next to mine with their yowling infant. I have never liked babies. For the most part they are horrible, ugly little Shrek-like beings, constantly bawling and, in my humble opinion, not quite human. This one was particularly obnoxious. He seemed to wait until I was in bed before starting his night-time caterwauling. However it was not this aspect of him that led me to do what I had to do.

It was his parents. Simon and Serena Jackson. They were far too young to have a baby and looked like kids themselves and not particularly bright ones at that. Most people had paid a small fortune to go on the cruise but they informed anyone within earshot that they had won the holiday in a Thomas Cook's competition. Being of such low intelligence they were unaware that this did not endear them to the other passengers.

'We'd never have been able to do a cruise if we hadn't won it,' Serena told my parents one morning as we sat at adjoining tables at breakfast.

'No and with young George we didn't even think we were having a holiday at all this year,' Simon added looking inordinately pleased by their change of fortune.

My father, ever the diplomat, asked what they had had to do to win. 'We had to answer two questions and then as we got them right our name was put in a hat and we couldn't believe it when it was drawn out.' I knew what was coming next and tried to do a Houdini act with my mind but to no avail.

Simon was in peacock mode by this time and said proudly, 'The first question was, "Is the capital of France Berlin, Paris or London?" And the second was "What currency do they use in America: Euros, crowns or dollars?"' Stone the crows, surely everyone on the planet would have been able to answer those two questions.

In many ways the Jacksons reminded me of my own parents. They were wrapped up in each other and seldom gave George (Gorgeous Georgeous I once heard them call him...yuk!) the attention he needed. I had my suspicions that the reason he cried so much at night was because he was left alone whilst they danced the night away in the ballroom, entwined in each other's arms. Some people are not fit to be parents.

Most days the ship docked and we disembarked and went sightseeing. Each time we stopped my father decided to go into "teacher mode" and deliver a lecture about the island we were visiting. Majorca, Ibiza, Sicily and Corsica are now a blur of long forgotten facts but on the morning of my next adventure we visited Sardinia.

'Sardinia is the second largest island in the Med, Sicily being the biggest and Cyprus the third. It has an area of almost twenty-four thousand square kilometres.' Why I was listening so carefully that day and even more strangely why I can still recall every detail of his diatribe is beyond understanding. Was I trying to concentrate my mind on something other than the afternoon's planned "extra"?

'Over the years Sardinia has been invaded and conquered by many nations: the Phoenicians, Romans and Vandals all ruled the island before it became Spanish in 1479, Austrian in 1718 and finally Italian in 1861 when it joined the newly established Kingdom of Italy.' There was no stopping him and mother and I stood under the scorching sun and tried to appear interested. The one redeeming feature was that he never produced a twenty question test on his torrent of information, though on second thoughts, how surprised he would have been when I would have achieved full marks following that particular visit.

Throughout the voyage George was left alone in his pram for hours at a stretch. He was obviously a nocturnal creature as his days passed in peaceful oblivion. Each day followed the same pattern. Mummy and daddy would arrive on the sun deck soon after breakfast and place the pram around the corner from the pool in a very secluded area out of the hot sun. The idea was that George would be watched over by one of the ship's babysitters but Sophie was far more interested in a certain rather handsome member of the crew and seldom checked on the baby.

His parents would spend the entire day lying by the pool, swimming, drinking copious amounts of alcohol and worst of all canoodling in full view of everyone. The last activity was totally sickening and made me feel rather nauseous. I realised that they cared more for each other than they did for their son. No child should have to live with that so I decided to remove him from the situation.

My plan was ingenious in its simplicity. The child must disappear. Over the side was the obvious solution. We were due to be on board for a fortnight so there was no urgency and I had the luxury of allowing myself many days of watching and seeing at what times of the day they bothered with young George. The parents were creatures of habit and they went nowhere near him for a couple of hours after lunch, a time when he was particularly settled. The decision was made. That would be the best time to ease him out of this world.

After the morning in Cagliari, 'The capital of Sardinia the ancient name meaning "castle"; population one hundred and fifty six thousand or four hundred and eighty if you include the outlying townships' (echoes of father) we were all back on board for lunch and our onward journey. My plan was to join in with the afternoon Otters' Club session, an off-shoot of the Jolly Roger, which organised activities in the pool. It was water polo that afternoon and I made sure that I was my usual fairly anonymous self for the first few minutes. I knew my absence would be of little consequence as there were so many playing that day. Just after three o'clock I left the pool, unnoticed as I had hoped I would be. George's parents were, true to form, sleeping off their lunch time excesses so would not be interested in their offspring for some time.

The baby was fast asleep and no one else was around as the ship had entered its afternoon hibernation. I picked the sleeping infant up very carefully and walked across the deck to the side of the boat. He was dressed in a pale blue sleeping suit and looked rather warm but was sleeping peacefully, one might say "dead to the world" which he soon would be. Oh the unspeakable joy of dropping him gently over the ship's railings. No sound came from him and I didn't bother looking over the railings in case I aroused suspicion should anyone appear unexpectedly. I was sure that the sea took him with such speed that he wouldn't have suffered. He had been saved years of heartache, of knowing that he was unloved. I had done him a massive favour.

I returned to the poolside and slipped into the water. It was then that I made sure others noticed me as I joined in the game with exuberance, making my presence felt by scoring a couple of goals. When all hell broke loose, as it soon must, I would have a couple of dozen witnesses to say that I had been in the pool all afternoon.

'Oh my God, where is he, where is George? Someone's taken him!' his mother's voice rang out, panic taking over at an amazingly dramatic rate. Why she should be concerned with his welfare was beyond my comprehension. She had not shown much interest in him up until then. His father, who had been dozing on a sunbed, leapt to his feet to see what the commotion was.

'What is it, what's wrong?' he yelled to his by now totally distraught wife.

'He's not here, Oh dear God, where is he?'

Pandemonium broke out with people rushing round searching for the missing infant. There was, of course, no sign of him, though every inch of the ship was searched, over and over. It all became rather tedious though my parents didn't find it so and discussed the various possibilities ad nauseam, as did every other passenger. The ship was turned round eventually, a long, slow process, and we returned to Sardinia where the local police boarded. All the passengers were divided into groups, each group going in turn to the main reception area where everyone was questioned individually. As this included the children I did not escape a brief interrogation. As a minor I had to have my parents with me.

'A baby has gone missing (tell me something I don't know, I thought). We are trying to find someone who might be able to throw any light on his disappearance, a person who might have seen something unusual,' the officer said though I doubt he thought he'd get much information from me. 'Can you tell me where it was you were this afternoon?' His accent was very strong and I had to concentrate to understand what he was saying. That, at least, made me appear to be taking the situation seriously.

'I was at the pool all afternoon playing water polo. The first I knew was when I heard the lady shouting.'

'He goes to the Otters' Club every afternoon,' explained my mother, helping me out without realising it.

'We're asking everyone this,' the officer continued, 'but did you see anything unusual, anything at all that might help?'

'No, like I said the first I knew that there was something wrong was when the noise started.'

I knew I wasn't likely to be a suspect, being of such tender years myself and having such a caste-iron alibi and that was indeed the only part I played in the proceedings. My parents answered the same questions and then we were asked to go to the dining hall where the Captain was waiting to speak to all the guests.

'Ladies and gentlemen, boys and girls, we appear to have an extremely serious situation on board. A baby has gone missing and has not, as yet, been found. I know that you have been questioned by the Sardinian police and it may interest you to know that the assistance of the British police has been requested and they will join us as soon as humanely possible. This is potentially the worst incident that has ever happened on board our ship as it is feared that the baby may have come to some harm. I would ask for calm and for our thoughts and prayers to be with the parents at this worrying time. I realise that until the baby is found life on board will be very difficult. Dinner will be served as normal but as a sign of respect all other activities will be curtailed for the time being. Thank you for your time.'

My goodness I thought everyone had been spared the embarrassment of a Karaoke evening though thank goodness none of my family had volunteered to take part in such a display of the untalented.

The passengers dispersed in a stunned silence, all fearing the worst. I alone felt the same sense of joy that had almost overwhelmed me when I first heard that Mrs Williams was dead.

My parents were poor company that evening, worse than usual, and I was glad to retire to my cabin. George's parents had been seen by the ship's doctor who had thankfully tranquilised them and their awful noise had stopped. I was to get my first good night's sleep since boarding.

By the next morning when George was still unaccounted for I think the general consensus was that he had been killed and as there was no body that he must have gone over the side. People were expressing outrage at the thought of such an event and most passengers were starting to suspect the parents. That idea had not entered my head and the notion that it was seen as a possibility only added to my euphoria. We were all re-questioned when the British police arrived and then Mr and Mrs Jackson the, by now, bereft parents, left the ship under police guard. There were no other suspects. After all why in the world would anyone, enjoying an innocent fortnight of sunshine, wish their son harm?

B.B.C. Ceefax: An incident has occurred on the Gloriana Cruise ship. A young baby, George Jackson, aged three months, has been reported missing. The ship returned late yesterday afternoon to the nearest port, Cagliari on the Mediterranean island of Sardinia, where the parents disembarked and are being questioned by both local and British police.

A spokesperson for Totally Cruises said that this was a unique event in the long history of the company and that their representatives would do everything in their power to assist the police. They offered their sincere condolences to the parents.

No charges were ever brought against Mr and Mrs Jackson as the CPS couldn't ascertain which of them had killed the child or who, if they had planned the act together, the main offender was and so the notion of joint enterprise was deemed inappropriate. Any judge would have needed the Wisdom of Solomon in that trial. However the press had a field day and they were certainly deemed guilty by the media. Unfortunately there were only two George and mummy and daddy Jackson free days left on the cruise but it will not surprise you to know that I enjoyed every last minute of them.

Once home the death of baby George had an adverse effect on mother who went into one of her declines. 'It's too awful; the death of a child. How will the parents cope?' she sobbed; so many tears coursing down her face and onto the living room carpet that I was tempted to look for a pool similar to the one created by Alice.

Father was tense, realising only too well how easily such an event could send her into one of her downward spirals, leaving her totally inaccessible. 'Perhaps one or both of them did it. The police certainly have their suspicions.'

'No, no, a parent could not do that to their baby and he was such a cute little thing and so good.' She had obviously been too far away to enjoy his night-time serenading!

Father's voice was becoming strident, 'Well there's no point in worrying about it, it's not our problem and you don't want to make yourself ill over it. Our fretting won't help anybody.' Mother had cried herself out and was entering the next phase: silence, stillness and a total physical and mental slump into her own tortured world. Watching her was like observing a computer after pressing the "shut down" sign. Everything disappears slowly leaving only a blank screen. Father helped her up to bed where she remained for ten days; incommunicado, followed by a lengthy trip to the local psychiatric unit.

'Now son, these things happen. They shouldn't but I don't want you worrying about it,' were his words of comfort to me. Was he talking about the baby or mother? Either way what was there to worry about? Why shouldn't things happen? How little he knew me.

Had I caused mother's latest depressive episode which was to last the best part of a year? No. Baby George Jackson was of no consequence in her life and she was creating a drama of Greek proportions where none existed. Homer would have been proud of her. I, most definitely, was not.

I have now acknowledged two killings and at the time I realised that, given the right temptation, I might strike again. On these occasions the murders had been planned and had been fully justified. The next one was a surprise, totally unpremeditated and, in my view, my least efficacious. But that was to be several years in the future and will keep.

Chapter 5

Daily Gazette

Forensic Evidence in Murder Trial.

It emerged yesterday that the defendant had thousands of indecent images on his home computer and the prosecution indicated that this has a profound bearing on the case against him. He was not however on the Sex Offenders' Register. The images are said to be the worst that even police officers hardened to such pictures had ever seen. Photos found beside the dead child are similar to the perverted ones downloaded on the defendant's hard-drive. Mutilations and dismemberment are said to be involved. Members of the jury were visibly shocked when they were shown the photos and several of the female jurors were in tears.

This paper will not rest until we have persuaded the government to introduce greater vigilance over the availability of pornography sites on the internet and to instigate lengthier sentences for anyone caught downloading such filth.

The jury was warned that future revelations may prove equally distressing. The trial continues.

Truly appalling images. Definitely amongst the most disturbing it has been my displeasure to see. The jury kept taking surreptitious glances at the defendant and I knew what they were thinking: how can a man who looks so normal indulge in such abnormal behaviour? My question, as always would be: how can anyone enjoy such depravity?

I was influenced by today's strong and well presented evidence and I think it had a profound effect on the jury.

Following my second foray into the delightful experience of killing another human being my time was fully occupied with academic studies. By this point I was well established at Preston Royal Grammar School for Boys. I cannot tell you how preferable this establishment was to my primary school for I was amongst my own kind: the clever, the gifted and the exclusively male.

It was a pleasant change to have specialist teachers for every subject and to benefit from facilities such as science labs, gymnasiums, art and music rooms which are not available in most state primary schools I was, if not happy, then at least very content there. The work continued to come easily to me and as I was now highly self-motivated I excelled in every subject area. Eleven starred A's in my GCSEs followed two years later by five top grades at A level. You may be interested to learn that I achieved the highest mark in the country in my Psychology exam. It was during my years in the sixth form that I was challenged academically for the first time and found that I adored the experience. I can't claim that the social side of school improved but that didn't bother me and my academic life was balanced by regular running and watching my beloved Preston North End.

Teachers can make a lasting impression on one, both positively and in some cases negatively. Mr Coward (a most unfortunate name at a boys' school) fell into the former category and was inspirational. I was fortunate to benefit from his exceptional teaching of English Literature during my final four years at the school. He had the ability to bring even the most obdurate text to life and was an incredible actor able to employ a huge variety of accents and modes of speech. His speciality was poetry and to this day I turn to W.B. Yeats, Lord Byron and William Wordsworth when I need to read something with substance.

'Poetry encapsulates life,' was one of his sayings, 'if you ever need to try to understand the traumas that life will send your way take down a book of poems. The answer will be in there somewhere.' No wonder I have the New Oxford Book of English Verse on my bed-side table. It was Mr Coward who introduced me to Shakespeare and reading the bard's accounts of bloody and gory murders has become a regular pastime. What joy there would be emulating some of those appalling deeds, but they would, without doubt, be detected far too easily!

Mr Hayden was a complete contrast He was abysmal. His attempts to drum some Religious Education into us were laughable. Perhaps he was too young but he was so easily embarrassed, a regular occurrence demanding little input from us. From the start he was easy pickings for the highly intelligent youths who found his subject boring.

'Sir, why was David watching Bathsheba as she bathed?'

'Could you please explain what circumcision is, we're rather confused.'

'What is adultery?' were just a few of the questions we asked in order to discombobulate the poor man. He would turn a tomato red and stutter, sounding like the hail pattering one memorable lesson on the flat roof of his room. That particular double period (yes, the poor soul had to endure our fourteen year old obnoxious selves for eighty minutes) must have thought he was suffering a foretaste of the hell that he had talked about the previous term.

The most unforgettable lesson was the one where the poor man was enlightening us about Joshua fighting the battle of Jericho. All was going well until Johnny Mitchell decided to read on and discovered the part where God tells Joshua to rescue the harlot. Mr Hayden's explanations of that old fashioned word produced smirks, giggles and finally gales of uncontrollable mirth at which juncture the poor man fled the room. Being reprimanded by the deputy head, Mr Hilton, whose tongue could lash with the ferocity of a force nine gale, and serving time in detention were as nothing when compared with the gleeful memories created that wet Thursday afternoon. I wonder if Mr Hayden is still teaching and whether he has grown a thicker skin, able to cope with adolescent humour.

With the one exception my time at Preston Grammar passed without incident. It is a strange phenomenon that the periods between my killings have varied from a few days to several years. This must tell you that I only kill when there is a valid reason. Yes, I get enormous pleasure from each event but every one of them has had a purpose, a justification. Given time I hope you will agree with me.

At eighteen I was offered a place at Balliol College, Oxford to read Law: Jurisprudence as it is called there. I chose Oxford for its academic reputation and Balliol as it claimed to be one of the top colleges. It was founded in 1263 by John Balliol, a loyal follower of Henry the Third. The first sixteen students who were enrolled that year received an allowance of eight pence a week. I doubt whether the four hundred undergraduates and the equal number of postgraduates studying there in the twenty-first century could live on such a pittance. Balliol only accepts six or seven scholars a year to study Law so I was fortunate to gain a place. Those completing their degrees successfully go on to become lawyers, solicitors, barristers and, on occasion, judges. Even more inspiring was the list of its alumni. These include former Prime Ministers: Herbert Asquith, Harold Mc'Millan and Edward Heath, authors: Hilaire Beloc, Nevil Shute and Graham Greene and the well-known atheist and prolific author Richard Dawkins.

The only disappointing aspect of this outstanding establishment was that it had become a mixed college, accepting females into its academic heights from 1979. I just hoped that my tutorial groups would be predominantly male. One claim in its prospectus was that it would guide the mind to go "beyond the superficial" not something that I have found comes easily to the female mind.

Oxford has a world-wide reputation as an outstanding seat of learning. Those fortunate enough to enjoy three or more years studying there also have the advantage of living in a beautiful city. Many of the colleges are amongst the most impressive buildings in Europe. Christ Church springs to mind with its magnificent central quad and grand Chapel which doubles as the Cathedral for the Diocese of Oxford and the college is a tourist attraction, with thousands flocking in each week throughout the year, blocking the pavements and the college quads. They cause traffic jams and annoy the scholars attempting to get to their lectures by the far more sensible mode of transport: bikes.

During my first year I lived in college in a set of rooms that must have housed generations of eager young minds. As I was near Exeter College I frequently attended Choral Evensong in its splendid chapel a glorious event which took place three times each week. The original chapel completed in 1624 was deemed to be structurally unsound and a new one was erected on the same spot in 1859, based on La Sainte-Chapelle one of the jewels of Paris. The chapel was, and no doubt remains a peaceful space of dark wooden choir stalls, candles and had the most superb acoustics. My atheism was tested on occasion as I sat transported by the beauty of the service. On those occasions nothing was further from my mind than murder.

Whilst at Oxford my home from home was the purpose-built Bodleian Law Library with its four hundred and fifty thousand volumes, covering every aspect of the subject. Being of a studious disposition I took my studies seriously and spent days beavering away in the magnificent rooms of that renowned library. I attended every scheduled lecture and tutorial benefitting from the input of some seriously clever people. My favourite tutor was to my great surprise a lady called Muriel Winterton. She was the archetypal "mad professor" with a shock of unkempt white hair and flowing clothes which looked as though they came from another era and which had almost certainly been purchased in one of the many charity shops to be found in town. Her appearance was unusual but goodness was she able to inspire her students. At first glance some aspects of the law looked deadly dull but were brought to life by her erudite lectures which included moments of joyful wit. She loved her subject and passed it onto us with the certainty of an accomplished athlete handing on the baton in a relay race.

The only relaxation I allowed myself was to continue my love of running. Running, during those three years, was a pleasure, through The Meadows and The Park. The Meadows is an ancient grazing land beside the River Thames, a great space for walking, running or for those so inclined, the back-breaking pastime of punting. However the Park was my favourite, seventy acres of open space with its claim to fame being the only first class cricket ground in the country where spectators can watch for free. County matches are played there and on a pleasant day crowds gathered to watch. I was seldom one of them, enjoying that game in very small doses. Seven large Sequoia trees and a Japanese Pagoda tree, all planted in 1888 continue to draw in the visitors. One amusing aspect of the Park is that it houses two secluded areas once used for nude bathing called Parson's Pleasure and Dame's Delight. No doubt they are used thus to this day.

My love of plants was satisfied by regular visits to the Botanic Gardens, established in 1621 for the study of medicinal plants. It has the most impressive greenhouses

I have ever seen housing numerous exotic plants and unusual flowers, though I never saw any Monkshood there! The Gardens were established in 1621 by the first Earl of Danby, Henry Danvers, who gave five thousand pounds (over seven hundred and fifty thousand in today's money) to set a garden which he said was "for the glorification of the works of God and the furtherance of learning". In the Walled Garden there is a set of beds that represent plants linked to modern medicine. How Pops, who revelled in both plants and medicines, would have loved to visit such an establishment with me.

All in all my years at Oxford proved to be a most amazing experience. They were, to date, the best years of my life. Maybe I should have stuck with academia as a career though even in that intellectual setting I succumbed, just the once you understand, just the once.

Chapter 6

Daily Gazette

Prosecution Witnesses Give Their Evidence in Murder Trial

Yesterday, during an afternoon of high drama in the haughty interior of Manchester Crown Court, the Prosecution presented their witnesses.

Mrs Albin, a widow aged 74, gave her evidence in an almost inaudible whisper. The lady was obviously distressed to find herself in court and had to be asked on several occasions to repeat her answers. She said she knew the defendant by sight as he lives near her block of flats on the Streatham Estate. She admitted that she had never spoken to him, "Not so much as a Good Morning," but that she regularly saw him on the way to or from the shops. You, the readers, will remember that it was from outside these shops that the little boy, Jamie Richardson, aged two was snatched and subsequently murdered.

Mrs Albin was adamant that she was remembering the right day, the day of the abduction, as it was her birthday and she was making a special visit to the shops to buy cakes and biscuits at Sam's General Store for the friends who were coming for a birthday tea.

It was very wet and she had her umbrella up but when she put it down before entering the shop she saw the defendant.

"It was then that I saw him, standing outside." When she was asked who she had seen she answered, "Him there, the man in the dock. The push chair was there as well and I remember thinking that little Jamie would get cold and wet if he was left there for very long."

Mrs Albin then became very emotional as she recalled that it was whilst she was in the shop that, as she so succinctly put it "All hell broke loose. There was such a to-do, Sharon, Jamie's mum, was shrieking at the top of her voice and everyone else was looking all over for the poor little mite." She added that by the time this happened the man had disappeared.

The next witness, Mr Robert Derby, aged 33, gave evidence that as he was driving towards the pelican crossing two hundred metres from the parade of shops where Sam's store is situated he saw a man, matching the defendant's description, hurrying along, pushing a small pram. However when cross examined he was not able to be a hundred per cent certain that the man he had seen was the man sitting in the dock.

The case continues.

Judge's Notes

Poor witnesses.

Both keen to help but neither strong enough to add much to the proceedings.

Mr Derby not one hundred per cent sure.

Mrs Albin better evidence but she didn't actually see anything of consequence.

The man was there, outside the shop, then he wasn't.

Was it even the defendant?

Not enough to convict him!

During my years at Oxford I was once again in my element academically and sailed through my time there, coming out with a First. I could have extended the degree to a fourth year, studying European Law but this did not appeal. I was happy to be qualified to work in England and Wales. I "Ran" for both college and university and having taken up rowing, was selected to represent the university, though, rather disappointingly never taking part in the famous Boat Race against Cambridge. However for me one of the most notable aspects of my years at Oxford was that it was the setting for my next murder. What a good job Inspector Morse and his side-kick, Lewis, were no longer detecting such crimes! I surprised myself (not to mention my victim) as this was a totally unplanned murder, an experience that has, so far at least, never been repeated.

Up to the age of twenty I had managed to avoid all female company finding them insipid, vacuous creatures not worthy of my time. My social life, if you could call it that, consisted of athletics and rowing practices and the occasional evening drinking in the college bar. It was one night following an unusually prolonged drinking session that, on walking down the Cowley Road back to the digs I rented for my second and third years, I was accosted by a creature, a lady of ill repute. She was well past the first bloom of youth and looked ridiculous in her skimpy clothes which revealed a great deal of not particularly enticing flesh.

'Looking for company?' she asked, leering most unattractively.

'How much?' The words were out of my mouth before I was aware I had uttered them.

'We can discuss that later love, depends what you want,' she replied, taking me by the hand.

'I'm Charlene and I'm sure we're going to have a good time.' That was in doubt. She smelt of sweat and the cheap perfume she was no doubt using to cover other bodily odours. I thought that if I breathed in a sufficient quantity it might work as an anaesthetic. She was skeletal and recent needle marks were evident on her arms. She was, taken as a whole, a rather unattractive sight. Her rooms were nearby so I didn't have far to walk with her. Being seen together would have been too embarrassing. I had been wondering for some time what it would be like to experience sex, the act that seemed to occupy most of the other under-graduates' minds for most of the time. This would be my chance. I would then know whether it was something for me - or not.

Charlene lived in the top floor flat of an early twentieth century house not far out of town. From the outside it looked highly respectable and I wondered what her neighbours made of the string of males who I imagined they saw visiting on a regular basis. As we climbed the communal stairs she kept up a mostly one-sided conversation asking me questions about my age, home town and what I was studying at the university. It was somewhat of a surprise to realise that she was extremely well spoken and not without intelligence. However the artificial light coming from a rather incongruous chandelier did little to enhance her looks and I found it hard to determine her age. If she was aiming to put me at my ease with her endless banter she did not succeed.

She led the way into a pleasant apartment and straight into the bedroom. I tried not to think about its numerous previous occupants and aimed at concentrating on the immediate future. The room was rather plebeian, definitely not the den of iniquity I had expected. No handcuffs or other items of bondage were on display and the walls were decorated with rather old fashioned flowered wallpaper. On the bedside table there was a shaded lamp which could have come from any high street outlet. I assumed that the low wattage bulb which gave a feeble light was a deliberate ploy. The bed itself, where I assumed the action was about to take place, looked comfy enough and was covered with a flouncy pink duvet. I hoped the sheets had been changed. No doubt most of her customers needed little to arouse them at this juncture however the room was such a disappointment that any courage I had left me but having come so far I decided to stay and see if the situation improved.

If only she hadn't laughed; if only she hadn't realised it was my first time; if only she hadn't mocked my feeble attempts to initiate proceedings, she would most probably still be alive. So many "if onlys". It was the one time that I lost control during a murder. Let's keep it simple. I throttled her. As I grabbed her pathetic neck my hands moved unbidden and squeezed the life out of her unappealing body. I was a black widow spider in reverse and luckily without the preliminary sex. Oh the ecstasy, the incredible delight that suffused every part of me. I had almost forgotten the rapture I experience when I commit such acts. It is a strange truth that despite the transcendent feeling I experience with each killing I am in no hurry to repeat the process. I am able to control the urge to exterminate another human being, and indeed as I have indicated years go by between my killings. Maybe it is their very infrequency that makes the episodes so rewarding.

Because it was all so spur of the moment, like a customer being tempted by the special offer at the check-out, the one that was not on her shopping list but is too good to resist, I had succumbed without due planning and had therefore taken no steps to avoid detection. Despite the fact that my fingerprints would not be on file I was careful to wipe down any surface with which I had come into contact. Anyone seeing me wiping the door handle as I left might have remembered such strange behaviour. Fortunately no one was about.

On reading the local paper a few days later I learnt that her body had been discovered by Sean, euphemistically referred to as her boyfriend. I had killed Amelia Westgate, aged thirty six, a prostitute well known in the area. The article said very little about her apart from the fact that she had been in court several times for soliciting. Police were making enquiries but so far there were no suspects. That was such a brief summary of a life. I almost felt cheated on her behalf.

However in the days following her death the papers, having completed their rather dubious research, were far more illuminating about the woman I had murdered. How they loved reporting the dirt they had dug up like pigs uncovering truffles. Amelia had begun life as the daughter of a wealthy banker. Reginald Westgate and his wife, Caroline, were socialites, famous in the more elevated echelons of the "London Scene". He had been a monetary adviser to various governments and was a familiar face on political programmes on the television.

Amelia's formative years had been spent at a selection of exclusive boarding schools, experiencing several permanent exclusions. Unfortunately she had become what one paper described as "a wild child, seeking ever more extreme thrills, often involving illegal substances". The principal at her finishing school in Paris said she was, "Out of control, permanently seeking attention but going about it the wrong way." Madame Beaumont added that Amelia was a kind-hearted girl, bright and with a lot of potential that sadly went to waste.

In her mid-twenties her parents disowned her after discovering she was living with Sean, a pimp and drug dealer. "We begged her to come home but she chose a different path," her distraught mother told one of the more sensational tabloids. Many of the papers bemoaned the fact that someone from such a privileged background should descend to a life spent as a prostitute. My sympathies were with Amelia; I knew, only too well, what it was to be on the periphery of one's parent's world.

What a sorry tale. Poor Amelia. All that and then she met me!

Nothing more ever came of that night and I continued with my normal activities which soon included Finals. Many undergraduates claim that their final exams prove to be rather traumatic. Finals, for those of you not au fait with the system, are the exams that are the culmination of three years of study, the results often determining the individual's future. The spectre of receiving lower class degrees or even of total failure is ever present during the long months leading up to the weeks in May when one's accumulation of knowledge and understanding are assessed. A First or Upper Second can lead to further study or excellent job prospects but the pressure to do well is such that some poor souls suffer mental breakdowns and suicide is not unknown.

Having experienced nothing but noteworthy success in my time at Balliol I knew that I had nothing to fear. My final term was spent alternating between long hours of revision and periods of joyful reflection. At a moment's notice I could re-live the exact instant my hands tightened around Amelia's throat. Sheer bliss. My First class degree came as no surprise and fulfilled several tutors' expectations.

I was expecting to leave Oxford a few months after my third killing. I knew I would be sorry to go as I had felt at home in such an exalted academic atmosphere. It had suited me and I had felt comfortable there. My tutor, Dr Edward Goldsborough, said I had a glittering future ahead of me and tried to persuade me to train as a barrister. That was not for me.

Being a specialist in advocacy and pleading my clients' cases would have meant hours ensconced with them, listening to their lies and formulating somewhat dubious cases. I would, like the majority of barristers have been self-employed and worse still would have had to endure the bonhomie of chambers. Standing in court on behalf of some random miscreant did not appeal. Even if I believed their stories and had the information with which to defend them, I would have lacked the necessary empathy, a characteristic which has never been in my repertoire.

During what I assumed would be my final year at Oxford I thought long and hard about my future. I wanted to work within the law in some capacity.

How truly wonderful it would be to be both maintaining and breaking the laws of the country. Then I happened to see an advert for a Legal Adviser in a Magistrates' Court and researched what that would entail.

Information received:

Court legal advisers in England and Wales (sometimes known as court clerks), are qualified lawyers who advise magistrates about the law.

Magistrates serve on a voluntary basis and do not need legal qualifications, so the main duty of a legal adviser is to explain the law and legal procedures to magistrates and others involved in the Youth Court, Family Proceedings Court and licensing committees. The legal adviser might assist with possible sentencing options, but they would never judge a case.

That sounded perfect. I realised that I must undertake specialist training and was delighted to read that Oxford Brookes University offered an appropriate course, a GDL, a Graduate Diploma in Law. Utter joy, another year in that superb city. It wasn't quite like being at Balliol but I was able to continue with my sporting activities and felt fortunate to be able to remain within touching distance of the pinnacle of academia. The year passed all too quickly and I became a qualified lawyer and was able to fulfil my aim of becoming a Legal Adviser.

The first post I saw advertised was in my home town. Whilst at Oxford the last place I wanted to return to was Preston but I decided to apply for the job as I thought I would save some money if I lived at home, the starting salary being rather meagre.

'Hello mother, I've got a job.'

'What good news Benjamin. Where is it?'

'In Preston, at the Magistrates' Court, I thought it would be a good idea to come back home for a while.'

There was a rather stunned silence broken seconds later as she relayed the news, in a rather unenthusiastic voice, to my father. Equilibrium was restored and she managed to tell me that it would be lovely to have me back at home. We both knew she was stretching the truth but at least she had attempted to sound positive. I moved back in a few weeks later and started my career on the right side of the law.

All cases are heard initially in the Magistrates' court. Only five per cent ever see their way to the Crown Court, those deemed too serious for the sentencing powers of the JP's. The vast majority are dealt with by a trio of local people who represent their community. My first day was spent with a delightful threesome, two men and a woman all of whom were far more experienced than I was. If they knew I was a new boy they certainly didn't let it affect the way they treated me and asked for my advice on several occasions. This was the power I craved. I could now influence the immediate future of each person to appear in my court room.

My effect was immediate. The very first case involved a man pleading special circumstances to prevent him from being disqualified from driving. He had totted the infamous twelve points through a mixture of speeding offences and the most recent misdemeanour of driving without insurance. The magistrates listened most carefully to his reasons.

'I drive for a living and if I were to be disqualified I'd lose my job.'

Mr Salmonds, the chairman for the day, a retired bank manager who must have spent an inordinate number of hours listening to a variety of pleas from his customers, asked him in a most benevolent voice whether he'd be able to find other employment that didn't involve driving.

'It would be hard as I'm not really able to do anything else. I'm a delivery man for Tesco's at the moment and I really need to keep this work.'

'Who apart from you depends on your salary, Mr Abbot? For us to allow you to keep driving once you have totted you must be able to prove that others, some dependants, would be adversely affected should you be disqualified.'

'My ex-wife depends on me to contribute to the upkeep of the children. They'd suffer if I couldn't give her the money.'

This was becoming rather tedious. I felt no sympathy for the man who should have thought of that before driving with so little regard for the law. His unemployment benefit would have to be directed towards the family he claimed to support. I hoped I would be asked to assist the magistrates as this was a most pathetic attempt to avoid his due punishment.

It was a good twenty minutes after they withdrew to discuss the matter that I was called through to listen to their reasoning.

'We are totally undecided. The man has given fairly solid reasons for not being disqualified but we are not sure they are strong enough. Have you any advice for us?'

It will not surprise you to know that Mr Abbot was duly disqualified for six months and ordered to pay court costs. Not a bad start to my legal career.

I have been working in Preston Magistrates' Court for the past twenty years, becoming the top man a few years ago. As I sit writing it feels very strange to be in a court playing such a totally different role.

After many years of retirement my father died of a heart attack. He was well in his seventies so had outlasted the Biblical "three score and ten" life expectancy. He loved cricket and would have been pleased to be "bowled out" so cleanly. Just like Pops there was no warning. At least I have a good idea how I will go when the time comes. My father was out playing golf the day before his sudden demise and according to mother he enjoyed an evening watching one of his beloved war films on television. For such a peace loving man he did enjoy watching hundreds killed in battles. He quit this life in a way many of us would choose. Just a few moments of, what I realise must be, rather agonising pain and that was it.

Dead, gone, all over.

The day it happened mother rang me at work. She knew she must only do that in the direst emergency so I realised something was wrong when Amy, one of the court ushers, came to find me.

'Your mum has been on the phone. She wants you to ring her as soon as you can.'

'Did she say why?'

'No, but she did sound a bit upset.'

I rang her immediately, no point putting off the inevitable. 'Hello mother, you rang me.'

'Oh Benjamin, I've got some awful news. It's your dad. He died as he was getting up this morning. Benjamin oh it was horrible, he was in such pain and I couldn't do anything to help. I rang for an ambulance but before they arrived I knew he was gone. Oh it's too much, oh Benjamin what am I going to do without him?'

I made the appropriate noises and said I'd go home as soon as possible after work, no point going before as the girls would be there and I would only feel like a spare part. As I put the phone down I felt unmoved. We had never been close and his departure wouldn't really affect me much at all. When parents die before their children it is the natural order of things, though it has to be acknowledged that there are those amongst us who enjoy disrupting this natural sequence of events.

If my father's sudden demise had little effect on me the repeated use of my name certainly exercised my mind for the rest of the day. To my parents I had always been Benjamin, never the shorter Ben or Bennie or a playful Benny Boo that Pops often used. Perhaps a name is as of little consequence as it was to Shakespeare when he wrote about the rose, but my full name is so formal, such a mouthful and can never be said with affection. But then endearments are only possible between people who share some love. My parents never teased me or indulged in the silliness that most families experience. Life with mother and father had always been a serious affair.

Not so when Pops was around.

'What are you two finding so funny?' mother would ask in a slightly disapproving voice.

'We don't know,' one of us would giggle, having honestly forgotten the cause of such side-splitting hilarity. I have never been anything other than Benjamin to anyone since Pops and I have certainly not enjoyed the realms of such helpless laughter. There are times I wonder whether I have missed out on some of life's lighter moments but then I reassure myself that I have done things that others haven't.

Father's funeral was a rather impressive affair. The minister was one of his best friends and long-time golfing partner, Reverend Michael Hughes, who stood and gazed lovingly at the coffin as he received it at the entrance to the church on a wonderfully bright but blustery morning. The full Church of England service with its time-honoured and rather moving phrases reduced most of the congregation to tears. I considered each of the phrases (no hanky for me) most carefully. Strange to relate it was my first experience of a funeral.

"I am the resurrection and the life, says the Lord, those who believe in me, even though they die, will live, and everyone who lives and believes in me will never die." How I wanted to believe that as it would mean Pops was still alive somewhere. He had certainly been a life-long believer and a truly good man so maybe, just maybe, Pops was in some wonderful new incarnation not yet revealed to mere mortals.

"We brought nothing into the world, and we take nothing out. The Lord gave, and the Lord has taken away; blessed be the name of the Lord." Did that mean that God had taken Pops? How could I believe in a deity who could perform such a deed? He should have given us more time together. Would things have turned out differently if I'd had my grandfather's support for longer?

"Blessed are those who mourn for they shall be comforted." What a load of arrant poppycock. Mourning does not bring comfort, quite the opposite. As you may have gathered the service did little to help me, thought provoking as it was.

The church, with the spring sunshine streaming through the impressive stained-glass windows, was full, which I found rather surprising. Former colleagues, ex-pupils and an assortment of his friends filled the pews and the rendition of his favourite hymn "How Great Thou Art" was sung with gusto at double forte.

'Dad would have loved that, I could almost hear him joining in,' Talia was so distraught that it was hard to tell what she was saying. I hadn't seen her for some time and was surprised at how she had aged.

As people spoke of Edward Richard Doyle I wondered if I was at the wrong service. Was this the man who had been my father? His steadfastness and dedication to duty I could recognise, but why had I never been privy to his sense of humour and generosity? We are all different things to different people but I felt an overwhelming sense of deprivation. I had missed so much that made him "him", a unique and apparently wonderful human being.

The crematorium was so different. Set in beautifully maintained gardens (some of the miscreants from court were assigned there to undertake their hours of unpaid work on a very regular basis) the building itself was ugly. It had a horribly modern edifice in grey stone with no regard for style or any attempt to provide solace for the people forced to use it. The entrance for the mourners was impersonal and was daubed in the obligatory magnolia which was at the stage where it needed repainting. The waiting room was totally impersonal, its only effort at trying to distract the mourners were four rather amateurish water colours showing country scenes one hanging on each wall. We were slightly early and were second in the unsought queue. The small group ahead of us were all seated in an uncomfortable silence, taking up the few available chairs. Everyone was careful to avoid eye-contact which suited me perfectly. Their service was over in fifteen minutes and then it was our turn. It was, all in all, rather like being on a conveyor belt of farewells.

We walked slowly into a bleak room decorated with artificial flowers (surely someone could have been in charge of providing a bunch of real ones every few days). The coffin was brought in and sat in solitary splendour in front of the crimson curtains. We have always been a fairly small family unit and it was just mother, the girls, four grandchildren and me who had gone to say the final goodbye. The short service was a sombre affair. No hymns, no eulogies, merely a rather formulaic prayer by a priest we didn't know and who had no knowledge of the man he was committing to God's loving care. The coffin rolled forward and the curtains closed. For a brief moment I regretted his passing; the man I had hardly known.

As we left the building we were greeted by an unexpected shower.

'Even the clouds are crying,' was the unsolicited remark made by an old gentleman dressed from head to toe in black, no doubt the appropriate garb for his generation of mourners. He must have been well over eighty but walked into the crematorium with a confidence and agility that belied his years. For a brief moment I wondered who was about to be sent on their way: wife, son, daughter or friend? His banal statement affected me and I had to pretend that the rain had got in my eyes. That was one of the very few times when I have felt empathy for a fellow human being, an experience which has, thankfully, seldom been repeated. The day had become overcast both literally and metaphorically. Feeling anything for someone else was something I would guard against in the future, I would be a medieval castle with the portcullis kept permanently down.

The girls had organised an impressive do at the hotel in the middle of town where my parents had gone each year, mother's health permitting, to celebrate their wedding anniversary. The buffet was excellent and I stayed long enough to enjoy it and be seen. I have no recollection of any conversation as I remained in a state of shock at the effect the day had had on me. Normally I was cocooned, unavailable to the effects of unwelcome emotions, but that day I needed to escape and regain my equilibrium.

I went home, changed and set off on a long run. There is always an answer and that was mine.

After my father died I continued to live with mother. That was a mistake, but we've all been to Spec Savers after the event. It was now just mother and me, my sisters having long since left to follow their separate paths. Life at home was fairly uneventful as my mother had her own world of WI meetings, church attendance and coffee mornings, even finding time for lunches with "the girls", none of whom would see sixty again!

There had never been much love lost between us and this did not improve once it was just the two of us. For the vast majority of the time we led separate lives, a situation that suited me perfectly. Occasionally I would wonder what it would be like if I were still loved and I would wish that Pops was there to remind me of that long lost feeling.

Mother was so different when one my sisters came to visit. She would become animated, smiling and laughing, a sound not often heard in our house. Helen, my eldest sibling, was a nurse, a Sister at Lancaster Infirmary in the Paediatrics' department. To this day she remains single but has always seemed to find her job highly rewarding and her many friends sufficient company. She was always the sister I preferred, taking, especially as time went by, a genuine interest in my life. She was the only member of the family who came to watch me run for Lancashire Schoolboys in Wigan, of all places, one wet Saturday morning when I was sixteen.

'Oh Ben, you were amazing. I didn't realise you were that fast. Winning your own race and really it was you that won the relay race, the rest were miles ahead when you took over. I'm really proud of you.'

In the months following father's death, Helen was a frequent visitor. When she came we would go out for lunch, nothing too fancy, a visit to the local Pizzeria or Chinese, but these were special events in an otherwise unvarying existence. Mother would never have dreamt of suggesting the two of us go out socially, for meals, to the cinema or even for walks. All joint holidays stopped once dad was no longer there to organise them. Maybe just as well on thinking about it, remembering the unfortunate happening on the cruise!

Talia was a very different kettle of fish as the saying goes. She was married at eighteen, a necessity as Thomas arrived six months later. She produced three more boys in quick succession but then mislaid a husband who'd had enough of family life and who probably wondered how many more boys would arrive if he stayed. Her visits were a total nightmare. I have said before that I hate babies and they don't seem to improve as they grow up. Mother, however, doted on the boys. They gave her an interest in life that had been lacking. Their photos littered every surface in the lounge and as time went by spread into the hall and kitchen. I don't remember my photos ever being so prominently displayed. She was forever buying them things: clothes, toys, sweets and as they grew older the latest DVDs and computer games. When Talia and her tribe visited I made myself scarce and went off for a long run.

My mother and I remained civil but there was no affection on either side. She continued to look after me physically. My room was cleaned, my washing and ironing done and an evening meal prepared. It was all bearable as I knew that my time at home was limited and that escape beckoned. There was also the knowledge that one day I would repay mother for the unfortunate part she had played in my life. My plan was to settle up with her in the best way I knew: the only way. Years were to elapse before that particular revenge was enacted. Life at home was plebeian and so disappointing following my glorious years away.

I lived at home until the Christmas after father died and perhaps the entry in mother's journal will explain the catalyst to my departure better than I can. Mother had always kept a journal though I was not to discover this uncharacteristic foible for many years. Her entries were more detailed than a diary and were written spasmodically rather than on a daily basis.

Mother's Journal December 25th

What a truly horrible day. It always happens when they all get together but not usually as awful as this. Talia's boys were over excited which didn't help and Benjamin was in one of his silent, morose moods. Thank goodness for Helen. Dinner was almost over, only the boys really making any conversation, mostly about what Father Christmas had brought. Then Talia did what she often does and started to tease Benjamin. She asked him if he had a girlfriend now he was working and earning a lot of money. We all know that he has never had a girl and probably never will. He just glowered at her and said nothing. That seemed to incense her and she asked how he spent his leisure time. What did he do in his room all day? Look at dirty images on the computer? Benjamin went mad, really lost it and stormed out saying he was going to find a flat and live on his own and have nothing to do with any of us. Thank goodness the boys were watching The Lion King in the other room by the time this blew up. Benjamin stayed in his room for the rest of the day and Helen and Talia left soon after. Oh happy families!

When the others had gone home I had such a headache I took one of Benjamin's sleeping tablets, I don't think he knows that he left a packet here. They are such a help I must ask the doctor for some.

I have all of mother's journals and they make for very boring reading although there are some interesting entries and they do at least prove my theory that she had few feelings for me as I seldom feature in them and on the few occasions I am mentioned it is usually in negative terms. They do however help to support my decision to do what I did. But more of that later.

Life in a Magistrates' Courthouse can be very interesting or, on occasion, excruciatingly monotonous. The good days involve a variety of cases, each one different with lively characters, both defendants and lawyers, appearing before the Bench. Since that first day when I had such influence I have loved the role of being an advisor. Admittedly much of the time the magistrates don't need much help as the cases can be very straight-forward and their Sentencing Guidelines tome suffices. However at times they need advice on points of law and that is where I come into my own. I have been told that I am very "clear, concise and helpful" so I must be good at the job. The days that are the most satisfying are when I am called out frequently to the retiring room to aid their decision making. It's strange that this is the only human contact where I feel comfortable. Perhaps it is because I am the one with the knowledge and the authority.

Defence lawyers are apt to annoy me. The lies they tell on behalf of their clients can reduce me to a state of almost uncontrollable rage. Being a total professional I never show my feelings and my court room runs as smoothly as a golf ball over a newly mown green. I tell myself that they are doing their job and doing it well, but it makes me glad that I didn't go in for that aspect of the law. I may be many things but I seldom tell anything but the truth ("the whole truth and nothing but the truth" may be a bit of a stretch!)

Our "clients", presumed innocent until proven other-wise, are a motley group; from the first time offenders who quiver and often cry in court and who look guilty even when innocent, to the "regulars" the recidivists, the ones who when asked for their address might as well give the Magistrates' Court as they spend so much of their useless lives with us. Most of the time I am almost unaware of them as individuals being more concerned that the details of the law are being observed. However, just occasionally, one of them cuts across my radar. One such individual showed disrespect in my arena and really made me take notice and no one wants to make me do that. My next killing became inevitable, as certain as the next tide in Morecambe Bay. It started the day Simon Bell, a young man with a lengthy record, appeared, yet again, in court and on this occasion made me aware of him.

Simon Bell was exceptionally good looking. In his mid-thirties he had retained a youthful appearance. He was considerably above average height with very dark hair and blue eyes, the proverbial "tall, dark and handsome" as one of the female ushers described him, adding that he would have no problem attracting the ladies. I told her that he had already sired two children by different partners but did not reside with either of them. Unlike many of the miscreants we see in court he was smartly dressed, almost certainly having been advised by his lawyer to make a good impression which indeed, as far as that went, he did.

Mr Bell was well known to the Magistrates having appeared many times, until the age of eighteen, in the Youth Court where he had received a variety of punishments from ASBO's to short stays in the Young Offenders' Institute in Lancaster. More recently the Adult Court had had the pleasure of his company on a very regular basis. On this particular occasion he was back in court for breaking his bail conditions by not observing his curfew. The previous bench had released him on bail, pending his appearance in the Crown Court for Aggravated Burglary. One of the terms of the bail was that he wore a curfew tag and remained indoors, at his place of residence, from eight p.m. to six a.m. He had broken the curfew on no fewer than five occasions in the previous two weeks. Thus it was that on a morning in mid-July he was brought up from the cells, where he had spent, I hoped, an uncomfortable night after being arrested, without bail, the previous evening.

'Good morning your worships, we have full day scheduled,' I said as I walked into their retiring room. It was my job to see the magistrates before court began at ten in the morning and give them the list of people who were due to come before them. We then had time to make sure they did not know any of the people due to appear or any of the witnesses in a trial. We could also discuss any special issues or points of interest. This was a time of the day that I enjoyed as they were, almost exclusively, friendly and keen to deliberate and learn as much as possible about the various cases. They were mostly of mature years, and all were there to do their civic duty, on a voluntary basis, no payment despite hours spent deliberating and deciding important issues. For the most part they managed to retain a sense of humour, despite the often appalling cases they were asked to deal with and it was the one time when I found myself laughing with other people.

'What a surprise, Simon Bell! It seems like only yesterday that I was on the Bench that gave him this curfew. It's not taken him long to break it,' said the Chairman of the day, Cecily Walters, a retired dentist and one of the kindest and most caring people on the magistrates' list. 'The question is how do we help someone like him? We thought a curfew might give him time to think about his behaviour as well as keeping the streets of Preston Simon-free for a few nights.'

'Can we help him? If he can't abide by the rules of the court then he must expect further, more stringent, punishment,' this was Nigel Lott, taking the words right out of my mouth. Nigel was ex-military and could be relied on to hand down the strictest punishments within the Magistrates' jurisdiction. He was never vindictive but thought that crimes had to receive their due penalties. A man after my own heart as the old saying goes.

'You have a few options,' I replied, 'you can re-sentence adding additional days to the period of his curfew; you can change his bail conditions so that he no longer has a curfew or you can retain him in custody until his hearing in the Crown Court.' Now the latter would have been my choice, but I wasn't the one with the ultimate say. However I thought he was long overdue to "face the music" and I hoped that the morning's J.P.s would agree.

Simon's first mistake was to swagger as he was brought, in handcuffs, into the locked-in part of the courtroom, the section partitioned and reserved for those in custody. What a prelude! He showed no remorse or understanding that his life was about to take a turn for the worse. The theme, definitely in B flat minor, was his continual scowl at the trio whom he surely realised had his immediate future in their hands. He had obviously been absent from school the day the teacher talked about winning friends and influencing people. The cadenza was the amusing excuses his lawyer, the rather inept Miss Ellis, attempted to make, everyone except young Simon realising that they were falling on deaf ears, not good for any music. The coda was the sentence that had been my final suggestion and he was duly remanded in custody until his appearance at the Crown Court.

'You can't do that. What gives you lot the right to take my fucking liberty away? Bloody stupid, you're just a load of old has-beens, past your sell-by-dates; don't know what you're doing. Fucking hell - keeping me in until my hearing. That means I've lost my job. Ta, thanks very much.' Simon was well spoken though his language left something to be desired. At that point his lawyer managed to interrupt the flow and indicated to the warders to take her client back down to the cells. The not so dulcet tones resumed and could be heard as he descended the steps.

I knew what the next part of his symphony would be. The second movement would be an adagio in jail, time moving very slowly then, oh joy, a lively, if brief scherzo with me. I had my next victim. He really should have shown a better attitude. After all, it was my court he was "dissing".

I met that day's Bench for a post-court review, usually a time when I could reassure the trio that their decision making had been appropriate, though as they sought my advice so regularly during most cases any hiccup was ironed out at the time. We spent a few minutes going over the day's proceedings and then got to the finale of the day.

'I don't think Mr Bell was very happy with our decision,' Cecily murmured, 'what a pity.'

'He had it coming, we've been very patient with him in the past,' David Cook, a long-serving and most able man added.

'I don't think you'll want to hear this Mr Doyle, but you and Simon look quite alike, in fact you could be mistaken for brothers. Sorry to say that as I know he is not your favourite client,' Cecily's statement was so ridiculous that it was all I could do not to yell at her, but I knew I had to hide my antagonism so I attempted an enigmatic smile. David Cook must have seen my discomfort as he added, 'At least you and he don't have law-breaking activities in common.' My goodness, how little the man knew.

Cecily was determined to continue the conversation, 'Mr Bell must be quite bright, he went to Preston Grammar, I only know that because one day last year Paul Denver was due to be the Chairman but when he saw Mr Bell's name on the list he had to be excused from taking part in that particular sitting as he had taught him. Paul did say that as a boy Simon was clever but was inclined to associate with the wrong crowd and was frequently in trouble, even then.'

I had heard enough. Bidding them a rather cold farewell I escaped to my office to complete the day's paperwork. That evening I needed a very long run.

I had plenty of time to plan this murder. A good thing as it was going to be the most difficult to date. So far the ones that I had performed had been undetectable, no direct links to me apart from the fact that I was in the vicinity for each one. I doubted that any police equipment, however sophisticated, would connect the death of an old lady in Preston (foul play was never suspected), a baby disappearing in the Mediterranean (parents deemed to be involved) and a prostitute found throttled in Oxford (dodgy client: unknown). However with this murder I had to be extra careful as it would be very close to home. Simon Bell lived near the house I had purchased on leaving home. There was the added problem that we had come into contact through the court. There must be no way the police could think that I was implicated.

A few weeks after starting to plan his early, but all too appropriate, demise I began to have palpitations. Given my family history I thought I ought to have a check-up so made an appointment at the local surgery. I had signed on when I moved to the area but had had no reason to see a doctor for many years, the need for sleeping tablets I had requested when living at home having abated. An evening appointment was made with a Doctor Wagstaffe. The lateness of the appointment meant there was no need for time off work or the need for any explanation.

As I walked into his room I almost turned round and walked straight back out. He was so young. He looked as though he should still be in a classroom and a Primary one at that! Two thoughts passed in rapid succession through my mind: either he was too young and inexperienced to know what he was doing and would be unable to help me, or he was fresh out of training school and would know all the latest thinking on heart problems. I went with the second option and sat down.

'Good evening Mr Doyle. I don't think we've met. My name is Hugh Wagstaffe. How can I help you?' His southern accent seemed out of place in the middle of Preston but he had certainly attended the bedside manner sessions.

'I've been having palpitations, a tight chest and it feels as though my heart is racing at times. We have a family history of heart problems so I thought I should have a check-up.'

It was then that I knew I shouldn't have come. I remembered why I avoided doctors like the plague, though even I would have sought help with that particular disease. He asked me, in great and I felt intrusive detail, what I meant by my family history. I told him about dad and Pops and to my utter horror I realised, quite suddenly, that I was weeping; that totally unbidden, a torrent of tears was coursing down my face. My throat was constricted and my breathing became laboured. I was out of control, a feeling I cannot abide.

Give him his due he didn't react or ask any questions, which at that juncture I would have been incapable of answering. No, the man just slipped a box of tissues quietly across his desk. After what felt like a very long time self-control was resumed.

'How long ago did your father and grandfather die?' he asked, his tone unbearably kind, re-opening the flood gates. This time they were less Niagara Falls force and more a Lake District cascade, but still they flowed.

'Take your time, there's no hurry. We can talk when you're ready,' he continued trying to be helpful.

My voice when it spoke was not my own, it was as though I was being controlled by a ventriloquist. 'My father died a few years ago and Pops when I was ten.'

'That is a long time for you to still be feeling so strongly about their deaths and for them to have such a profound effect on you. Have you ever thought of counselling?'

Oh dear God not that again.

'I saw the family doctor and a psychiatrist at the time,' I said, mentally adding "and it was a total waste of time".

'Well things have moved on a lot in the intervening years and many people find talking to someone helps. I can suggest a six week course with our Practice counsellor. Some people need more and others require fewer sessions. A lady I sent recently had one meeting and because of a suggestion the counsellor made said that she was able to deal with her problems and never went back. It's probably worth a try.'

I said that I would think about it and get back in touch, which of course I never did. If truth be told, and as you must be beginning to realise I always aim for that, I have never had any desire to get over Pop's death. That would mean that I no longer cared, that the future was bearable without him. To keep him close I have to continue to suffer, to re-live his demise every day. People might say that my suffering is therefore self-inflicted but it keeps me focussed, it keeps me in touch with him.

The doctor then examined me physically and found nothing wrong. He said he would send me to the hospital for further tests and again I asked for time to think. Throughout the following months planning the next murder the symptoms continued but I forced myself to ignore them.

The one thing I asked for were some more sleeping tablets. I hadn't taken any for years and didn't need them. This prescription was not for me. Temazepam was the most popular and widely prescribed hypnotic at the time and Dr Wagstaffe seemed happy to provide a prescription for twenty-eight of the ten milligram tablets. On returning home I looked Temazepam up on the internet and was interested to discover that an overdose can be fatal, especially if taken with alcohol. A study showed that the drug has the highest number of deaths per million prescriptions. If taken with alcohol death by alcohol poisoning becomes more likely. I doubt whether I will need to explain why I started to order a repeat prescription every six months. One cannot be too well prepared.

Chapter 7

Daily Gazette

Tragic Mother Tells Her Story

Tears were the order of the day as Sharon Richardson took the stand to give her evidence in the trial for the appalling murder of her tiny son, Jamie. She wept as she said how guilty she felt for having left her "precious, darling little boy" outside the shop. She added that she was only inside for a few minutes and was "totally freaked" when she found he was missing.

Ms Richardson was adamant she had seen the defendant approaching the store as she parked Jamie's pram near the entrance. She acknowledged that she only knows the man in the dock by sight as they had never spoken. The packed courtroom was then told that her suspicions were aroused when the man was no longer anywhere around by the time she came out and realised that Jamie had gone and she was sure he had not entered the shop.

Under cross examination Sharon admitted that she has an older child in care and that Social Services were monitoring Jamie's progress. There followed a few moments of uproar as Sharon's mother informed the court that busybodies were always interfering and that her daughter was an excellent mother.

The judge, Sir Cecil Montgomery, restored calm and instructed the jury to ignore the last few comments. He said that Sharon was not on trial for her skills as a mother. The defence lawyer, the impressive Mrs Deidre Hannigan, was asked to change her line of questioning.

Under further cross examination Ms Richardson remained adamant that the man she had seen outside the shop was the man in the dock.

Judge's Notes

I recall laughing when I saw who the defendant had as his defence counsel. Deidre and I go back a long way and I have presided over many cases where she has defended both the innocent and the obviously guilty with equal relish. She has a superb track record and if anyone can get this man off she can. Many a criminal has walked free thanks to her inestimable skills.

It was obvious what she was doing today, one of the oldest tricks in the almost legal book. Put doubt in the jurors' minds as to the credibility of a witness. Sharon is shown to be an inadequate mother ergo she is a poor witness and her testimony is unsound. Good try Deidre!

By the time I spoke to the jury the damage was done. Very little point asking them to ignore what they have just heard.

Richardson senior, a formidable woman, hardly helped her daughter's cause with her raucous outburst. Bet the paper's don't quote her verbatim. She used words I haven't heard for a very long time!

I realised that the method I would use to kill Simon Bell was almost impossible to determine until he was released from prison and resumed his normal (if anything about that worthless individual could be deemed normal) life. Through my contacts at court I knew I would hear about his release date though I must not appear to be taking too much of an interest. Because he couldn't control himself in prison he served almost all his sentence, no remission for good conduct for him, and it was almost three months before he came to live amongst us again.

They say that serial killers don't commit their crimes too close to home. There is the obvious danger of being recognised by someone who knows them. However I knew that Simon Bell's murder needed to be committed in Preston. I no longer had a car as the property I had purchased had no parking facilities and the garage where I had kept my old Ford became unavailable. Had I attempted to kill Simon beyond the precincts of Preston I would have had to use public transport and taken an even more prolonged risk of being seen.

On leaving prison Simon was found employment with the invaluable aid of the Probationary Service. It was not a particularly desirable job, but one that his probation officer hoped might keep him out of trouble. I had severe reservations. The infamous Mr Bell was bound to reoffend given sufficient time and temptation. He reminded me of one of our previous "clients" who, on release from the nick, had been given a job in a Kentucky Fried Chicken outlet. He decided to take a large amount of money from the safe in the office, in full view of the CCTV camera and using his own code!! Needless to say that particular miscreant made yet another appearance in court and was returned to jail.

Simon was given the job of stacking shelves at our local Asda store. As these need replenishing when there are fewest customers he started work at ten p.m. and finished at six in the morning. Finding this information out was straightforward as one of the Legal Advisers in my department was married to Philip, the probation officer in charge of Simon's welfare.

'Philip said that he was lucky to get that job and hopes that he appreciates it,' Marie stated one morning as we met in the staffroom.

'I doubt whether that particular villain appreciates much that is done for him,' I replied.

'Strangely Philip seems to quite like him and says there is a good man in there somewhere and he thinks that Simon just needs help to stay on the straight and narrow.'

'With his track record? I remain to be convinced. To me he's a bad 'un through and through. Waste of the public's money trying to sort that villain out.'

'I'll pass on your words of encouragement to Philip!'

'Please do, I admire him for trying but I wouldn't have his job at any price. Do keep me informed of any developments.'

I thought that I needed a break and that an extended respite would afford me the time to devise the best method to use on Simon. Little did I think that it would lead to a new, totally unexpected, and of necessity quickly planned ending of a life. The holiday was to provide my next, extremely satisfying, murder. Holidays do one such good.

As well as my twice weekly running sessions I have always gone walking on my own. By going alone I have no need to converse with others whilst enjoying the mental and physical exercise a walk provides. Striding out my head fills with thoughts that I have no desire to share. Unaccompanied, I can stop whenever I want, to look at a view or for some refreshment. I can go at my own pace and walk as far as I see fit. So why, oh why, did I decide to join a hiking group? The advertisement in the "Walker's Weekly," a magazine to which I have subscribed for years in order to discover new routes in the North West, looked interesting. It was for a fortnight's "walking in the amazing and life-affirming scenery" of Switzerland, a country that I had sometimes thought about visiting. The maximum group size was twenty five, minimum age ten. I loathe groups but at least there would be no young children. My thinking was that it would be an excellent way to experience walking in the Alps, something I would not have felt brave enough to try on my own. So I signed up and paid the extortionate fee, due in total as the holiday was just a few weeks off. I actually enjoyed buying new waterproof trousers, strong boots, and a pair of ski-type sticks. I changed a huge amount of English money into Swiss Francs as I had heard it was a very expensive country. I was ready.

The group, twenty one of us, met at Manchester airport early one Saturday morning in mid-August. Our flight was due to leave at just before eight but was delayed. That gave me a chance to study my fellow travellers. There were six couples, one with a boy who sat constantly chewing and who remained plugged into his iPod. The rest of us were "singles", five men, including me, and three women. Our ages appeared to range from the boy, who looked too young to fit the company's profile, but who I later learnt he had just had his tenth birthday, to a couple in their late seventies. Looking around I didn't feel that I would have much in common with any of them and I had no desire to sit and participate in meaningless conversations. One of the single women, of indeterminate age, thought otherwise and talked at me for an hour before we were allowed to board the plane. To this day I have absolutely no recollection of a word she said. For the next two weeks I was careful to avoid her as much as possible.

The flight was uneventful and I was able to sit apart from the group, there would be more than enough time to socialise over the next fortnight. Zurich airport was highly efficient and enjoyed many original features including a wall of cascading water, a prelude to the numerous waterfalls the country boasts. Once through passport control there was just a short walk and two escalator rides down to the railway station situated most conveniently below the airport itself.

We validated our rail passes and got on the first of the many trains we were to travel on that holiday. Swiss trains are famous for their efficiency. They run as meticulously to time as the country's equally renowned cuckoo clocks and should one be even a few minutes behind schedule an apology is delivered in four languages over the intercom. The trains leave their stations at the same time every hour, departing not just to the minute but to the second. Travelling by Swiss Rail it was amusing to watch the platform clock and observe that, as the second hand moved to the vertical, and the minute hand to the allotted time, the doors clanged shut and the train would move off. Eat your heart out, British Rail!

Once we had passed through the city of Zurich the railway journey to Grindelwald, our base for two weeks, was truly spectacular. The Bernese Oberland must have some of the most beautiful scenery on the planet and for the three hours that the journey took there wasn't a single view that disappointed. We were undertaking the longer, even more beautiful train journey that goes via Lucerne. It was there that we changed to our second train, a swift and easy transfer. After an hour we went over the Brunner Pass. They say the Swiss have no sense of humour but the carved wooden bears, goats and birds that stood beside the line were surely meant to amuse. The gradient of the pass necessitates the use of rack and pinion rails and strange noises emanated from beneath the train as it caught hold and lumbered up then sauntered down the sides of the pass. The views were amazing but were surpassed as we were transported beside Lake Brienz to Interlaken. I was in the lakes and mountains!

From Interlaken we took our final train up to Grindelwald, the train dividing in Zweilutschinen, the front half going on to Lauterbrunnen and Wengen and the back portion travelling via more rack and pinion tracks to the ever popular resort of Grindelwald, famous as both a winter and summer resort. It was most entertaining at Zweilutschinen to watch people dashing along the platform, in both directions, to get on the desired part of the train, a surprising number having got it wrong.

'Collect your cases and I'll meet you in reception in a few minutes,' Dan, our guide for the next fortnight, bellowed at us as though we were a party of rather slow school children. The hotel, the Derby, was at the side of the small station, practically on the tracks. In England it would, almost certainly, have been called "The Railway Hotel". It looked comfortable enough though I hoped my room would face the famous Eiger, the mountain of legends. Sadly, for the next fourteen days, my single room faced the endless procession of trains, though I must add that the mountains beyond were rather grand with snow covered peaks even in summer.

Dinner time that first night was horrendous. Fortunately the food was delicious and the dining room was most comfortable and welcoming and very Swiss, with gingham curtains and identical table clothes covering the carved wooden tables. Happy Swiss music played in the background and the whole affair should have been exceedingly pleasant. The problem was that there were too many jolly people all being ridiculously friendly and attempting to share every last boring detail about their lives, whilst at the same time trying to learn as much as possible about everybody else. Not my scene at all. If they considered me unforthcoming they didn't show it but then I rather doubt that most even noticed me, keen as they were to chatter mindlessly on and on. The evening lasted until well after my normal hour of retirement, by which time I was almost at screaming point.

Dan informed us that breakfast would be at half past seven with the morning walk commencing at eight forty-five. He amused others, but not me, by saying that he was keeping the first walk a secret, a surprise. 'It's a beautiful route. I know you'll all love it. Not too strenuous for the first day, but walking boots and sticks are recommended. Oh and don't forget your cameras, lots of photo opportunities.' Once again he sounded as though he were addressing a group of Special Needs children.

Going up to my room, without wishing anyone a 'Good night' or as Henry, the father of Marcus, the ten year old, insisted on saying, 'Gutten nacht,' I realised that I had made a huge mistake coming on this holiday. I would go on the morning walk then decide whether I spent the remainder of the time discovering my own hikes. I was capable of reading a map and surely anything was preferable to a fortnight spent listening to inane conversations. Small talk has never been my forte.

I slept surprisingly well, only waking as the first train left the station just before six thirty. I got ready very quickly so was able to go to the dining room and finish my breakfast before most of the others came down. Anthea, a retired teacher and on her hundredth trip to the Alps, was already eating when I arrived but I pretended not to see her and sat at the other end of the room. I hoped that people would soon realise that I had not gone on this trip for company and would leave me alone.

'Good morning, I trust everyone feels refreshed and ready for an amazing day. We're leaving in ten minutes, I'll meet you all on Platform One.' Dan was determined to make sure we got the most out of the holiday and we invariably set off before most holiday makers were even up which was most fortuitous as by mid-morning the trains were packed.

The introductory walk that Dan had arranged for us was delightful. We caught the train back down to Zweilutschinen, so named as two rivers meet there, the White and the Black. They are aptly named and do appear to be different colours though grey and cream might be more apposite. There is an interesting spot just beyond the station where they meet and merge, the two colours blending. At that point the, by now, single river enjoys a steep descent and the water broils and bubbles like a witches' broth as it begins its long downward journey to Lake Brienz.

We were rounded up and began the two hour hike up to Lauterbrunnen, an exhilarating walk beside another fast moving river that bounced and danced over huge boulders.

'Do you do a lot of walking?' Jenny, a middle-aged lady who I had so far managed to avoid, asked obviously wanting to engage me in conversation as we walked. I muttered a very brief reply. She was not to be easily deterred. 'I think I should have broken my new boots in before we came. They are already starting to rub, so silly of me.' That surely didn't warrant any response. Just as well as I would have used a far stronger word than silly! I then made sure I accelerated to the front where Dan was already talking to Marcus's dad so I could proceed in peace.

It was as we left the village that there was a communal gasp as we turned a corner and saw a spectacular waterfall plummeting down the side of a mountain. 'That is the Staubbach Falls, at two hundred and seventy metres it is one of the highest in Europe formed by a single unbroken descent.' There were to be many times when Dan sounded rather like a talking extract from Google but he was knowledgeable and kept us well informed.

Anthea had to let the rest of us know that she was equally well informed and au fait with the area. I could hear her teacher's voice as she declared, 'That waterfall is probably one of the most impressive in the Bernese Oberland. Not many have such an uninterrupted drop.' Were others hoping that she might suffer one of those before too long? No don't get excited the old girl was not about to become my next victim, that privilege would fall (pardon the pun) to a far younger member of the party.

The walk seemed to get better with every step and I was truly delighted by the remainder of the morning's hike up the valley looking at the most breath-taking scenery which included the famous Jungfrau.

Dan "Googled" us again.

'The Jungfrau has been called the most beautiful mountain in the world,' he informed us with an enthusiasm that was never to waver. 'She is the highest of the famous trio, the other two being the Eiger and the Monch, and she is four thousand one hundred and eighty-five metres high. The nuns of Interlaken are supposed to have named her. She was at the time unclimbed and was snow covered and white all year. They said that as she was both inaccessible and virginal they would name her the "young maiden".

The mountain was first conquered on August third 1811 by two brothers Johannes and Hieronymous Meyer from Aaran. Soon mountaineers from all parts of the world were opening up new routes to the top. In 1893 work began, that was to last sixteen years, to construct tunnels carrying trains up to the Jungfraujoch or as it is now known "The Top of Europe" reaching an impressive three thousand and fifty-four metres. The journey from Kleine Scheidegg takes fifty minutes and today tourists make the ascent in their thousands.' So much detail, and all quite interesting - though her beauty alone would have sufficed.

The weather that first day was perfect. The one thing that spoilt the excursion was Marcus. What an obnoxious child he was. From the start he was complaining.

'My feet are sore'

'How long is this boring walk?'

'When are we having lunch?'

He droned on and on. He would, without doubt, have been made the captain of the England Schoolboy Moaners, should such a unit exist.

On the optional afternoon walk back down the valley, the alternative being to catch the local bus which no one did, we were encouraged to visit the famous gorge, the Trummelbach waterfalls. A memorable experience. The water, twenty thousand litres every second, gushes, rumbles and explodes through a series of incredible gorges inside the mountain. The torrents transport the glacier water from the incomparable trio of the Eiger, Monch and Jungfrau. Nature at its most spectacular. The one unfortunate aspect of the visit was that Marcus was in full voice, albeit sounding reasonably enthusiastic to begin with then reverting to type and demanding sustenance. I had an almost irresistible urge to push him over the edge into the dramatic deluges below. Coming straight from the glaciers the water remains at an extremely cold temperature and I doubt whether the lad would have survived very long. It was there, gazing at those unique glacial waterfalls, the only ones in the whole of Europe that are accessible inside a mountain, that my next murder became as inevitable as the first fall of winter snow.

It would be him! No child should be allowed to spoil an adult's pleasure and so far he had done exactly that. What should have been a truly awesome experience was blighted by the raucous caterwauling's emanating from his almost permanently dissatisfied mouth.

'What time are we going back? This is dead boring.'

'I've seen enough and I've eaten all my chocolate.'

'Why did we have to come on this stupid holiday? I'd rather have stayed at home.'

I suspect I was not alone in wishing he had got his last wish. With what vehemence I loathed that child but maybe you are getting the picture. Yes you probably worked it out before I did that dear little Marcus had to be the next and perhaps the perfect murder.

Chapter 8

Daily Gazette

More Evidence Presented in Murder Trial

The prosecution questioned Mrs and Mrs Kemp, the owners of the shop where tragic toddler, Jamie Richardson, was snatched in May this year. Mrs Muriel Kemp, aged fifty six, was questioned at length. She said that she knew the man in the dock as he was a regular who for many years had popped in several times a week.

In her evidence she said that she had seen him near the shop on the day in question as she returned from her weekly visit to her Cash and Carry outlet. There was laughter in the court when she said that she always noticed him and her husband regularly teased her about him and said she was looking for a "toy-boy"!

When cross examined Mrs Kemp had to admit that she couldn't be one hundred per cent certain that the day she was thinking of was the day Jamie was snatched but said, "I am pretty sure as I had collected stock on the day all hell broke loose."

Mr Roger Kemp, aged fifty nine, was confident that he saw the defendant in his shop on the relevant day. He said he remembered the day in question as the papers were full of the weekend's football and his club, Blackburn Rovers, had won six-nil which had helped their chances of staying in the Premier League. "Didn't work we were relegated two week later," he added and was asked, by the judge, to make sure he kept his answers relevant to the questions asked and not to add irrelevant information. Mr Kemp said that although he'd seen the defendant wearing a Preston shirt they had never discussed football as the man wasn't one to chat. When questioned further he repeated that the day the boy was abducted was the day when the big football score was headline news.

Both Mr and Mrs Kemp gave vivid accounts of the moment when Sharon, a regular customer in the shop, discovered that Jamie was missing. By this time they thought that the defendant had left the shop but when cross examined neither witness could say for certain if that was the case or how long he had been gone before Jamie's mother realised her son was missing. They said that the shop was busy and it was impossible to be sure exactly who was there at that moment. Several of the customers started to search for the toddler. It was Mr Kemp who phoned the police and they arrived on the scene within a matter of minutes.

The case continues and we as a responsible paper will keep you fully informed of all future proceedings.

Judge's Notes

The jury looked confused by today's witnesses.
Fact: both Mr and Mrs Kemp know the defendant
Fact: he is a customer in their shop
Fact: they saw him outside the shop

Disputed information: did they see him on the day in question and did he enter the shop?

Collecting stock and Blackburn Rovers distorted their evidence until it was as clear as the proverbial mud.

Neither remained certain (amazing how swearing on the Bible concentrates the mind and one is careful not to commit perjury) and the evidence is poor when witnesses admit that they cannot be one hundred per cent sure.

I think that the jury has, in my opinion quite rightly, been left with strong doubts as to the validity of their evidence.

What pathetic evidence, if that is the best the CPS can come up with the verdict may not be a foregone conclusion.

Back to Marcus. It did seem a shame to mar such glorious scenery with such a dire act. But it had to be done. I prefer to plan my killings, down to the last miniscule detail. Two reasons for this: less chance of discovery and, for me, infinitely more satisfying. As the old saying goes "If a thing is worth doing it's worth doing well". But meticulous planning is not always possible and this was one of those occasions. I had days, twelve at the most, not only to prepare but also to accomplish the deed.

As you will be aware, the trouble with the annihilation of a child is the parents. They are ever watchful, aware that the world is a dangerous place, hidden perils lurking around every corner. Henry and Margaret Parker were no exception. I learnt that Marcus was an only child, born long after they had given up hope of having any offspring. Oh that that had remained the situation. But no, along came Marcus in all his obnoxious glory. The boy was thoroughly spoilt.

Thesaurus words for spoilt: failed, substandard, ruined, inferior, indulged, pampered, cossetted pandered to, blighted, impaired etc.

Need I go on? Have you understood? He was all of these and therefore his existence must not be allowed to continue. The world would be a pleasanter place without his presence and the holiday would have passed without any tragic incident.

But how to rid the world of him? After seven days I was beginning to think that it was an impossible task. Then came the day when we all trooped down to watch the Interlaken/Jungfrau marathon. I have taken part in a few English marathons but this one was a new experience and I was thankful that I was just watching. It was far more challenging than any race I had ever entered.

The Swiss marathon has an entry limit of four thousand runners and the event is so popular that all the available places are snapped up months in advance. Over four hundred countries are represented and in the past there have been British winners. Each year the race begins at half past nine, on the dot, in the main street of Interlaken. The first part is relatively easy; once round the town then along to Wilderswil. After that it is all, and the word is most definitely all, uphill. The gradient to Lauterbrunnen is fairly gentle unlike the remainder of the run, to Wengen then the final climb to Kleine Scheidegg. Most impressively the winner that day took less than two hours to complete the gruelling challenge.

All twenty of us watched the start and then took the local trains up to the finishing line. We had the easy part. It was whilst we were waiting for the first runners to appear that I noticed how often Marcus left the group. Each time one of his parents would search for him and return him to the fold. They were ridiculously patient with his wanderings and never chastised him, just seemed to find his meanderings amusing.

'Oh Marcus, Minikins, where have you been?'

'Stay with us dear boy, don't wander off. What would mummy and daddy do if they couldn't find you?

'One of these times you might be taken by the mountain trolls,' were just some of the endearments he received, from his oh so indulgent parents.

I had my plan. Should he remove himself from the group whilst on a walk I could pounce, the predator could dispatch his prey. What a shame the Pied Piper's mountain opening wasn't available. My mind went in to overdrive as I knew I had the beginning of an idea. As soon as Dan talked us through the next hike I would consult the map, work out the route down to the tiniest detail and start to work out places where the child might absent himself in a gloriously dangerous locality. It was so deliciously simple, so unbelievably obvious that I couldn't understand why I had not thought of it before.

'Gather round folks,' our endlessly cheerful leader said, wanting to tell us about the following day's walk. I have to give him his due and say that he was an excellent guide and the walks were unfailingly impressive, though that was at least partly due to the wonders of the Bernese Oberland.

'Tomorrow we are going on a walk of walks and I know you will all love it. We're getting the train down to Lauterbrunnen then the cable car up to Grutschalp and then we'll hike along to Murren. The views along that particular path are breath-taking, so do remember your cameras. We will then have lunch in Murren before walking on for a further two hours down to Stechelberg. You'll be glad to know it's then the local bus back down the valley,' at this several of the group smiled.

'How long will we be out?' Anthea asked, 'if it's longer than normal I'll need to take my pills.'

Dan's reply made me smile, 'Most of the day, we might not be back until very late in the afternoon.' Plenty of time, yes surely plenty.

The route was a clarion call to action. Oh how wonderful those Germanic names sounded: Grutschalp, Murren, Stechelberg. All I had to do was study the map and find some suitable places, spots where the, to me, inevitable extinction of Marcus might occur.

The afternoon section of the planned hike looked the most promising with a path that meandered through thick forest. Perhaps, once there, I could suggest to the boy that we went on ahead, lead the way, forage through the undergrowth, forge a path; that might appeal to him. There appeared to be sufficient bends in the path to create places where we would be unobserved. I also noted that a lot of the track was beside rather steep drops. The elation I feel when a plan starts to fall into place was present and was almost uncontrollable but I knew that the following day I must remain calm and appear to be part of, and blend in with, the crowd.

Dinner that night was a special affair: a Swiss Gala evening. The country's red and white flags adorned every surface and a trio of musicians were adding to the jolly atmosphere. The double bass player was excellent though the accordionist was rather amateurish and the gentleman who alternated between the clarinet and a caterwauling yodelling did little for me. The meal was certainly delicious and typically Swiss with a thick barley soup followed by an exceedingly filling rosti or roschti as the natives spell it. Rosti was originally a traditional dish of grated potatoes which farmers ate for breakfast. Our version was far more sophisticated and included bacon, onions, cheese and apples. Had I not been almost unable to conceal my excitement, and thus draw attention to myself, I would have indulged in seconds. The selection of sweets, presented on three groaning tables in the dining room's alcove, would not have been out of place on a cruise ship. Marcus took full advantage of these and for once I didn't begrudge him, thinking of the apocryphal condemned man and his last meal.

That evening I forced myself to be sociable and engaged in conversations with most of our company. It did not come easily but as they were more than happy to talk about themselves I was able to say very little. Anything I did add to the conversation was pure fabrication. I was slightly perturbed to realise that I quite liked Marcus's parents who came across as decent folk. Henry was the manager of a Sainsbury's store and obviously took his responsibilities very seriously. His wife had left her job as a secretary when Marcus was born in order to look after him. I was almost sorry that their lives would be altered so dramatically the following day. But, and it was a huge but, Marcus stopped me from prevaricating as he was his usual loathsome self.

'I want more chocolate log but there's none left,' was one of his characteristic self-indulgent moans.

'Oh dear, I'll ask the waitress if there's any in the kitchen,' his mother replied, instantly losing all the respect she had accrued.

As the evening ended the weather turned very cloudy and then the rain started, a veritable deluge, not uncommon in the mountains after a hot, sunny day. During the night there was the most amazing thunderstorm which lasted for hours, an alpine extravaganza with lightening that turned the sky from black to silver and thunder loud enough to wake the dead. By morning the storm had abated but it had left the roads running with water and the streams overflowing. The white-water rafting planned by another group in the hotel had to be postponed. Health and Safety ruled, but hopefully not for Marcus.

The conditions were most helpful. Marcus could easily slip on a sodden path and cavort down one of the many, almost vertical banks, a veritable Dance Macabre! All that was needed was one opportunity and the repulsive youth would be no more.

The day remained cloudy with periods of rain and the promised views were disappointing, mostly lost in thick mist. I am pleased to relate that a couple of days later I repeated the walk, on my own, in glorious sunshine and was able to admire the celebrated peaks. Dan had been correct. The scenery was so perfect it seemed unreal. The post cards I purchased as mementoes did not do it justice.

During the morning the group stayed together, Marcus only leaving his parents' side when others were in the vicinity. I was never alone with him, but that was not part of the pre-lunch plan. We ate our packed lunches on rather soggy seats in Murren then went to a café to dry off. The day was fast disappearing, unlike my target. After our extended sojourn we were all ready to begin our descent. It was a short way out of the village when fate smiled upon me. We all began the route together, on a reasonable path which led out of the village. My map reading had been accurate and we were soon on a rougher track which meandered through the dense forest. This path was rather steep and slippery and after a very short time the group started to spread out. A few of the more energetic and confident hikers marched on ahead whilst others, mostly the more mature members, were going slower in the increasingly adverse conditions. Marcus was somewhere in between but gloriously out of sight of his parents. Only I was with him.

I had my opportunity.

'Shall we dash on ahead and make sure the path is alright for your mum and dad?' I asked, trying to sound innocently enthusiastic.

Marcus gave me a strange look which did not surprise me as I had never before addressed a single comment to him.

'Yeah, suppose so,' was his almost insolent reply.

Little did he know that those were to be the last words that he would ever leave his mouth.

There was a place where a stream, which eventually joined the more major Weisser Lutschine, cascaded under a bridge. Following the rain of the previous twenty four hours it had turned into a torrent.

'Shall we play Pooh Sticks?' I asked producing some suitable twigs from my pocket. He gave me a look that suggested that such games were rather too juvenile for him but making it appear that he was doing me a massive favour (as indeed he was) he took one of the sticks from my hand. We threw our pieces of wood into the water on one side then ran across the bridge that formed the road, to watch them reappear.

As he stared over, sure, of course, that his twig had won, all I had to do was launch the unsuspecting boy over the edge. Luckily I am very strong and he was a puny little wretch and totally unprepared. It was so easy to grab him from behind and negotiate him to his demise. Moriaty sending his archenemy Sherlock Holmes over the nearby Reichenchbach Falls must have had a much harder time of it. Marcus was dispatched in a matter of seconds and as luck would have it, as he entered the stream, he hit his head on a huge boulder at the side of the water. A glorious sound. Death was instantaneous. His body was shipped downstream, with the speed of an Exocet missile, to reappear days later in Lake Brienz having travelled the eight point six kilometres undetected.

I walked on and after a quarter of an hour caught up with the trio from our group who were striding out at the front and as we were at a division in the path we decided to wait for the rest of the party.

To create my alibi I pretended to be out of breath and muttered, 'Thought I'd test myself and catch up with you fit people.'

'Path's a bit slippery in places, bet some of the others are finding it hard going,' Chloe said sounding her usual smug self. She was a most experienced hiker but wanted everyone to know it.

'Yes they were a bit too slow for me, so I got a move on,' I added.

After what seemed like an eternity the rest approached us, stumbling down the wet path. Oh the elation I felt when Mr and Mrs Parker realised that Marcus was not with us. Any empathy I had felt for them the previous evening had dissipated overnight. They had apparently been calling his name for some time and had assumed that he was walking with the confident members who had forged ahead and that he had, as was his wont, become detached from his parents.

'Where is he?' the whole of Switzerland must have heard Margaret yelling. Why her crescendo had to be on an orchestral scale was incomprehensible. The hullabaloo was gloriously reminiscent of the one on the boat many years before. No wonder people enjoy holidays so much!

'Has anyone seen him since we left Murren?' Dan asked attempting to keep the group calm.

Of course no one had; only me, and no one would suspect me, the loner in the group, of having any knowledge of his whereabouts. I had made it very obvious that I had no time for children. Why would I have had anything to do with him? Fortunately in the chaos that followed people were unsure of exactly where others had been when Marcus disappeared. It was assumed that I was with the people at the front and the energetic threesome thought that I had been with the majority until my spurt to join them.

Dan and Chloe volunteered to retrace our steps and look for the missing child. We were advised to go on ahead all the way into Stechelberg. There was just a chance that he was ahead of us and would be waiting in the village.

'Someone ring me when you get there, you've all got my mobile number,' Dan said, trying to maintain some normality. 'If we find him I'll give you a call, someone is sure to have seen him. He must be either ahead or behind somewhere. Don't worry he'll turn up.'

The final part of the path down to the village is extremely steep, probably the most precipitous we encountered on the whole holiday. By this time Margaret was despairing. Apart from her shrieks of terror and the constant calling of his name there was little sound. All, barring me, were hoping to see the young man around each corner.

Stechelberg was a dreary place that afternoon: an empty, rather damp, road; a dilapidated inn and a few bedraggled souls waiting patiently for the next bus back down the valley. There was, of course, no sign of Marcus and no phone call from Dan. Margaret went into hysterical overdrive, weeping and wailing in a most unladylike manner. Henry did his best to console her and kept up a mantra telling her that it would be alright, their beloved son was undoubtedly hiding somewhere. I rather suspected that he was probably starting to doubt his own words.

At first we all huddled in the soggy bus shelter but then went to the inn and waited for Dan and Chloe. As they had to go all the way back to Murren it took hours for them to return to our party in the valley: with no news, no sighting of the missing boy, nothing to report. It was at that point that the police were informed and give them their due, they arrived surprisingly promptly.

'We have the helicopter looking. He will be found. He may have slipped and fallen off the path, but we will find him,' the officer who was obviously the senior partner, said in impressively good English. He added that it was not unknown for someone to become separated and perhaps be unable to seek help, but with several hours of daylight still available he was not unduly concerned and was sure that Marcus would be safe.

A special bus had been ordered to take us back to Grindelwald. The Swiss efficiency was commendable but I knew that no amount of competence could help Marcus now.

It was a sombre journey. Some of our group managed to retain a modicum of hope that he would be found whilst others feared the worst. That evening each of us was asked about the walk and when we had last seen the missing child. Everyone appeared to be telling the same story.

'I know he was with the rest of us as we left Murren,' I said, keeping to the truth for as long as possible. 'Then I decided to stride out and keep up with the keen ones at the front. I never saw him after that.' Oh with what ease I was able to lie. I can do it when needed and practice does indeed make perfect.

Fortunately for me there was no suspicion of foul play and no one was interrogated. The assumption was that he had either gone off the path, into the woods, and got totally lost or that he had fallen down one of the many steep sides that descended from our route. As the hours passed and darkness fell the search was called off, to be resumed at first light. It was then that the severity of the situation hit home. The women all became tearful and the men assumed an air of resigned composure. The Parkers had retired to their room so I was unable to observe their suffering. The rest of us parted in a subdued manner. I, however, lay on my bed elated as I relived the moment Marcus fell to his death. The sound of his head hitting the rock lulled me to a deep and utterly restful slumber.

It was on the final morning of the holiday that the police came to the hotel to break the tragic news to Mr and Mrs Parker. Marcus's body had been found amongst some rocks at the side of Lake Brienz. They were, to say the least, inconsolable. Although they had, quite naturally, feared the worst as the hours then the days passed they had, as human beings do, managed to maintain a small degree of hope.

'Marcus had damage to his head's side. We think he his head hit on a boulder when he fell. He would have not suffered,' said the policeman not quite managing to observe the nuances of the English language.

It was assumed that his death had been accidental; a slip on the wet path and a fall into the stream that carried his body down to the lake. There was little surprise that no one had seen the incident. Everyone agreed that the group had become dispersed and that Marcus was inclined to venture off during the walks. The inquest confirmed a verdict of Accidental Death. Not yet my perfect murder, rather too easy, but it has to be noted that it was unspeakably satisfying.

Chapter 9

Diary entry of Mrs Samantha Turner, member of the jury.

I have always wanted to do jury service as I thought it would be interesting but I hate it. It is a truly terrible case and the details we are asked to listen to are so upsetting. Jennifer, the lady who sits next to me, was in floods again this morning. That poor little boy. The photos were bad enough but today we listened to the forensic expert describing how Jamie was killed. And even worse what the fiend did to his body afterwards. What kind of monster does that to a tiny child? The defendant looks normal. I would have passed him in the street without giving him a second glance. If I'm honest he is rather good looking but with a cold manner and staring blue eyes. He sits day after day hardly paying any attention to what is going on. We all say that we can hardly bear to look at him.

We have been told that we have only heard part of the case and we are not to make up our minds before we have listened to all the evidence both for the prosecution and then the defence. We are not even half way through yet. The sooner this is over the better.

Judge's Notes

A harrowing day with extremely unpleasant evidence. Sado-sexual behaviour; the removal of

Jamie's penis and balls. Apparently post mortem, so one wonders about the reasoning behind the act. Perhaps there were no reasons that anyone normal can understand. The defendant continues with his, almost incessant, writing. Is he even listening to the case that is stacking up against him? Of course if he is guilty he already knows it all.

Watching the jury is proving to be a fascinating diversion. The twelve have sworn, under oath, to render an impartial verdict. How incredibly difficult that will prove. The trial is sensational news on an hourly basis on the television and the tabloid newspapers' headlines are becoming more and more lurid.

The concept of a jury system is one of the abiding triumphs of civilisation and has its antecedents in Ancient Greece. The Greeks delighted in using their ordinary citizens to consider and judge the crimes committed by their peers. In those distant days when each individual reached their verdict they voted by secret ballot. I recall being told, probably by Mrs Walters, my excellent history teacher in Year Nine, that in the City State of Athens there are records showing the use of juries and so the system goes back to at least 500 B.C.

Being a member of the court service I am ineligible for jury service, a shame as I would find it most pleasing to be able to determine a person's immediate future, though you could say I've practised doing that in other ways both legally in my job and ....well I think you can finish that sentence.

Some people try to avoid jury service and do not see it as a civic duty and it would perhaps be advantageous to re-adopt the rule formulated under the 1730 "Bill for Better Regulation of Juries Act" whereby all those liable for jury service were listed somewhere public in each Parish and so individuals were prevented from evading their responsibilities.

Sometimes things do go awry and there is the funny story of the cat, Tabby Sal, who was called for jury service in Boston, America. Apparently her name was on the previous census in the pet's section. Her owner, a Mrs Esposito, claimed that Tabby Sal was not qualified to undertake this duty as she spoke no English and would have to utter a loud "Miaow" when asked for a guilty or non-guilty verdict.

Each jury needs to appoint a foreman, a leader, one of the twelve who will act as their spokesperson. Despite the fact that this is not done until they retire, many days if not weeks off yet, I have a good idea who this group's spokesperson will be. I have named her Mrs Organised. She has an air of authority, doesn't miss a thing and is forever writing copious notes. She is probably in her forties, a good looking woman with highlighted blond hair and always smartly dressed. Each day there is a different outfit, her wardrobe must be enormous. If I had to guess I would say she worked in some professional capacity: a teacher, dentist or civil servant. None of the others are quite as dedicated. Yes I think it will be her.

But I digress..........back to Preston, back to the problem of Simon Bell.

On returning from Switzerland and the holiday that for many different reasons, not all of them legal, I had adored I realised that I must start to make plans for the demise of Mr Bell. My font of all wisdom, Marie, informed me that he was as she put it, 'keeping his nose clean,' and that his night-time job at Asda was working out well. It wasn't exactly what I wanted to hear as I don't believe in Road to Damascus moments or giving people second chances so was not prepared to believe that he had reformed and become a worthwhile citizen.

'Philip still seeing him?' I asked as casually as possible. I knew Simon must remain under the watchful eye of the probation service.

'Yes I think they've got to stay in contact for another few months. He says that he still has hopes that Simon won't reoffend this time, but then he always has been an optimist.'

'I rather think we'll see that young man again, it's only a matter of time.'

'I agree people like Simon usually succumb given enough temptation. He'll manage to keep out of trouble whilst he's seeing Philip then we'll probably have the pleasure of his company again.'

How was she to know that I intended having that particular pleasure sooner rather than later. Unfortunately I was still unsure about the method needed to end the miserable existence of Mr Bell. A morning in court gave me one or two ideas.

The first was a sad case. It involved a Jack Morrison, a gentle looking man in his mid-fifties. Unlike most of our clientele he had never been in trouble before and had certainly not seen the inside of a court room. He had kept a clean driving licence for well over thirty years but was in front of the Bench for causing the death of a young motor bike rider. Poor Jack wept from beginning to end. The relatives of Tom Michaels, the eighteen year old biker, found the proceedings overwhelming and also sobbed noisily throughout the trial.

Jack's lawyer spoke of his client's shame and remorse and added that he was taking medication to help with the depression that had developed as a result of the accident. When he took the stand Mr Morrison admitted that the fatality was his fault.

'I know I looked right then left but I don't remember looking right again,' he paused to regain some composure, 'the next thing I knew was that there was a loud bang and a body was flying over the bonnet of my car. I know it was my fault and I can't say how sorry I am.' He muttered his last comment through loud sobs and he was shaking so much that I asked him to be seated to give the rest of his evidence and gave him some water. It was one of the few occasions when I surprised myself by feeling some pity for a defendant.

'I will never drive again and I realise that I deserve to be punished for what I did.'

The two witnesses said that the biker appeared to be going rather faster than the permitted speed limit of thirty miles an hour and both added that once Mr Morrison pulled out on to the main road the biker could do nothing to avoid contact with the car. The police officer who was first on the scene said that in all probability Tom Michaels would have been dead before he hit the ground.

The Magistrates dealt with the case with great benevolence which probably didn't suit the victim's family. In his summing up the Chairman, Mr Welkins, a most experienced J.P., said that Mr Morrison had caused a death whilst in charge of a car but that it had been an accident and one that would haunt him for the rest of his life. The mitigating factors were his immediate guilty plea, his remorse and the fact that this was his first driving mistake in many years behind the wheel.

He expressed tremendous sympathy for Mr Michael's family and said that the loss of a child is the worst thing that any parent can experience.

'We do not feel that a prison sentence would serve any purpose. Mr Morrison will continue to punish himself and will have to live with the knowledge that, due to a momentary lapse of concentration, he took a life. We therefore order that he undertakes one hundred hours of unpaid work and he will have six points put on his licence. Our sincere condolences are extended to all concerned in this tragic case.'

The second case was far more prosaic. A hit and run. Plain and simple. Knock her down and leave the scene.

Hit and Runs happen with disgraceful regularity and the police almost invariably put them down to a lack of citizenship, rather than premeditated violence. The number of such accidents has continued to rise over the past ten years. I know I have dealt with several in my courtroom and the government has asked for zero tolerance when dealing with them. One in ten personal injury claims are down to callous accidents where the perpetrators don't stop. The majority occur between nine in the morning and six at night with very few in the evening. All facts that I thought that might prove useful.

In court such cases are under the heading of "Fail to stop/report accident" the maximum available sentence being six months in prison. The case that week fell into one of the more minor categories as the injury sustained by the victim was negligible. She was a young lady called Sally Hopkins and she had spent the evening drinking in several pubs in the town centre and had then decided to make her own way home. As she was crossing Windsor Avenue the car driven by Stuart Sanderson had dealt her a glancing blow, knocking her off her feet. It was the fact that Mr Sanderson had not stopped that was the serious issue. A passer-by had witnessed the incident and noted the car registration and contacted the police.

'I knew she was O.K. as I looked in the rear view mirror and saw her get up,' was Mr Morrison's rather feeble excuse, 'so I didn't think it was worth stopping. I was in a hurry as I was late for work. I do nights as a hospital porter.' If he thought that being a member of the caring profession would help his case he was wrong. His punishment was a hefty fine, payment of court costs, victim's surcharge, compensation to Miss Hopkins and six points on his licence. The good news was that this meant he had totted over the allowed twelve points so was, to other people's advantage, disqualified for six months.

Having observed these two cases I had found my solution. Simon Bell would meet his end with a road accident.

Have you ever noticed how fate can lend a helping hand? Kismet can provide aid at the most auspicious of moments. That very evening as I was returning home, far later than normal having been delayed catching up with the many items that had accrued whilst I had been away, I saw him. He was waiting at our local bus stop. I realised that this was the time he must set off each evening to go to work. He looked at me without any sign of recognition.

Alone at home I had the rest of the night to work on a plan, to devise a strategy. It all needed careful and meticulous preparation. There had been no one else at the bus stop. Should I change my mind and go for a surprise attack with a knife? I had an impressive array of kitchen knives so would not have to worry about purchasing one. I was slightly taller and, with my running regime, I assumed far stronger than he was but somehow the idea of a knife attack didn't feel right and it was definitely not a foregone conclusion that I would be able to outmanoeuvre him. Too many things could go wrong. Just because he had been alone on that occasion didn't mean others wouldn't normally be there. What if he was strong enough to resist? I didn't object to physically inserting a knife into him but I rather wanted an ending where he would, at least for a slightly longer period of time, know what was about to happen. Knifing would be far too quick. A collision with a car would, hopefully, cause far greater suffering as I hoped, if I was skilful enough, he would not die too quickly.

The following evening I got home early and decided to try to discover his route to the bus stop. I knew his address, given so often in court, so was waiting for him when he emerged a few minutes before he was due to catch the bus. His flat was in one of the blocks that were erected, with no regard for style, in the 1960's. He had a ground floor flat and I wondered briefly whether this would be to my advantage as it would be easy to observe. Being October the nights were just beginning to draw in and I saw the light, that I assumed was in his living room, go out just before he emerged. He didn't see me standing across the road and I was able to follow him until he reached the bus stop.

His route was past three other blocks of flats, then two streets of semi-detached houses. It was as he approached the bus stop that the inkling of a plan emerged. He had to cross a very busy main road and didn't bother to use the pelican crossing.

Whilst I was living with mother I had a car, an ancient red Ford, whose milometer was well into six figures. At home I was able to keep her in the garage but when I moved there wasn't one with the house, only most unsatisfactory on-road parking. For several months I used an empty one nearby that was left open until the owner got wise and started to check each garage fairly regularly. Living close to my work a car was not a necessity and my old banger was starting to cost a lot in repairs so it went to the nearby scrap yard.

No car was readily available to carry out my plan. That night I thought about various options. I could hire a car but if Simon caused any damage to the body work it might be hard to explain when I returned the vehicle. I could steal one but I am no car thief and wouldn't know how to open a lock and what's more I realised I could very well be caught. My only other option was to "borrow" one. Most of my colleagues drove to work and parked in the staff car park, but of course they took them home at night. My dilemma remained unresolved.

To my horror on Court Two's list the following day the name Simon Bell jumped out at me. This time he was appearing as a witness in a GBH: A Grievous Bodily Harm case. It was certainly a change for him to be assisting the police. I have to admit that he gave his evidence in a most clear and concise manner, with none of his usual foul language, and helped to convict the assailant in a nasty assault that had happened one Sunday lunch time outside a rather notorious pub in the middle of Preston. Was I getting soft? Was I being misled into thinking that he had a more honourable side to his character? Would this spoil my plans? Fortunately for me, but not for him, he then reverted to form and gave a two finger salute to the Bench as he left the room. I was the only one who witnessed this. He would have been back in the dock himself if others had seen the uncouth action. As I wanted him out and about in the community I pretended not to notice. That one moment did however seal his fate. His end was necessary but I needed more time to plan this murder, one that was so close to home. This one had to be perfect.

Little did I know that a set of circumstances were about to send me down a totally different route in my inevitable dealings with that particular man.

Chapter 10

Mother's Diary

What a turn up for the books. To think that Benjamin, always so law abiding, would be detained at a police station. How the girls laughed when they heard.

He was released, without charge, but was up in arms that his fingerprints had been taken. There was a fracas after the game yesterday afternoon. Preston's and Oldham's fans met outside the ground. Honestly it's only a game, fancy letting it lead to that.

Benjamin said when I phoned him that he just happened to be a bystander and was taken into custody in error. He kept going on about a Simon Bell who was there as well and who had been involved in the incident, but who, much to Benjamin's disappointment, had also been released.

Benjamin has always had such a strong sense of right and wrong; life is forever black or white. Teasing him about it went down very badly but we all think it's highly amusing. Benjamin in trouble with the law!

"In trouble with the law", no, not true: one of mother's facile statements. It was mayhem outside the ground that Saturday afternoon, surprising as the game was a poor one, not one to raise any emotion. Two mediocre teams had played out a goalless draw really nothing to get excited about.

'Bloody awful game, it'd still be nil-all if we played till tomorrow,' Bill, my long-time neighbour at the ground, summed up Preston's dismal performance perfectly. Like many long-time supporters he sounded resigned to his fate as he added, 'Oldham didn't contribute much to the match either and never looked like scoring. All in all, a match to forget.' Unlike the post-match happenings.

'We can play better than that, even Johnson was off his game today,' was all I could add to the conversation. Bill was in his late eighties and had supported his home team for over eight decades. Did remembering the good years make the present dire performances even harder to watch? After wishing each other well we walked out with the other die-hards in a miserable silence.

Normally at the end of a game the home supporters leave first, the away fans being kept in their section of the ground until the coast is clear. Something went wrong that Saturday and within minutes of the game ending there was a free for all as the two sets of fans met.

'Preston, those pansies for promotion? You've got to be bloody brain dead to believe that. More like relegation on that fucking form.'

'Can't even sodding score against us and we're bloody bottom,' were two of the cries I heard from the Oldham fans. The language, as always, left something to be desired but I was quite impressed by the unwitting use of alliteration. Seconds later fists were being used and blood was flowing. I started to get worried when I saw a couple of knives appear. The police seemed to take an age to intervene and then when they did they arrested the wrong people. Me included.

As soon as I realised that the violence was escalating I had started to walk away but just at that moment I felt a hand on my shoulder and the next thing I knew I was being loaded into the police van. Having one's fingerprints taken when one is entirely innocent (at least of football hooliganism) is an assault on one's civil liberties. Unfortunately the police did not take kindly to my protestations and kept me in the cells for three hours. Being detained in police custody was horrendous. I was not with my own kind. To my chagrin Simon Bell was released at the same time as me, though in all probability he had been involved in the fighting.

All in all an incident I would rather forget though given time it would turn to my advantage. Our personal belongings were returned to us by a rather surly custody sergeant who had spent the night on duty and who murmured comments about grown men who thought that football was worth fighting over being a total waste of his time. I managed to keep quiet and collected my belongings, thanking him most politely. However there was a mix up with rucksacks. It was an easy mistake as they were identical Preston North End ones with the logo on the front. I was given Simon's and I presume he got mine. He inherited an empty thermos flask and a sandwich box containing one, by then, stale cheese roll and I gained his gym equipment: shampoo, hair gel, towels and shorts. But more of that later.

Chapter 11

Daily Gazette

Death of Football Supporter

The young man killed following a home game at Deepdale last Saturday has been named as Micah Robert Lee, aged eighteen. Mr Lee lived in Oldham and had travelled to the match with his parents and two younger brothers, all season ticket holders at Oldham Athletic. It was the first time the family had been to an away match.

His devastated family were too upset to speak yesterday but a family friend told our reporter that Micah was a wonderful lad who had never been in trouble in his life. He was described as extremely bright and had recently started to read Engineering at Manchester University. Fighting broke out as the two sets of fans met as they left the ground on Saturday afternoon.

Police Constable Roger Parker, aged forty seven, told our reporter that he had not seen scenes like Saturday's at a football match for decades. It appears that Mr Lee was leaving the away stand when he was attacked. There is absolutely no suggestion that he was involved in the fighting and the poor lad seems to have been in the wrong place at the wrong time. P.C. Parker sent police condolences to Micah's family who had the misfortune to witness the death of their beloved son.

The incident is being treated as murder and a description has been issued of a man they wish to interview. He is white, of above average height, aged between twenty and thirty and was believed to be wearing a blue top and dark blue or black jeans. Anyone with any information is asked to contact their nearest police station.

Several supporters, involved in the appalling incident, are due to appear at Preston Magistrates' Courthouse today and we are sure that you, our readers, will expect them to receive severe punishments. No one wants to return to the dark days of football hooliganism.

No, I know what you are thinking, but this was one murder I played no part in. Honestly.

As a Legal Adviser I have often been called upon to assist in other courts in the North West. Blackpool has never been my favourite as it is always so incredibly busy and full of unsavoury cases, often involving holiday makers who over indulge on sun and alcohol with unpleasant consequences. However I have always liked the days when I am asked to work in Lancaster, a most pleasant place as long as one disregards the architecture of the Court, a squat unattractive edifice which, although not very old, has not worn well. The people who work there make up for the building's shortcomings. They are excellent at their jobs and unfailingly welcoming. How strange that my next murder should be associated with those most capable professionals.

I had completed almost a week in Lancaster when Sophie Drummond appeared on the scene. She was one of the defence lawyers and it was soon apparent that she was a most accomplished operator. Sophie won all three short trials that day, though I suspected that on at least one occasion this allowed the guilty to walk free. After the courts had finished for the day we were the last to enter the staffroom and found ourselves alone. I complimented her on her handling of the last witness. She had basically torn his evidence to pieces with the speed and efficiency of a paper shredder. She smiled and asked if I had time for a drink after work. It has probably become evident that I have little time for socialising, deeming it a frivolous and inconsequential activity, but for some reason I was tempted as I wanted to know if she had any conscience about getting miscreants "off".

It was a lovely warm evening and we walked along the canal path and sat outside the Pack Horse where we had several drinks. I kept to fresh orange juice but Sophie had three large glasses of red wine in quick succession. She was a cheerful girl, newly qualified, and in her mid-twenties. Many would have deemed her pretty, with her curly brown hair and hazel eyes. That day in court she had been smartly dressed in a dark grey suit and white blouse though with rather too much flesh on show especially once she undid a couple more buttons. Her patent leather black shoes had the highest heels I had ever seen but did not seem to impede her progress, probably due to years of practise.

The female of the species has never appealed to me but I did enjoy her company and we amused each other with court anecdotes. Her favourite was the lady, of very limited intelligence, whom she was defending for none - payment of fines and for breaking her curfew on several occasions. Sophie said that when the lady in question was asked why she had not paid her fines her reply had been that she couldn't leave the house due to her asthma. In the very next breathe (which Sophie said came very easily considering the lady's alleged respiratory difficulty) her excuse for breaking her curfew was, 'Well I have to get out, I can't stay in the house all night.' Needless to say that was one case that she lost.

'I don't lose many and I have no qualms about releasing the guilty. It's my job and I want to do it to the best of my ability. I've been told I could have gained Harold Shipman his freedom.'

Everything was going so well. Anyone observing us might have thought we were long-time friends or even lovers. As the light faded the evening was just beginning to get chilly and it was then that Sophie made her big, and I am pleased to add, fatal mistake.

'Would you like to come back to mine? I could make us a meal and some coffee.' As she said the word "coffee" she gave me a look that implied that there was a lot more on offer than just the drink. I thought back to the prostitute in Oxford and was sorry that I would be forced to revisit a past killing. I always prefer to be original, so much more interesting. Each assassination should, in my ideal world, be unique, but a woman who would offer herself after such a brief acquaintance is as the phrase goes "no better than she should be" and detracts from the moral welfare of society.

'That sounds wonderful,' I heard myself reply, giving her a positive and I hoped suggestive smile. As I am unpractised at these I suspect my look was more comical than sexy. After so much wine she didn't appear to notice.

Fortunately her flat was quite nearby, in one in the new developments overlooking the canal. By this time it was growing dark and the area was quiet, still too early for the night-time revellers, mostly students who during term-time account for a large percentage of the city's population. The last thing I needed was a witness. People must have seen us outside the pub but hopefully not by anyone who knew me.

Her top floor flat was small and functional. The kitchen was an extension of the living room and the space was made to look bigger than it really was by the extensive use of white paint and well placed mirrors. I decided that I would allow her to prepare the promised meal. No point her dying with an empty stomach; it was the least I could do for her.

Sophie proved to be an adequate cook, though Delia and Nigella were in no danger of being usurped, and she produced a cheese omelette and a mixed salad. She opened a bottle of wine and proceeded to drink at the speed sought by the Hadron Collider. Unsurprisingly she was soon noticeably tipsy. As this was an unplanned demise I had not decided on the method. Strangling would make it a copy-cat of Oxford and as I said I like to be creative and wherever possible for each murder to be unique.

Not being accustomed to the seduction techniques of women with, or indeed without, dubious morals I have no idea whether or not her attempts to lure me to the bedroom were skilful or not. I played along and acted the part of a man who was keen to enjoy what was obviously on offer. As we entered the bedroom Sophie asked me to close the curtains. This was a surprising request as she was definitely not the shy type. It was as I started to draw them that I realised that there was a balcony. Instead of closing the curtains I opened the French windows leading on to it. What a ridiculously simple idea. The baby had been despatched over the railings of a ship, Marcus down a ravine and now Sophie was to fall from her balcony. All alike - but each one sufficiently different to keep me amused.

'Come and look,' I said in a voice that I hoped sounded seductive, but even to my ears sounded less than convincing, 'there's a full moon, most romantic.'

She staggered across and was happy to be led out onto the small veranda. The next part was far more difficult than I had expected. If you have ever tried to lift someone over a railing, even a small one, you will be aware that it demands immense strength, some agility and the surprise factor. Despite her inebriated state I knew that if she realised what was about to happen she would fight back. I prefer my victims to be docile. So much easier.

Though I say it myself I do keep myself in peak condition and with an extra lift and forceful push I was able to dispose of her onto the concrete below. No sound escaped from her and as she landed there was only a dull thud to indicate that she had reached the ground. A head hitting concrete is a most rewarding sound, like a muffled beater connecting with a drum. I was delighted with my evening's work.

I washed and dried the dishes we had used and wiped all the surfaces I had touched. On the way up I had been careful not to touch anything in the lift but I thought it advisable to walk down the stairs to the rear exit. Once outside I made straight for the Red Rose in the middle of town and watched the football match they were showing. When I went to the bar to order my sparkling water I commented on the game and the amazing first ten minutes that I had heard the Sky presenter discussing in glowing terms. When those minutes had been happening

I had been otherwise engaged. My alibi felt secure so I left before Arsenal completed the double over their local rivals, Chelsea.

I walked through the busy town centre and out to the railway station where I caught the last train back to Preston. Being mid-week it was an extremely quiet journey and I was able to sit and review my evening's work. I felt the inordinate pleasure that I invariably feel after I have rid the world of a person not deserving of life. There are so many millions on this planet at any one time that I have always been able to reassure myself that the occasional one making a slightly premature exit is of little consequence when viewed in the great scheme of things.

On arriving home I saw that my answer machine was flashing. Few people phone me so I was not surprised to hear my mother's voice. Not the exultant end to the evening that I would have chosen.

'Hello Benjamin. Hope you've got over your incarceration! I've not seen you for ages. Why don't you come for lunch on Sunday? I'll expect you at one unless I hear from you.'

Hell and damnation I thought. But it would be alright to see the old girl again. I knew it was fast approaching the time to seek my revenge for her years of uncaring coldness. Dear me, I remember thinking, this killing lark might just be becoming a habit. A few brief hours after one homicide, I was considering, the next. Would this be the perfect one? Was I capable of committing such a crime? Would I ever achieve the total, all-encompassing satisfaction I craved? Would any ever match up to the very first, the one that for the time being is the one to which I alone am privy.

Chapter 12

Daily Gazette

The body of a young lawyer was discovered late last night beneath the balcony of the canal-side flat where she lived in Lancaster. A man taking his dog for its evening walk along the canal path saw the body lying beside the newly built apartments. It is not clear whether she fell accidently or intended to harm herself. Her name will not be released until her next of kin have been informed. Police are keen to hear from anyone who has any information.

I was back in Lancaster that day and the scene that greeted me as I entered the rear door of the court was like an episode of an irritating soap on the television. Grown women were weeping and wailing and asking, repeatedly, what could have happened?

'Oh! Mr Doyle, have you heard the news?' asked Jenny, in a voice rendered almost inaudible by the tidal wave of sobs coming from the other females in the room. Mass hysteria at its worst. Whatever happened to the British "stiff upper lip"? Tears were streaming down her face. She was normally a mature and eminently sensible member of the same local firm of lawyers as Sophie, the one employed by most of the defendants who appear in the Lancaster court, but at this moment she was totally distraught. 'No one seems to know exactly what happened,' she continued, mangling a paper hanky that had seen better days. 'I was mentoring her and she was such a delightful girl and had the makings of an excellent lawyer. I met her parents recently and they are a lovely couple. They must be totally devastated.'

'The police are saying she must have meant to fall as she would have had to make an effort to get over the railings on her balcony,' Steve muttered. I was horrified to see that he was fighting an inclination to cry. I hoped his battle would prove successful. Poor lad, I was to learn that he had a soft spot for her but had never plucked up sufficient courage to ask her out. On learning this I was very tempted to tell him that she would have been easy pickings.

'I can't believe that she did it deliberately, she was such a happy girl, always so full of life,' this was Jenny again who had thankfully gained some self-control. I really have no time or patience with women who fall apart at the first sign of something going wrong. 'She did like a drink, so maybe didn't know what she was doing. Maybe we'll never know. It's just too awful, too awful. Poor Sophie and her poor, poor family.'

Fortunately no one seemed to expect much of a reaction from me. I stood trying to look suitably distressed and made the appropriate noises, agreeing with the various over-the- top silliness that was filling the room.

'Have the police been here?' I asked, thinking that we would need to be interviewed, being the last people to see her.

'They phoned and said they'd be along some time this morning,' Steve said, his voice still wobbling in a most unmanly way.

As the old adage goes "life must go on" and defendants were starting to arrive and be signed in. They needed to have discussions with their lawyers prior to their appearance in court. It seemed that I was the only one capable of organising the morning and as I had absolutely no intention of cancelling any trials, of which there were many assigned that day, I came out with the irrefutable, 'Sophie would have wanted us to carry on as normal. She loved the law and would have wanted to see justice done today, just like any day.' Well no one could argue with that. Mr Bickerstaff, the top lawyer in the firm, arrived within the hour and took on Sophie's list and so the day's proceeding began, only slightly later than normal. The government is forever saying that court proceedings should be swift and completed in the shortest time possible and despite the unfortunate demise of one lawyer that is exactly what happened.

I was in Court Two with a trio of magistrates I particularly liked. They were a sensible group, all nearing the enforced retirement age of seventy, who must have witnessed many of life's tragedies and all three agreed that they would be able to sit as usual.

The police did not appear until late in the day. They had obviously got their priorities right and had been dealing with the living. There were two of them and they saw each member of the court staff individually. I was slightly apprehensive when it was my turn, but felt some reassurance when the ones who had already been said that all they wanted to know was how Sophie had been recently and when the last time was that they had seen her.

'I don't work at this court full time. I'm based at Preston and only met Sophie for the first time this week.

She was a most accomplished lawyer and I admired her work in court. She seemed very pleasant but I can't say I knew her or could comment on her state of mind. The last time I saw her she was downstairs talking in the office at the end of the day.' I felt quite safe with this approximation of the truth as I was confident that no one had seen us leave together. The younger policeman was busy writing down my comments. 'What do you think happened? People are saying she might have taken her own life.'

'We're not sure at the moment, sir, but it's a sad business.'

They seemed to be satisfied with everyone's answers and left shortly afterwards. As far as I know foul-play was never suspected and no alibis were required.

Daily Gazette

The woman whose body was found beside the canal in Lancaster on Tuesday evening has been named as Sophie Drummond, aged twenty six. Her family have said that they have lost, "the light of their lives." They described her as vibrant and intelligent with her whole life in front of her. Sophie was a successful lawyer who had worked for a large firm in the city for the past eighteen months. Her body was found below the balcony of the flat into which she had recently moved. Police do not suspect foul play and say it was most probably a dreadful accident. She does appear to have consumed a large amount of alcohol prior to the fall but her family and friends do not think that she was suicidal. No note was found at the scene and she had not used her mobile phone that evening. The case has been referred to the coroner's office.

Another successful murder. It may interest you to know that, several weeks later after reviewing all the available evidence, including our witness statements, the coroner gave an open verdict as she said there was insufficient evidence for her to be sure exactly what had happened on that tragic night. She was most sympathetic with Sophie's family and added that not knowing the details leading up to their daughter's death must, inevitably, add to their distress. She extended her sincere condolences to them and hoped that they would learn to live with their loss.

It wasn't until the coroner's verdict had been announced that I felt able to visit my mother. I had put her off several times and avoided her predictable Sunday lunches. However the day finally arrived and there I was back at home. Nothing, and I mean nothing, had changed. Even the predictable apple pie tasted the same. It was not a successful meeting. We had so little in common. We didn't read the same books or newspapers, watch the same films or television programmes and certainly never shared hobbies or interests. I sometimes used to think that it would have come as no surprise to find out that I was adopted. It was just the two of us and the conversation was stilted.

'How are you Benjamin? You're looking well. It's been ages since we met,' was about as exciting as it got. As you may have gathered I am not much of a conversationalist at the best of times but with her I found it almost impossible. I learnt that my sisters were both well and that the horrendous grandchildren were becoming more obnoxious now they were in their teens. Unattractive pictures of them as spotty youths now adorned the sideboard. They had not been blessed with my intelligence as none were gaining good results. I made an effort and told her about my Swiss holiday (well obviously not in its entirety) and she enthused about the coach trip to the European capital cities from which she had returned recently.

'I had such a good time with a very friendly group of "Golden Oldies" and we saw such a lot: Vienna, Budapest and my favourite, Prague.' She was in full flow by now and, most unusually for her, was sounding really enthusiastic.

'The Charles Bridge in Prague was so beautiful, especially in the setting sun and the buildings you can see from it, well, you must go some time. The food was wonderful. I love the goulash and the continental gateaux. I'm sure I've put on several pounds. It was a great holiday and no awful happening like the time we went on the cruise.' "Good job I wasn't there" slid through my head, like a winter Olympiad on skis. Lunch passed and after a suitably short period I was able to make my escape.

'Don't leave it so long; it's always good to see you.' I had no answer to that particular lie.

Mother's Diary

Not the best of days and I feel really tired and depressed. Sleeping pill tonight.

Benjamin came for his lunch today. I haven't seen him for months. He looked well and I'm always surprised how good looking he is, strange to forget what your own son looks like. What a pity his personality doesn't match his looks.

It wasn't an easy meeting but it never is with Benjamin. He's so negative about everything. I wonder whether there is much joy in his life.

The girls are such good company and we have a gossip and a laugh but everything is strained with him. If I'm truthful it always has been. He was never a baby who wanted to be cuddled and was a difficult, awkward child. As far as I know he has never made friends. I wonder if it would have been different if we'd allowed the school to run the tests on him when they suggested them. They suspected he was on the Autistic spectrum, which was becoming more spoken of at the time, but Edward didn't want him labelled and said that even if they decided Benjamin had a problem there would be very little help available in a busy mainstream classroom. I bet it's different these days.

We never know what to say to each other and I wasn't sorry when he left straight after lunch. Next time I must have a store of things to talk about, but not his grandpa, he went up the wall when I mentioned him. When I think back Henry (dear Pops) was the only one with whom Benjamin really interacted.

I know when it went wrong and that I should have dealt with it better and not given in to the periods of depression. I just wish Edward was still here to help. His dad was always better at handling him than I am.

Helen is popping in after work tomorrow. That will cheer me up. If only I'd stopped having babies after the girls my life would have been so much better. No regrets, no tragedy to relive each day, No Benjamin to worry about.

Visiting mother made me agitated. I needed to take my mind off her selfish ramblings and inane comments.

What did I care about her boring neighbours or the dog that lived across the road and barked all night and listening to other people's holidays is either tedious or makes one jealous. Stories of my sisters were told to show up my own inadequacies. According to mother they both lead such full, exciting lives and she has invariably made it clear that she finds mine mundane. I knew the answer to my disquiet but wanted to deal with Simon Bell first; fortunately for him, my planning was leading nowhere.

A few weeks later I was back in Lancaster overseeing a particularly tricky case. The government had brought out new guide lines (they do so on an incredibly frequent basis on a whole range of issues) for dealing with anyone who allows their premises to be used for dealing drugs, emphasising a huge range of punishments depending on the type of illegal drugs involved. George Hinterland, a regular in the Lancaster Court, was found guilty but I was the only one to spot that he had been charged with the wrong class of drugs, a detail that would greatly alter his sentence. There had been a simple error on the paperwork, probably made by a busy clerk at the CPS, but the misinformation needed to be addressed. As it was a Class C drug and not as on the form a Class B, the magistrates had no option but to send the delightful Mr Hinterland to Preston Crown Court for sentencing. No doubt he continued his lucrative business whilst at Her Majesty's Pleasure.

Things were still tense behind the scenes and every conversation seemed to include Sophie Drummond. I ignored these as I had no viable contribution to add, though I was very aware that I could make a most interesting and jaw dropping one if I so desired. Instead I sat and completed the crossword.

'I can't believe you can finish the Guardian crossword so fast,' said Jenny.

'Doesn't surprise me, he's got us all beaten in the old brain-box department,' was Steve's rather pleasing comment, 'he was the only one to notice the mistake in Court Four this morning over the classification of the drugs. You ought to join Mensa, bet you've got an incredible IQ.'

'It's 168,' I said trying not to sound too proud of the fact, 'we tested each other at university.'

Steve had given me an idea. Joining things has never been my idea of a good time but to be challenged intellectually seemed like something I might enjoy and it would keep my mind occupied. Keeping my brain busy would, I surmised, help me to work out the finer details of the next murder. Simon Bell was starting to bug me and maybe doing something completely different would help clarify my thinking.

Mensa, for those of you who do not have the intellect to become a member, is an organisation for the very brightest people. Its purpose is to provide stimulation for the clever-est brains and to encourage those so blessed to use their incredible intelligence to the fullest. To become a member of this elite club one needs to be in the top two per cent of the population. I wasn't so keen on their aim of meeting with other members to participate in social or cultural activities which, according to the information I received, happened somewhere in the UK every night of the week.

I was attracted by the monthly magazine with its articles, news from the Mensa world and members' letters. I did not intend to have direct contact with any of the others but took the tests and was soon a fully paid up participant of the intellectual elite.

If only I had stuck to my sensible plan of not associating with other "Mensas" Amanda Albright would still be alive. Dear Amanda was definitely not one of us; in fact I suspect that she was in the bottom percentile as far as intelligence went. The Good Fairies had, however, certainly given her looks as she was, even to my inexperienced eyes quite stunning: light blond hair, deep blue eyes and a wonderful figure with curves in all the right places. Unfortunately that was where her assets stopped. Each time she spoke her broad Mancunian accent made her sound like the latest recruit for Coronation Street (not that I watch such drivel, but I've had the misfortune to catch the end of the odd episode when waiting for a decent programme to be shown). The content of her conversations was on a par with her appalling accent.

How you may be wondering did I come into contact with such a person when I had just been selected as a member of Mensa? Amanda, like many beautiful women, had married well. She had been a dental assistant and had, rather prosaically, married William, the boss of the large, and particularly lucrative, orthodontic practice in Preston where she had worked. The fact that he had left his second wife and four children for a newer and much younger model did not seem to bother either of them.

William was one of the most able people I have ever met and one of the few I deemed to be on my elevated level. He was an ebullient figure, the life and soul of the party type. From his size it was obvious that he enjoyed his food and I was to learn that he was also rather partial to a few drinks. I never saw him drunk but whenever I was with him he almost invariably consumed a large quantity of alcohol. He had been born into wealth, his father being the Managing Director of a large bank in London and he took it as his right to enjoy the privileges that this brought. I doubted he had ever wanted for anything in his life.

Meeting William, who was in his early fifties, opened up my life to the possibility of friendship. As the Chairman of the local Mensa Bridge Group it was his role to welcome new members. It was a cold November evening when I decided to go along and see if it was for me. I had learnt to play Bridge at Oxford but had not played for well over a decade. The room set aside for these meetings was in the rather grandly named Excelsior Hotel near the bus station in town. I went with some trepidation as I do not find it easy to meet new people and there was also the concern that my skills at the game would be rusty. There was no need to worry. The evening was a delight.

'Good evening everyone. I'd like you to welcome a new member, Benjamin Doyle,' William's voice was loud and authoritative and certainly silenced the fours, several of whom had commenced their games.

'Come and meet Jeffrey and Paul. They need opponents so why don't we give them a run for their money.'

That first evening passed quickly and I was relieved to note that I hadn't lost my ability. I knew I was good but William was exceptional. We were partners, having both cut higher cards than Jeffrey and Paul. We sat at the table as North and South and our opponents were East and West. I soon discovered that whilst all four of us were proficient, William had all the necessary skills of clever tactics, silent communication and an auspicious understanding of probability to a somewhat amazing degree. Best of all he appeared to have an utterly phenomenal memory, a great asset in Bridge. We won hands down and laughed afterwards about our almost telepathic ability to communicate via imperceptible glances or tiny movements.

It was the first of many enjoyable nights and William, though many years my senior, was a most affable companion and we soon became friends. He had studied medicine at Barts and had opted for dentistry as the most lucrative career. He never boasted about his wealth but, having amassed a small fortune through his work and as an only child having inherited well, he must have been a millionaire, probably many times over.

'Amanda was wondering whether you would like to come to a little party we're having on Saturday evening? Do bring a friend along.'

'I'm not really into parties; never know what to say.'

'Do come, Amanda has heard so much about you and wants to meet you. Actually I've just had a better idea, why not join us for supper one evening, more informal, less pressure?' That sounded preferable and so we arranged an evening the following week.

Their house was definitely in the mansion category. It was a double-fronted detached house, about twenty years old, and built in the Georgian style. The gravel covered front drive curved round to an impressive entrance. Once there the quiet road was no longer visible. The house was surrounded by manicured gardens and I was not surprised to learn that they employed a part-time gardener who spent three days a week maintaining its impressive appearance. I had never set foot in such a place and wondered whether it had ever featured in the magazines placed in his waiting room, the kind that are usually several years out of date, but keep patients' minds off their immediate future.

Entering the front hall was like visiting a National Trust property, though with more modern décor and furniture. Huge vases of the most opulent flowers I had ever seen bedecked every surface and the walls were filled with gilt edged mirrors and works of art that looked, even to my inexperienced eye, extremely expensive. The wooden floor had two Persian rugs artistically positioned and the overall effect was of faultless taste and enormous funds. Amanda was there to greet me and she did not look out of place.

She was, without doubt, one of the most beautiful women I had ever met and she looked, that evening, like a film star on the red carpet at the Oscars. Not a single strand of immaculately styled hair was out of place. Clothes have never been high on my list of priorities but I was aware that I was staring at hers which was behaviour in those meeting her for the first time that was probably not uncommon. She was wearing a most becoming turquoise dress that shouted designer label. Amanda was a "stunner"!

Unfortunately her conversation displayed a shallow mind. She had absolutely nothing to say that was of any consequence. She wittered on, at length, about the holidays she was planning, to Antigua and St Lucia, and the excitement of a newly opened trendy boutique where she could buy clothes for the aforementioned trips. How William could bear to live with such a vacuous creature was to exercise my mind for many weeks. However, she was the third wife and definitely in the "trophy" category.

I believe they never knew what I thought of her as the invitations to supper, barbecues and pub lunches kept coming. William and I played Bridge with increasing regularity, sometimes three or four times a week. We almost invariably won, thanks mostly to his skill.

It all changed when the Mensa Bridge Tournament was announced. It was to take place in the Majestic, a well-known hotel in Bolton on the third Wednesday of the following month. Teams had been invited from across the North West.

William looked slightly abashed and muttered something that I didn't quite catch.

'Could you repeat that?' I asked, though from the look on his face I had an idea that I wasn't going to like it.

'Sorry old chap, but you'll have to find another partner for that. Amanda has started to object to my being out so much.'

'But it's the tournament,' I heard myself whine.

'Yes but it is a Wednesday and that is the night we always go out to eat.'

'Can't you go another night?'

'If I tried to change a Wednesday there would be all hell to pay.'

'But we have a good chance of winning the whole thing.'

'You'll find another partner and do brilliantly.'

I knew that was untrue. I had never played as well as I did with William. Never. But there was to be no changing his mind and I realised that not only was Amanda an irritant but also that she was a threat. I could imagine that soon she would be stopping our Bridge evenings altogether. That would not do. It would not do at all. Already with her incessant demand for holidays William was to be away four out of the next six weeks. He had confessed that he didn't particularly enjoy their trips, preferring more cultural weeks in cities with historical buildings and art galleries. He found lying on a beach boring but it was his wife's idea of heaven and so he went along with it. If she was not on the scene William and I could enjoy civilised ventures to Paris, Venice or Rome.

If she was not on the scene. Now what could I do about that?

How planning a murder, and one as potentially tricky as this one, cheered me up. The Bridge Tournament paled into insignificance compared with the extinction of Mrs Albright. It was during the planning stage that I chuckled out loud at the inappropriateness of her name. What a misnomer. She was anything but bright and soon I would extinguish what little light she possessed.

Amanda had stopped working the day she married William. Her time was filled with such trivial activities as shopping, going to the gym, booking appointments at the beauty parlour and meeting her equally inane friends for lunch. None of those destinations seemed like a suitable place for a killing so it would have to be somewhere in her home, there were enough rooms to choose from. I would have to make it appear that she had disturbed a burglar who had attacked her and left her for dead. My prints were, quite legitimately, all over the house so unless I was seen in the vicinity on the day of the burglary I would not be a suspect.

'How is Amanda?' I asked the next time I met William.

'Fine, she asked if you wanted to come for a barbecue, weather permitting, otherwise it's a kitchen do, on Saturday. Come about seven.'

'That would be great.' As I said this I was thinking that, with a bit of careful questioning, I could ascertain

Amanda's movements for the following week. I hoped the murder would be done that week as after that they were off for their fortnight in the sun. Planning is fun but one can delay the actual event too long. Simon Bell was starting to be a prime example of that scenario.

Saturday evening was surprisingly warm. It had been a lovely late spring day and the Albright's patio benefitted from the evening sun so we were able to have the promised barbecue. Amanda was looking wonderful in a red top that left little to the imagination and a pair of white trousers that were so tight they would probably need removing surgically. There was a brief moment when my resolve to kill her almost deserted me but then I remembered that she was curtailing William's life. He would be a free soul without her and able to indulge in his academic hobbies and cultural holidays. I would be doing him a massive favour.

'Are you going to be very busy before you go away?' I asked trying to sound as though I was merely making conversation.

'Well I've got a dress fitting on Monday afternoon, lunch with the girlies on Tuesday and the hairdresser on Thursday. Then we leave on Friday. I can't wait, two delicious-wiscious weeks of sun.' She wittered on about the forthcoming holiday but I had stopped listening. There was only one thing on my mind.

Having ascertained that it was a gardener-free day I knew that it would have to be Wednesday!

The evening was pleasant enough. William was a dab-hand at cooking food over hot coals and we were able to stay outside until the light had gone and the midges started to bite. Once inside I made my excuses and left, wishing Amanda a wonderful holiday.

'We'll send you a post card and tell you all about it when we get back. You must come round and see the photos. We always take too many, but it's so easy to look at them when they're loaded on the computer.'

Yet again I had to ask myself why anyone thinks that people, who weren't there, want to look at holiday snaps. It is another of life's great mysteries. Do other people find as many of those as I do?

Chapter 13

Daily Gazette

Garage Owner Questioned.

Mr Greg Walters, aged fifty two, gave lengthy evidence yesterday in the trial for the murder of Jamie Richardson. Mr Walters was initially questioned by the police immediately after the toddler's abused body was discovered in one of the garages he owns on the Streatham Estate. He was suspected of playing a part in the toddler's murder but was released on bail pending further enquiries. We were one of the few papers not to profile him adversely at that time. This is to our credit as, after his alibi was proved to be reliable, the police knew him to be innocent and looked elsewhere for the killer of the tiny boy.

Whilst in custody himself, Mr Walters had been able to give the police valuable information which led to the arrest of the defendant.

In his evidence Mr Walters said that he knew the defendant as he had at one time used one of the garages to house his vehicle. This arrangement had lasted for nearly eighteen months when Mr Walters decided to give all the garages a "clean out". It was during this process that he found pornographic photographs and sex toys hidden at the rear of a garage, the one that was being used by the defendant. He said that he hated anything like that and immediately told the man that the garage was no longer available.

When Mr Walters asked the defendant to vacate his garage the defendant had become angry and tried to assault him. This had led to an appearance in court but the case had been dropped as Mr Walters had not been willing to press charges. He added that he had not seen the defendant for over two years. He was not aware that his garage was being used again and would have carried out his threat to call the police about the pornography if he had caught him there. When asked how he thought the defendant had gained access to the garage he admitted that he seldom locked any of them as the kids on the estate did more damage breaking the locks than they did once they were inside.

When Mr Walters was asked to look at the photographs found beside the body he said that they looked similar to the ones he had found. He said that both sets were of young boys in highly sexual poses and both showed signs of torture. As a responsible family paper we are reluctant to add greater detail.

The case continues.

Judge's Notes

Mr Greg Walters: a credible witness. Stuck to his story during the prolonged cross examination. For once the admirable Deidre made no inroad and was unable to get him to change a single word of his testimony. However I am not convinced that his vital evidence made a sufficient impact on the jury. One feels they are growing weary and it was a long day and stuffy in court.

I knew the significance of Mr Walter's comments but surprisingly the defendant looked unperturbed. Had I been him I would have been worried, but he is such a cold fish and appears to have distanced himself even further from the details that are emerging (which as far as he is concerned appear increasingly unfavourable). Most peculiar.

Deidre Hannigan arrived home later than usual. The journey through Manchester's rush hour had been particularly tedious. She had been married to Walter for almost thirty years and for most of those they had lived in Alderley Edge, fifteen miles to the south of the city. The village was famous (or infamous depending on one's point of view) as a haven for Premier League footballers and the house prices were beyond most people's means. Walter had accrued his wealth as an entrepreneur, joining the computer and later the internet explosions at the most lucrative times. He was almost two decades her senior and had been retired for many years, providing her with a "house-husband" and enabling her to pursue her career without the worry of domestic duties. There had been no children, a disappointment at the time, but Deidre realised that she would not be where she was today had she not been able to take advantage of the promotions that had come her way.

'How was your day?' Walter asked, handing her a cup of tea. Deidre never drank alcohol thinking it might inhibit her thinking processes.

'Not good, not good at all, not that Mr Casual (her name for the defendant from day one) appears to agree with me. When I saw him at the end of the day, after some pretty damming evidence, he just smiled and said it would be alright. He repeated that he was innocent and the jury were bound to agree.'

'Still telling you he had nothing to do with it?'

'Yes, and more so as the trial goes on, he's like an areoplane set on auto-pilot.'

'How are you going to play it now?'

'Do you know, for the first time in my life I'm just not sure, a feeling that is most disquieting. Talking to him is like ploughing through a muddy field wearing the wrong shoes. He just bogs me down with his constant repetition of his innocence, but gives me very little to work with.' They were sitting in their conservatory looking out over the Cheshire countryside, the daily pattern when Deidre arrived home. She was in the habit of discussing her cases with Walter, who she knew would never divulge any details to his cronies on the golf course, but this trial was hard to talk about.

'I can hardly sum up today. There is evidence that Mr Casual is into pornography but he is adamant that he has never looked at any as he put it "deviant children's pics". Even he looked a little nonplussed today when it was suggested that he was into that sort of thing. I have to say none was found on his hard drive though there were plenty of other images.'

Walter listened without comment as his wife reviewed the day's events. He knew from long experience that using him as a sounding board often helped her to organise her thoughts and plan the next day's strategy.

'Do you recall how when I first met him I was convinced by how adamant he was that he had nothing to do with the murder? I know that, on occasion, I am *required to put my client's case even when I suspect they are telling me a pack of lies, but this man is so different and until today I believed him. The trouble is I'm not so sure any more, but I am duty bound to continue to provide the best possible defence for him.'*

'Knowing you my dear, that goes without comment. It sounds to me as though he is lucky to have you.'

'Just another cup of tea then I'd better go and study my notes to know how to advise him, though he is so strong willed that I doubt he'll take much advice from me. I have a feeling he would rather have a man defending him, but I did opt for this high profile case and he has said that he knows I have an impressive track record.'

'Dinner can be ready when you are,' Walter said, thinking it might be in the oven for some time.

How excruciatingly tedious the trial is becoming. The prosecution is soldiering on manfully but some of their witnesses give evidence that feels like clutching at the proverbial straws. Sir Cecil looks rather like a small child who, excited by an unexpected fall of snow, is becoming more and more frustrated by his inability to keep any of the snowflakes in his hand. I suspect he is beginning to think that the evidence he has been given to use is rather flimsy. But the case is a long way from over and some of the jury look confused even when he makes telling points. Were they really aware of the importance of Mr Walter's evidence? Few of them were taking notes and might have forgotten the salient points when the time comes to discuss the case and they were reminded that it is the prosecution's duty to prove guilt. Nevertheless I am sure that at least some of them will have understood the value of his evidence.

Back to my writing. Ah, yes, Amanda Albright, soon to be no more and thus allow William to become a widower, a very happy one. I needed some pretext to pop round to see Amanda on the Wednesday though I knew she was not clever enough to think that there was anything strange about my turning up uninvited. No element of surprise was necessary but there should be a reason for her to invite me in.

I had in my possession a particularly classy Parker pen which I had received as a present many years before but had never used. I would take that. It would gain me access more readily than any key.

'Hello Amanda, just thought I'd come round with a little going away present. You promised to send me a post card on your holiday so I've brought a rather posh pen to use. No excuses now for not keeping me informed about the vacation.' (A somewhat tricky word for her but she appeared to understand.)

'Do come in. I was just popping the kettle on. Have you got time for a cuppa?'

'Thanks I'd like that.'

'You are a sweetums to think of a pressie, thank you so much.'

One of the things that had always grated was her constant use of such immature words. "Sweetums" and "pressie", for goodness sake, she sounded about eight. I followed her into the state of the art kitchen where modern appliances stood to attention, like soldiers on parade, waiting to do battle with a range of foods. I doubted whether they were used much but they looked impressive which I suspected was the main idea. She was, as I had thought, totally unsuspecting.

I had brought the pen in a plastic bag, too large for it but ideal to place over a head. She had her back turned, and was placing the cups on a tray when I sprang into action. The bag was perfectly in place within seconds and her air supply cut off. Naturally she struggled but I was several inches taller and many pounds heavier. I suppose these days I should use centimetres and kilograms but the old-fashioned units are good enough for me. There was little she could do and as she started to lose consciousness her body, once so gorgeous, crumpled to the floor. All so delightfully straightforward. Definitely one of my less traumatic killings: no sound, no mess, nothing to clear up. All over in a few, utterly glorious, life-taking moments, the kind I spend weeks anticipating.

Removing the bag from her head was like unwrapping a birthday present, the sort one has asked for but had little expectation of receiving. She looked very little different in death, still beautiful and with her usual uncomprehending expression.

I put away the cups; mustn't let the police think that she had invited her killer in. Having been to the house so many times there was no fear of my fingerprints being identified so I didn't need to clean the kitchen. I knew I had to make it look like a robbery so I put on some gloves and spent a short time riffling through and emptying the contents of several drawers in the living room and bedroom. I left her jewellery lying on the bedroom floor, hoping the police would assume that Amanda had disturbed a burglar who had then fled after killing her. The bedroom was as palatial as the rest of the house with a huge four-poster bed placed against one wall. Flounces and frills added to it and the entire room looked unquestionably feminine with various shades of pink assaulting the eye. Did William feel out of place there? In future he would be free to sleep in a more masculine setting.

From my years in a courtroom I know that nothing is fool-proof but I thought it most unlikely that I could possibly be in the frame for this one. I had covered my tracks and anyway, as far as anyone knew, I had no possible motive to kill her, no reason to want her dead. She and William had become my best, indeed my only, friends. On returning to the kitchen I retrieved my pen and the plastic bag.

I went outside and smashed the glass section of the kitchen door hoping it would look as though that was the burglar's point of entry. I had heard William chastise Amanda for going out and forgetting to set the alarm so I hoped that both he and the police would assume that that was the case on this occasion and that the intruder had entered without too much noise.

Feeling deliriously happy I went round the back of the house and exited through the side gate. It was, as always, unlocked and I was soon on my way.

The road was quiet and no one saw me leave. I was attired in an outfit I would never normally wear: denims, a hoodie and dark glasses. Amanda hadn't noticed how different I looked or if she had she had not commented. The outfit was rather prosaic and if I had been seen I truly believe no one would have recognised me. The whole thing had lasted less than an hour so I was able to run back to court and be ensconced in my room, pretending to be catching up with paper work before anyone needed to speak to me. I had made my presence felt at the beginning of the day but had then asked not to disturbed as I informed them that I had a lot of work to do.

I found it almost impossible to sit still and kept leaping up and dancing a jig around the room. Anyone who had come in might have sent for a straightjacket. As lunch time approached I went to the staff room and heard the usual out of court discussions.

'Maggie Hendrix was in again this morning. That's the third time this month. We should issue her with a season ticket,' Jill, one of the other legal advisers was saying as I walked in.

'She needs help. I thought the Probation Service was involved,' Barbara, my deputy replied.

'Well they are now.' Jill turned and saw me.

'Hi Ben, had a good morning with the paper work?'

'Yes thanks, I got a lot done. Not quite finished but nearly.'

Johnnie Saunders, one of the most unlikeable lawyers, perhaps soured by years of defending the obviously guilty, was lounging by the window. The man was attired as per usual in one of his many flamboyantly striped three piece suits and a brightly spotted dickey-bow tie. The general consensus was that he would have been more at home at the Old Bailey. He and I rarely exchanged many words but on this occasion he addressed his unwelcome comments in my direction.

'You look pleased with yourself. Have you been doing something more exciting than paperwork?'

I knew he was being his usual irritating self and that I mustn't rise. This was not the time to have any display of emotion, or to let anyone think that I had been otherwise engaged.

'I'm merely thankful to have done sufficient to break the back of the work. An afternoon should have it completed.'

'Do you ever use one word instead of ten?' was his rather nasty rejoinder. I was tempted to ask him why he repeated himself ad nauseam in court, boring both myself and any magistrates unlucky enough to have him as the defence lawyer for the day, but thought better of it. Today was not the time to draw attention to myself. Managing a smile I excused myself and duly spent the afternoon finishing off the backlog of forms.

It was late in the evening when the phone rang. The voice on the other end of the line was almost unrecognisable. William was blubbing! He was not the man I had thought he was. How could a grown man, of his background and education, allow himself to give way to such embarrassing emotion?

'She's dead, Amanda, she's been murdered.' He had to repeat himself several times before I was able to understand a word he was saying. The man was out of control. Something I cannot abide.

'Someone broke in and killed her. I found her when I got home. The police have been and say it looks as though she disturbed a burglar. Will you come round?'

Now to be honest with you I have never felt comfortable revisiting the scenes of my misdemeanours. I am afraid that I will give myself away either with an outburst of unwarranted pride or an unsuitably cheerful comment. However I had no viable reason to refuse William's request and was with him within the hour.

'Oh thank God you're here, it's all too awful. She's dead Ben, she's dead. What am I going to do?'

'This is terrible, William.............' I was about to say more but he interrupted me by breaking down and weeping in my arms. After a suitable period of time I put on my most caring voice and asked, 'Can you tell me what happened?'

'I was late home, oh dear God if only I had been earlier I might have saved her, oh my poor darling Amanda.'

'Do you feel up to telling me exactly what happened?' I asked softly, doing my best to keep the irritation I was feeling out of my voice. In retrospect he was probably too emotional to register such vocal nuances.

'She was murdered, oh bloody hell, what a word, murdered..............no, no, I can't bear it, my beautiful, adorable Amanda.' The man was now yowling like next door's tom-cat looking for some action. He was still almost impossible to understand but I persevered, if only to get the official thinking on the incident.

'You said on the phone that the police suspected a break-in.'

'Yes, yes, that's what they think happened; that when she came home she disturbed a burglar. ....he killed her............ why do that? ....why not just leave? ....she'd have given him anything he wanted. ....no need to kill her.' He appeared to be making a monumental effort as he uttered each phrase.

'Maybe he panicked and thought she would be able to ID him. Do you mind me asking how she died?'

'They think she was smothered.....there has to be an autopsy...........oh hell, hell, hell, to think of her beautiful body being cut up..............oh dear God.'

I had to agree that Amanda had been a most attractive woman, but any suspicious death results in an official investigation and part of that process is an autopsy to ascertain the cause of death. Why the fact that she was pretty should have any bearing on the matter was beyond me. By now she was a cadaver. We all become equal in death. I surmised that I was probably better to keep these thoughts to myself.

'If they think it was a burglar, did he get away with much?'

There was a long pause as William seemed confused by the inappropriateness of such a question. When he spoke it was with a coldness I had never heard him employ. He then appeared to regain a modicum of self-control as he replied, 'I have absolutely no bloody idea and at this moment it doesn't even come in to the bloody picture.' He had never, in our many months of friendship, spoken in such a brusque manner, nor had he ever sworn, an aspect of communication that I abhor as it displays such an inadequate regard for the English language. I felt slighted and was unable to speak for many minutes whilst he resumed his unmanly caterwauling. The William I had thought I had known would have retained more dignity.

Had I really known the man?

'Is there anything I can do?' I asked using that so oft repeated vacuous phrase. 'I could plan a holiday for us; we could go somewhere to take your mind off all of this.'

'All of this? What in God's name does that mean? All of this is the death of my wife, the woman I adored. My soul mate, my best friend; the woman I wanted to spend the rest of my life with. That's what "all of this" means.' The dramatic crescendo that accompanied each phrase would not have been out of place in a Verdi opera. I wondered whether I had broached the idea of a holiday together too soon. But really the man was a wimp, a total wimp. What better way to overcome an unfortunate occurrence than by doing something different? Why could he not see that?

'Well maybe when you're ready I could plan something for us. I know you like holidays and you'll be missing the one next week.'

William exploded. He ranted, his face turned a most unattractive and, I feared, an unhealthy red. 'Next week! Next week! Yes my beloved Amanda and I were going away but if you think for one iota of a second that going away with you could possibly...........possibly make up for that you are a complete and utter bloody moron.'

I had heard enough. There was to be no reasoning with the man when he was in this mood. I had thought better of him but what a state he was in. There was no point in staying. However if I left it might look bad. I decided to stay.

William was no longer worthy to be called my friend and that truth was utterly devastating. A man who could behave with such little regard for propriety was a poor specimen of humanity and I wanted to have nothing further to do with him. My dreams of our shared holidays evaporated as swiftly as the early morning mist I had seen disappear in the Alps. Throughout the long hours of darkness he alternated between an excruciating weeping and a humiliating whimpering. Oh William wherefore art thou?

He was given sedatives by the doctor and, just as dawn was breaking he passed out on the settee. I left him there and enjoyed several hours of peaceful slumber in the extremely comfortable spare bedroom, a room furnished much more to my taste in muted beige and cream. The police returned later in the morning. I contacted the court to say that my friend's wife had been murdered and that consequently I would not be at work. I seldom have time off but thought that this was probably a reasonable excuse to be absent.

How can twenty-four hours seem like an eternity? That was how long I remained with William. That was how long he continued his crying. I was amazed to hear that he was under suspicion, but I reminded myself that when a spouse dies the partner is usually one of the prime suspects. He told me later that they had even considered the possibility that he had hired a "hit-man"; definitely not William's style. Amanda had been his third wife, but far from killing his former partners he had, rather more mundanely, merely divorced them.

Needless to say the police had absolutely no leads. They never charged anyone and I rather imagine that the case remains "open". No doubt he will, by now, have found wife number four. A pathetic man like him needs companionship and he had rejected mine.

I had hoped that this would be my "perfect murder". It had many of the hallmarks necessary for such a title: it had been well planned, easily accomplished and had rid the world of a feeble woman. Unfortunately, because of it I had lost William and my hopes of future adventures. So no, not yet perfect.

Chapter 14

Daily Gazette

Impressive Forensic Evidence in the Jamie Richardson Case

The jury in the trial for this horrendous murder heard evidence from Professor Alex Parkinson, a world-famous forensic scientist. The Professor stated categorically that the defendant's DNA was found in the garage where the youngster's body was discovered.

When questioned he stated that he could assure the members of the jury that the defendant's DNA was found on the towels placed above and below Jamie's body and on the camera, found in a nearby waste bin, where the graphic photos remained on its memory stick.

Professor Parkinson added that he could say, with absolute certainty that the evidence was incontrovertible. The likelihood of unrelated people sharing the same genetic profile is one in one hundred and thirteen million and even siblings share only a tiny amount of genetic markers.

During cross examination the witness remained adamant that the DNA could only belong to the defendant but his testimony was interrupted when the man, who normally sits so passively in the dock, became distressed and started shouting that it wasn't possible that it was his DNA as he had not been anywhere near the garage for years. It was when he added that the whole thing was an utter fiasco and that he wasn't being given a fair trial that the judge called for a short recess. The defendant's lawyer was asked to remind her client that should there be any more outbursts the trial would be continued in his absence.

Judge's Notes

Well, well, well, the man is human after all. What an outburst. Did he realise that the DNA link was damning him?

His claims of innocence, that the DNA couldn't possibly be his, sounded so sincere. Does he believe that he is blameless, that he had nothing to do with the murder, or is he a consummate and incredibly believable liar? Did he hope to influence the jury?

Things certainly became more lively as evidence from experts can be so long-winded and at times almost incomprehensible.

I expect he will be back to his usual calm self tomorrow, though his outburst did add drama to the day's events.

Normally I am not given to depression, a ridiculously self-indulgent illness, but after the disappointment of William I was extremely low for several days. I did not return to work immediately, taking a very long weekend, an indulgence I rarely feel is necessary. The football season was over so no chance of taking my mind off things at a match. Cricket, never my favourite sport, was the only alternative. These days it is easy to travel to Old Trafford to watch Lancashire play. Train to Piccadilly then tram straight to the ground. I was able to do the former but as this was pre-tram days had to suffer a slow crawl by bus out of the city along Oxford Road and through to the cricket ground.

Rain had been forecast but the day remained dry if a little cloudy. The world-famous ground has been the home of Lancashire Cricket Club since 1864 and became extremely popular after the Roses match of 1875 when Lancashire beat arch rivals Yorkshire by ten wickets. The legendary W.G. Grace played there for Gloucestershire in 1878 in front of twenty eight thousand spectators, many more than most football clubs can expect to attract today. The ground was closed during the First World War and it is hard to visualise its use as a transit camp for soldiers who had escaped from Dunkirk during the Second. It was badly damaged by a bomb in the blitzing of Manchester in December 1940 and it is ironical that German POW's were employed to restore it when hostilities ceased. The "Victory Test" between England and Australia was played there in August 1945 with over seventy thousand (including my father and Pops) attending over the three days. Internationals have been played at Old Trafford for well over a century though it has the rather dubious reputation as the wettest Test venue. Many Mancunians, loyal to their city, dispute the validity of this accolade.

Lancashire was playing Somerset, a five day endurance test for those stalwarts who attended each session. I was sorry that the game wasn't a One Day event, the sort at which Lancashire has excelled since its introduction in the 1960's. The shorter games tend to be more exciting and have the added bonus of seeing a result on the day. The Saturday in question was the third day of a rather plebeian affair. Lancashire was batting having bowled Somerset out the day before for a mere two hundred and five runs. Perhaps it was a poor batting wicket but the northerners didn't fare much better and by close of play had managed a rather disappointing two hundred and twenty five. The day served its purpose in that it allowed me to forget William but it didn't tempt me to go on a regular basis.

For some reason I have absolutely no recollection of the remainder of the weekend.

The thrill of Amanda's demise had worn off far more quickly than I hoped but as I walked to work on that glorious Monday morning in late May I little thought that my next murder would occur quite so soon. It was however, as always, utterly necessary. The sky that morning was a deep cloudless blue, the type we seldom enjoy in the North West of England, and by eight o'clock the temperature was already approaching the high sixties.

Unfortunately the Court List did not match the weather and looked most unappealing. The weekend's "Drunk and Disorderly" reprobates were in the cells along with several who had committed assaults or had managed to do some criminal damage. Many of the names and faces were familiar, the individuals who by the time they progress from the Youth to Adult Court, at the age of nineteen, are as well- known to both the Magistrates and the Legal Advisers as they are to their own families, indeed they must sometimes feel that they see more of us than them.

I was in Court Two. I knew all three of the Magistrates who were sitting that day and I was pleased to see that the Chairman was Mr Timothy Wellbrook, a retired Managing Director and a stickler for protocol. The morning's business began with the appearance of a certain notorious duo, Sharleen and Chelsea Froom. We saw them so often that I began to wonder if they enjoyed our company. My spirits rose as they were always a challenge and I felt that that was what I needed. Most people in court are on their best behaviour as they know they must make a reasonable impression and have been given sensible advice on how to do so by their solicitors. Not so the Froom duo. Over the years they have been in court for a variety of offences and are most unsavoury characters.

The charge that day was "Harassment - putting people in fear of violence". The obnoxious pair had been involved in the more serious racially aggravated variety and both were alleged to have committed the offence on several occasions. As they pleaded not guilty (no surprise there) a trial date was set. Now it was by no means the first time that I had encountered such a crime, but it was the first that I had witnessed such a lack of propriety. They smirked, chewed gum, chatted between themselves and exhibited a complete lack of respect. Lawyers advise their clients to dress appropriately in court but Silvia Mander's advice to her twosome had obviously fallen on very deaf ears.

Both were dressed in the style of overgrown teenagers and today's outfits of matching skin-tight leopard skin leggings and lurid pink boob tubes did nothing to add to their allure. Their appearances were not helped by their rather ample bosoms which resulted in quite a lot of boobs spilling in every direction around the tubes. Pictures of them could have featured on not only page three of the Sun but also pages four and five! They looked ready to audition for a second rate "sister act" caterwaul on one of the many atrocious and misnamed talent shows that abound in the less salubrious night clubs in Preston.

'Miss Mander, your clients appear to be taking the court proceedings with an unacceptable degree of levity. The magistrates are going to withdraw for ten minutes whilst you remind both Miss Frooms how to behave in a court of law. Should their behaviour not improve they may find themselves detained in the cells for the duration of the day's work.'

As the JP's retired to deliberate Sharleen made a rude gesture which amused her sister. Their lawyer did her best but I felt she was not succeeding. She was a fairly forceful woman and an excellent defence lawyer, but in the Froom sisters she had more than met her match.

I decided to intervene, 'Miss Froom and Miss Froom unless you start to behave in a respectful and polite manner not only will you be kept in court all day but you are also likely to be given additional punishments for appalling behaviour and showing disrespect to Her Majesty's Court.'

'Who are you, Granddad? You can't tell us what to do.' Sharleen's voice was full of unwarranted bravado. I did not respond knowing I would have my revenge. What an ignorant girl, the sooner she was out of all our miseries the better. This one would take very little planning but would be so inordinately satisfying. Everyone associated with Preston Magistrates' Court would be forever in my debt.

Neither Sharleen nor Chelsea heeded the advice they had been given and after being fined were informed that they would spend the rest of the day in the court buildings and were sent to the cells for their total lack of respect. Chelsea was the lesser of the two evils and would, I thought, probably be a better person without the influence of her older sister. I would, therefore, also be doing her a massive favour.

It was very soon after Amanda's death and, as you must have realised, I am not given to committing my annihilations too close together. I allow myself time to appreciate each deed and do not feel the need to kill before a suitable length of time has elapsed. This time it was different. The intense disappointment of William's reaction continued to rankle. There was an appalling sense of anti-climax.

Sharleen would help; she would suit my needs very well. She could no longer be allowed to besmirch my courtroom so I would deal with her. At the end of the day she was released with her sister and they headed straight for the nearest pub, their natural habitat. My idea was simple. Follow them, wait for them to become drunk, to imbibe the proverbial "skin- full" and follow them home. Farewell and good riddance Miss Sharleen Froom.

They could certainly drink. Beer, wine, vodka and goodness knows what else was poured down their throats. Eventually, after a few hours they became raucous and were asked to leave. Having given the poor landlord a mouthful of most unsavoury language, they staggered out onto the street. Imagine my joy when they parted company almost immediately. Chelsea headed to the taxi rank and Sharleen lurched along the road, clutching the wall in order to remain upright. She turned down an alley, no doubt destined for whichever friend would lend her their settee for the night. I was reasonably sure that she had never done a day's work in her miserable life and existed, as so many of our "clients" did on benefits and the generosity of friends to provide shelter for the night and allow people like her, those euphemistically referred to as of no fixed abode, to "sofa-surf".

She was a scrap of thing - her body having been ruined by years of alcohol and substance misuse. She was in her early thirties, but as is so often the case when the body has been abused in that manner she looked about two decades older. Her extremely high heels made any movement difficult and with the added constriction caused by too many drinks I knew she was not about to escape.

It could have been over in seconds but I was determined to make her realise exactly why her days were about to come to a premature end. I never carried a knife normally, knowing that to have one in one's possession on the street was an offence, but I had picked a huge carver up from the staff kitchen just before I left. There were so many in the drawer that I knew one would not be missed. It felt enormous and rather unwieldy but I hoped it would serve its purpose.

Overtaking her was easy. Swinging round I faced the miserable specimen. She didn't recognise "granddad" and merely snarled, 'What the fuck do you want?' I was almost overcome by the alcoholic fumes emanating from her.

'Don't you recognise me Sharleen? I was in court today when you were such a naughty girl.' Her reply was unprintable and contained the foul language that was her normal style of speech.

'You really cannot be permitted to behave like that so I have come to make sure that it doesn't happen again.'

'You a fucking gob-shite? Get the bleeding hell out of my face.'

'What a shame that those will be the last words you utter; so uncouth; so unladylike; but then you really aren't much of a lady are you?' To give her some credit she was standing her ground, swaying slightly but looking me in the eye.

The knife slid into her side so easily, like a well-oiled key into a lock; it felt like the sole purpose for which it had been created. A look of total amazement sullied her face which became marred by the dark rivulets of black mascara that streamed down. She was too shocked to speak which was a blessing, one that would have been beneficial on many previous occasions.

'In a moment you will take your final breath. I am about to kill you. If I don't you will be back in court within a very short time and I really cannot allow that to happen. I do hope you understand. You see Sharleen all actions have consequences. Your action was to behave unforgivably in my court room today. The consequence of that action is that you are about to die. Goodbye Miss Froom.' Unlike hers my manners remained impeccable.

She had no time to reply. Being careful not to come into direct contact with her clothes for fear of fibre remnants I re-applied the knife, this time to her heart. Death came all too quickly. I left the blade in situ and I had taken the precaution of wearing gloves, though why anyone would suspect me of having anything to do with her demise I couldn't imagine. She had been a notorious character with more enemies than Genghis Khan and there would be a plethora of suspects. Few I thought would mourn her passing.

As I walked home I felt an unusual calm. I knew, beyond doubt, that I had done the right thing, the only possible thing in the circumstances. I was suddenly ravenous. The only establishment that was still open was an Indian take away, not normally my preferred food but I loved every mouthful of my chicken curry and rice. I had served the gods well and earned my ambrosia. That night I slept for nine hours and woke refreshed to face the new day, the first one minus the abominable Sharleen.

The local news was on as I ate a well-earned breakfast. Killings give one such an appetite. I had recently purchased a small portable TV for the kitchen and enjoyed what felt like an indulgence each morning.

The body found in Shorewell Alley in the centre of Preston, in the early hours of this morning, has not yet been identified. The police are treating the death as suspicious. The victim is believed to be female and between the ages of thirty and fifty.

I laughed at the death being called "suspicious". A knife protruding from the chest would make it look like that. Elementary - even for Doctor Watson. There was no talk of the news item at work that day. No one realised that it was Sharleen. The day passed without anything untoward happening and I was pleased that my demeanour remained totally professional. I continued to experience the most delightful feeling of serenity and an almost surreal superiority over my colleagues. I knew things they didn't. I had done things they hadn't. I had the power of life and death.

That evening both the local and the national news had Sharleen's murder as their lead item. I felt as though I had reached the big time. Matthew Green, the reporter for BBC North West, was given the task of reporting the incident. I sat transfixed as he spoke from the entrance to Shorewell Alley.

The body, discovered in Preston in the early hours of this morning, has been identified as that of Miss Sharleen Froom. Miss Froom was of no fixed abode and was well known to the local police. She was last seen by her sister, Chelsea, at ten o'clock yesterday evening after they left the Bull's Horn public house in Preston. The sisters had spent the day in court and had been bailed pending a trial for harassment. Sharleen was due to spend the night at her friend's house but did not arrive. The event is being treated as murder and police are anxious to interview anyone in the vicinity of Shorewell Alley between the hours of ten o'clock and midnight. If you have any information please ring 01772 455677.

The murder made the headlines in all the tabloids the next day and was page two in the rest.

Chapter 15

Judge's Notes

A weekend away from court. Jane and I should be enjoying two days of relaxation, but I can't switch off.

After so many years presiding over numerous disturbing trials, too many to recall, I wonder why this one is invading my every waking thought, like an army laying siege to a city. Cases involving children are particularly harrowing, and I have sat on several before, but this is the first to dislodge my equilibrium to quite such a degree. I feel utterly weary but am unable to enjoy a good night's sleep and when I do nod off lurid dreams disturb my rest. Jane is, as always, a reliable and trustworthy pair of ears but even she is losing patience with my endless obsession with the case.

The unpalatable evidence would appear to be stacking up against the defendant who yesterday returned to his silent self, and appeared once again to have removed himself mentally from the proceedings.

His note taking is becoming more and more frantic and one is left wondering whether his writing will ever become public.

Two murders in such a short time were so unusual for me that I decided to take a break from any thought of more slaughter. Life resumed its normal pattern: work, running and watching my beloved Preston North End. Deepdale was a happy place. The new season started well and for many months we were in the play-off positions. Another couple of wins and one of the automatic promotion spots would be occupied by us. Stay there for the next six months and we would be in the Premiership for the first time. Football is the one area of my life where I am an optimist! My Saturday afternoons were most enjoyable as not only were we winning all the home games but winning them in style. A new player, Jamie McDonald, had signed for us in the summer and was making a difference and scoring at will. Glorious hat-tricks witnessed in the previous two games. The defence was stronger than it had been for a while so all in all the fans were happy.

Sharleen's murder had helped me come to terms with the disappointment of Amanda's and I was feeling reasonably content, so much so that I wasn't in a hurry to deal with Simon Bell. How strange, just when he was not intruding on my life, that I should read his name on the court agenda one cool October day. I immediately made sure that he was on my list in Court Three. His misdemeanour this time was "Theft from a Shop".

He was second on the day's agenda. As usual he entered the room with an arrogant swagger. The case against him was that he had stolen goods in excess of eight hundred pounds from the Comet store on the outskirts of Preston. It was in essence, a very straightforward case of stealing fuelled simply by spur of the moment greed. He had taken three cameras which had been left on the counter by an inattentive assistant who had forgotten to put them away after showing them to a genuine customer. Simon didn't need three cameras and, no doubt, intended to sell them on in his local pub.

'Mr Bell took the cameras, succumbing to a moment of temptation. He did not go into the shop intending to steal and has shown remorse for his actions. The cameras have been recovered and he has pleaded guilty at the first opportunity.'

Do the defence lawyers actually believe the rubbish they spout? No intention? Remorse? Simon Bell? I didn't think so. He had been caught on the CCTV cameras in the shop and as he was so well known to the police was apprehended the same evening.

The Chairman was Miss Stewart, a retired head teacher, and a magistrate whom I knew would, with the assistance of her wingers, pass the maximum sentence. I could imagine her, in times past, with the black cap perched neatly on her grey curls.

The court rose as the J.P's took their seats. Miss Stewart stared at Simon and spoke in a voice that was so cold that it even sent shivers down my spine. I wondered how many pupils, over the years, had become quivering wrecks when sent to her room.

'Mr Bell, you appear before us yet again. Your list of misdemeanours is so extensive that it may one day be entered in the record book named after the Guinness breweries. There is absolutely no doubt that you committed the crime with which you are charged. The CCTV evidence is irrefutable, showing you very clearly taking the cameras from the counter and leaving the shop without paying. You targeted high value goods and although this may well have been an unpremeditated theft you knowingly broke the law, as you have done so many times before.

We have considered a custodial sentence but past incarcerations show that in your case this is an ineffective punishment. We are therefore issuing a High Level Community Order. You will undertake two hundred and fifty hours of unpaid work. We considered three hundred hours but we have reduced this in recognition of your early guilty plea, though it was obvious that you had little choice in the matter. In addition you will have a two month curfew between the hours of seven p.m. and six a.m. As the cameras have been recovered there will be no compensation to the Curry's store. You will, however pay the costs of this trial, three hundred and fifty pounds.'

Simon stood impassively; he had been here so many times before and had known what to expect. He was told to see his probation officer.

'You made me laugh when you told Simon to see his probation officer. They must be becoming quite good friends by now,' was my comment to Miss Stewart once he had left the room.

'Philip has the patience of a saint and often performs miracles with his clients, but even he must be despairing of Simon by now. Hope he tells him that it's another spell in prison next time,' was her quiet reply.

'We're expecting a next time?'

'Without a doubt, such a pity as I think there is some potential in there somewhere. I wish I'd had been able to have him at my school for a few years, an impossibility as it was all girls, but it might have been interesting to see if our style of regime could have influenced him to lead a more productive life.' Knowing her I rather suspected that that might well have been the case.

The morning's business finished eventually, the usual array of chaotic lives having been witnessed and dealt with ad nauseam.

'Anyone seen Mr Bell's rucksack?' Simon's lawyer, the long suffering Mr Rogerson was doing his best to sound concerned. 'He says that the police don't bother when something goes missing that belongs to him. Reckons he never got it back after he was arrested following the fight at the footie a few months ago. Makes a song and dance about it every time I see him. Claims it had his new trainers and towels in and that he was planning a visit to the gym after the match. What a shame the police interrupted his keep - fit plans.'

'He can always replace the items in his own inimitable fashion, shouldn't cost too much!' I retorted feeling satisfied that as I was the one with his belongings I had caused the odious man some disquiet.

The curfew that had been imposed meant that any plans I had would have to be put on hold. However when I went into the staff room at the end of the day all three of Simon's erstwhile cameras were sitting in an open box on the coffee table prior to their return to Curry's. I helped myself to one (an unpremeditated theft) thinking that it might come in useful one day. I had missed having a camera in Switzerland and knew that I would never spend that much money on such a state of the art piece of equipment. There was, quite naturally, a brief investigation as to the whereabouts of the missing camera but in a busy establishment that soon died the death, unlike Mr Bell. To think there was a thief in the Magistrates' building! Was I becoming as much of a scallywag as the miscreants I dealt with each day?

It would be many months before I thought of him again. There was a prolonged period where I had no desire to commit another murder and I wondered whether I had done enough. They had all been most satisfying and some had proved positively exhilarating and for a time the desire for the perfect one abated. I came into contact with few people outside work, most weeks talking only to my fellow supporters at the football. I enjoyed the articles and puzzles in the Mensa magazines but was not tempted to join any more of their activities. Recovering from the disappointing consequences of the one associated with that group would prove be a slow business.

Had I committed sufficient murders? Typing the words "Serial Killer" into a search engine produced almost eleven million results in zero point one nine seconds. One definition was:

- A minimum of three to four victims, with a "cooling off" period in between;
- The killer is usually a stranger to the victim — the murders appear unconnected or totally random;
- The murders reflect a need to sadistically over-whelm and dominate the victim;
- The murder is rarely "for profit"; the motive is psychological, not for material gain;
- The victim may have "symbolic" or personal value for the killer; method of killing may reveal this meaning;
- Killers often choose victims who are vulnerable (the immature, prostitutes, runaways, etc.)

Yes all are true. I am also a white male, middle class and was in my twenties and thirties when many of my murders were committed, again all facts that fit the general profile. The sites speak of the killer being the product of a dysfunctional background where he or she lives in isolation, given little love or attention and they enjoyed little bonding with their parents. Some killers say they felt they were viewed as the "black sheep of the family". It is agreed that the majority of serial killings might have been avoided if the killers had been treated better in their youths. I wondered whether they were writing about me?

Some statements are not relevant: an apparent lack of motives (every one of my murders had a purpose), an inability to be accepted socially (I hold down a job where I am dealing with people at all times), disorganised thinking (my First Class degree from Oxford would seem to abolish that notion) and a resentment towards society (no, only certain individuals).

The site I particularly liked was the one that spoke of serial killers as seeing themselves as dominant, controlling, powerful figures with the power of life over death. The infamous Ted Bundy summed up the situation perfectly when he said, "Most serial killers are people who kill for the pleasure of killing". Exactly!

For the next twelve months I was a responsible citizen. Life was, all in all, quite pleasant, until the day Preston was forced to remain in the second tier of the football leagues having lost two-one to Burnley in a thrilling Play-Off final at Wembley in late May. We were the better team throughout the match. Yes, I am biased but the reports in the papers the following day confirmed my opinion. We were one-nil up at half time, a glorious volley from Johnson just before the break, the ball screaming into the top corner of the net, giving their goalie no chance. We had several opportunities to increase our lead but the Burnley defence was rock solid. I truly believe the score would have remained one up to us were it not for the so called assistant referee.

It is easy, when one's team lose, to blame the officials and I would hate to think that they got decisions wrong deliberately, though rumours of bribery make one suspicious. However so many glaring mistakes are made by the men in charge that the sooner modern technology comes into the game the better. The linesman that day, the one with the bright yellow flag, was incompetent. During the entire game he indicated very dubious off-sides, though for both teams in equal measure so, for most of the match, they evened themselves out. It was late in the proceedings when he lost us the game. Burnley's eightieth minute goal was allowed to stand though the scorer was blatantly off-side when the ball was passed to him.

With ten minutes remaining we had time to recover but not from the killer blow of an extremely dubious penalty a few minutes later. Neither the referee nor the thirty thousand Preston supporters saw any incident but the spot-kick was awarded, totally erroneously, after consultation with Mr Yellow Flag.

We lost. End of story. No dizzy Premiership heights for us the following season. No promotion money. No away-day trips to the likes of Stamford Bridge or The Etihad. The journey home was a miserable one. I had gone by special coach with other Preston supporters and the journey down had been full of expectation. We knew we were the better team and the promotion was ours by right as we had finished third in the league, just a point behind West Ham who gained the second automatic promotion spot. Burnley had scraped into the last play-off place on the final day of the season finishing several points behind us. We had already beaten them home and away and were confident of doing so again.

We were a subdued group on the return journey which was completed in abject silence. The linesman, alias assistant referee, came in for a lot of much warranted criticism. He had ruined it for us. It should have been us celebrating a glorious victory. How could one incompetent fool wreck it? He simply could not be allowed to get away with it. I had the match programme, a glossy affair that had cost a small fortune. The names of the officials were printed near the back. Referee: Keith Vicars; Patterned flag: Sam North; Yellow flag: Nigel Montgomery Fitzsimmons. Ye gods and little fishes I remember thinking what a moniker for a football linesman.

Arriving home in the early hours of the morning I was tired and depressed and knew I wouldn't sleep so decided to look at Nigel's details on the internet. He was easy to find. Wikipedia have lists of all the referees in England. I knew that Nigel would be a registered referee as for the top games referees are often used as linesmen or assistant referees, though the fans often have other, less polite, names for them. I learnt that he had been on the referees' official list for six years, being accepted at the age of thirty, and there was an impressive record of the major matches in which he had been involved. He was so well respected that he was on the FIFA listing and had refereed internationals. Little wonder England hadn't won anything since 1966 if his decision making was anything to go by.

Personal details were added: he was married with two children and was a teacher of chemistry at "a prestigious school in the North West". Obviously his address was not included but with that last detail I knew he wouldn't be too hard to find. Each school has its own web site with a list of teachers and it didn't take me long to find his.

St Steven's Grammar School is famous as a centre of excellence and has been lauded as a "Beacon" school by successive governments. The fees are extortionate and the parents coughing up such a vast amount each year expect great results. They are seldom disappointed. The school has been top of the secondary league tables on many occasions. I had an idea where it was and soon found it on a map on the ever useful internet. It was a few miles outside Blackpool, so not too far way. Easily accessible by train.

I now knew where Nigel spent his working week but felt a school was not the correct venue for murder. Some of the pupils might have retained some degree of innocence and I have never wanted to impinge on blameless lives. Even I would draw the line at allowing children to witness a brutal murder and more to the point there would be too many witnesses. Ideally the execution should take place somewhere that the public would associate with football but a stadium would be far too public with thousands of fans present and I would not be able to avoid detection. This one required planning of the highest order.

This murder would be committed for all PNE fans. They had been cheated of their moment of glory at Wembley, and far more importantly the chance to see Preston back where they belonged in the top division. Football is crucial to the people who go week in and week out to follow their team and Nigel had hurt us, the loyal fans, beyond measure and must pay the ultimate price. I was going to do this for the thousands whose second home is Deepdale.

Chapter 16

Daily Gazette

Shocking Details of Jamie's Final Hours.

The jury, in the case for the murder of Jamie Richardson, sat looking horrified as Doctor Michaels, a forensic pathologist, and a renowned expert in her field, gave further details about the toddler's murder. It appears that he was killed almost immediately after being snatched from outside a local shop though it is not clear where his body was kept until it was placed in the lock-up garage where it was discovered over a week later.

The defendant's house was searched but there was no evidence of Jamie having been there. The little lad's body had been mutilated; his sexual organs removed and placed beside the body. Photographs of the disgusting injuries were laid out beside the body in the garage and the camera containing these and other repugnant photos of the horrendous scene was found in a local waste bin. The doctor was one hundred per cent certain that all the damage to the body occurred post mortem. She added that it was most unlikely that he was tortured in any way prior to his death.

Further sadomasochistic images were discovered on the computer's hard drive and pen stick found at the defendant's house, though none involved children.

During questioning Doctor Michaels stated that Jamie appeared to have been in reasonable health prior to his death but she added that he was rather mal-nourished and slightly underweight for his age. Death was due to smothering and the towel used to do this was the one found underneath the body. Fibres from the towel were found lodged in Jamie's mouth and wind pipe.

Judge's Notes

What a good witness. Carol Michaels is clear and concise. She speaks with such conviction and appears to be unmoved by the horrific nature of the evidence, rather unusual in one so young. Unfortunately such well presented evidence from an "expert" has been known to convict the innocent. The natural instinct when listening to such lurid and despicable detail is to want to find someone to take the blame; someone to find guilty. For the jury the man in the dock is the obvious target, but were they influenced by his calmness and unusual passivity throughout the day? Did this indicate his innocence?

Deidre did her best and highlighted the undisputed fact that no child pornography was found on her client's hard-drive. She said that pornography between consenting adults was very different to the type where children are involved. She then quoted some bamboozling facts: seventy-five million people visit adult websites each month; twelve per cent of all sites on the web deal with pornography and one estimation is that at any one time there are over *twenty-eight thousand people on-line viewing it. She added, in her most authoritative tone, that none of these figures were for child pornography which was thankfully far more rare and was not the choice of her client so it was erroneous to use the images discovered to link Jamie's murder with the man in the dock.*

The defendant sat calmly throughout the day, apparently unmoved by either the doctor's evidence or his lawyer's protestations on his behalf. Time will tell how today's gruesome details affect the outcome of this dreadful case.

The weekend was spent on my writing, utter bliss: so good to have two days away from the confinements of the court room. The daily tedium is starting to irritate me but I decided to review the trial so far. Each day the evidence is presented so painstakingly and precisely and is then subjected to endless and repetitive cross examination. Have the CPS got a strong enough case? At the start I assumed that the verdict was a foregone conclusion, but after days of listening to them droning on I am not so sure. They appear to have minimal evidence and the eyewitnesses for the day of the abduction have been poor and unsure of their facts and have been made to look inadequate by the probing interrogation from the defence lawyer, the delectable Deidre. However the case continues and I am losing interest; thank goodness for my writing.

The promotion that never was. Nigel Montgomery Fitzsimmons needed to die before the next season began in mid-August. I had two months in which to stop him officiating at any more games. Never again must he be allowed to spoil results with his erroneous decisions. I needed to make it obvious that his death was as a direct consequence of his lack of ability as a referee. I had an idea but this murder would need to be carried out with the utmost care. He was the only one of my "subjects" to be, if not a celebrity, quite well known, at least in the football world. His death would probably be reported, not only in Britain, but also abroad. I was rather looking forward to that. Developing a taste for fame could become habit forming.

How to kill him was the next issue. I had strangled, stabbed, smothered, thrown people to their deaths and I wanted a new method. Then it came to me: Pops rifle. The Lee Enfield, No. 4 MK1. It hadn't been used for almost three decades but I had it still, safely hidden, in the loft. Waiting. This time it wouldn't be employed on rabbits but for its original purpose, to kill a human being. The enemy.

At the Magistrates' court I am able to work the occasional flexi-time. Some days are exceedingly long when a trial overruns its allotted hours. When this happens I can accrue the extra time and take some leave. I did this on a dull, extremely overcast afternoon in late June, the type we have become accustomed to in the so called "summers" of Lancashire. I caught the train to the station nearest St Steven's.

It was a pleasant area. Quiet roads lined with well-established trees added to its air of calm. There was a mixture of semis and detached houses, the vast majority kept in immaculate condition, probably benefitting, as had the Albrights from the attention of avid gardeners, the paid variety. As I neared the school I wondered whether the time of day was a good one. Cars were being parked ready to take the little Hermiones and Oscars home. Several parents were arriving on foot to collect their offspring and blending in with the crowd appeared to be the best option. If anyone spoke to me I would say I was moving into the area and looking for a good school for my children.

A whirlwind exploded through the school gates. Children everywhere: the ninth circle of hell. For many minutes ebullient youngsters escaped from the confinement of the day. The noise was horrendous and I pitied the people who lived in the nearby houses and had to endure this cacophony on a daily basis. Finally only the stragglers were left; the older ones, the teenagers, many of whom looked too mature for the decidedly unfashionable brown uniform. They were too busy texting and talking on mobiles to move with any great speed.

Having no idea how long teachers remained after their pupils had left I was aware that I might be in for a prolonged wait. Marking, meetings, chatting to colleagues could all take hours. Patience prevailed. There was no one left to notice a man standing beneath the trees. Waiting: merely waiting.

I knew from his personal details, published for the whole world to read on the internet, that Nigel, being a keep fit fanatic, jogged to work. I was wearing my running outfit so hoped to be able to follow him home. I had decided that I would kill him in some secluded spot. Somewhere not overlooked. Somewhere I could derive maximum enjoyment from delivering his final moment. Somewhere I could rid the world of a man in dereliction of his duty. That somewhere would, I hoped, be on his homebound route.

Mr Fitzsimmons was obviously more dedicated to his teaching than he was to his football duties and there was a long period between the end of the school day and his appearance. It seemed like hours before he emerged suitably attired for running. I let him set off and followed at a careful distance. I cannot tell you how excited I was when he veered off the pavement and headed through a rather overgrown area of rough ground. This was a superb location. There were dog walkers in the distance but one area caught my attention, a few hundred yards of thick scrub. He covered it in a matter of seconds but that would be sufficient for my needs. A bullet can travel so much faster than a man. This was my somewhere.

Transporting a rifle was not an everyday experience for me. I knew I must be able to travel with it undetected. It was whilst I was shopping for new running gear that I saw just what I needed. I always shop at Sports' Leisure, an outlet with an excellent variety of kit in the proliferation of stores all housed together to the south of the city. The area has been appallingly named " Preston Mall: the ultimate shopping experience" (why we have to adopt so many American phrases I do not know; after all we invented the incomparable English language which has more than twice the vocabulary of any other).

I took ages to choose new trainers from an almost overwhelmingly wide selection. Next to them there was a display of sports bags of every shape and size, the kind used by athletes to carry their spare clothes, towels, bats, racquets and other paraphernalia. I bought a large black one; a colour that I thought would prove so boring as to go unnoticed. How surprised the young, rather spotty, assistant would have been had he known the bags intended use.

Unfortunately the young man in question had either been on a charm offensive course or had a form to complete on his customers' shopping satisfaction – I was already more than happy with my purchases and hoped that my pleasure would be increased, but I could hardly explain any of that to him.

'Good afternoon sir, thank you for shopping with us today.'

'Yes, good afternoon, I'd like to buy these trainers and this bag please.'

'Can I ask why you chose Sports' Leisure for your purchases?'

'You've always got a good selection of sports' equipment,' I muttered hoping that the flattering remark would suffice.

'Just one more question sir, to help with our stock evaluation, exactly why have you selected this particular bag?'

Oh the temptation to tell him that it would accommodate a rifle which would then be easy to transport to the scene of my next murder, (would he believe me? would he call his manager? would he tell all his friends? or would he just laugh?).

'Well it's a good size, should hold all my gym equipment,' was my more prosaic reply.

'It is one of our more popular bags; I hope it serves its purpose.'

'I have absolutely no doubt about that!' I managed a brief smile, hoping the conversation was almost at an end.

'Thank you for your time sir and we at Sports' Leisure hope your purchase proves successful.' I certainly concurred with that. It proved to be an excellent choice as the rifle fitted perfectly. It was all falling into place and I knew that the Football Association would soon need a new referee..........hopefully one who knew the rules.

How naive I was to think the rest would be easy. There were two weeks left until the school term ended, after which my opportunity would be lost. The football season would have started several weeks before the new school year meaning that Nigel would once again be ruining some dedicated fans' dreams with his dubious decisions. Last week a Premiership manager was pontificating about poor decisions by the officials evening out over the season but any fan will tell you that this is seldom the case, unless one happens to be one of the top teams.

As we approached the final week I took some leave. It was imperative that I was there every day: appropriately attired, mentally prepared, and armed. I knew there would be one, just one moment, when I would have the opportunity to shoot him, to extinguish his errant life. I was getting extremely worried when he didn't appear on the first three days. Was he ill? Was he taking a different route? Would it be necessary to re-plan the whole thing?

Travelling on the train each day was a nerve-wracking experience. I dressed in the most unremarkable outfit I could muster: grey jogging pants, a pale blue sweat shirt and my old trainers. The new ones looked too showy and I didn't want to draw any attention to myself. Fortunately the weather had changed and the bright sunshine allowed me to wear sunglasses. The aim was to look innocuous, just another passenger and as the trains were reasonably busy I hoped no one would notice me. Most people are too wrapped up in the minutiae of their own lives to pay much attention to others and that, thankfully, proved to be the case. The bag containing the gun was on the large side but looked ordinary. What would the other passengers have thought if they had had an inkling of its contents?

Each day was spent waiting in the small copse. As I arrived I removed the rifle and loaded it as gently as a mother dressing her new born baby. It was strange to sit holding a piece of metal that can take a life in a milli-second. It felt surprisingly heavy and rather unwieldy and I hoped it would not prove too cumbersome when the moment arrived. However it was wonderful to realise that I had such an instrument of destruction at my fingertips.

I sat and waited: Monday, Tuesday, Wednesday. Each day I obliterated any footprints and was careful not to brush against the small bushes or drop any litter. By Thursday I was starting to despair. I knew there would be only a matter of a few seconds between seeing him approaching and shooting the bastard. Just in case anyone else walked through that part of the field I had to keep the rifle concealed. It was hidden but ready. Ready for action - and what action. Part of the thrill was the waiting, dreaming of the moment of extinction and the knowledge that he was no more.

Thursday was the day. It all seems surreal now. It was over so quickly. Too quickly. I was surprised that there was so little time lapse between seeing him approaching and meeting him in the secluded copse. The look of surprise on his face when he saw the gun will be with me forever. It was wonderful, a moment of pure delight.

Unfortunately I knew that there wasn't time for conversation though I would dearly have loved to tell him why he was being shot. For my own satisfaction I yelled 'Preston North End' as I pulled the trigger and ended his errant existence. One shot sufficed. It sounded loud, almost deafening, the noise there should have been when Preston won the game, but no one was near enough to hear it. In order to tell the world why he had to die I left my copy of the Play-Off Final programme on his body. Let them work that one out! Most football fans would understand. The programme had, of course, been cleaned meticulously. The rest was easy. Pack up the gun and walk back to the station.

I wanted to skip, to cavort, to leap in the air and shout my success to the heavens, but that would, to say the least, have caused unwanted interest. On the return journey I sat in a paroxysm of happiness. I had done it; again.

Returning to work on the Friday was tempting but as I had requested a week's leave I thought it better to stick to the original plan and have the final day off. I spent it happily reading all the newspapers on line. Alone with the reports I was able to savour every last word. The body had been discovered by a dog walker about ten minutes after I had left. Was I becoming careless? That was a bit too close for comfort.

Chapter 17

Daily Gazette

Top Football Referee Found Shot Dead

The body of Nigel Fitzsimmons, aged thirty eight, a Premier League and world acclaimed FIFA referee, was discovered late yesterday afternoon in an overgrown area of a field near his home. He had been shot in the head and the experts say he would have died instantly.

Nigel, a keep fit fanatic, was believed to have been attacked as he jogged home from the school where he taught. A colleague, Sue Street, a geography teacher, aged forty, said she remembers seeing him leave school at about twenty to five. She added that it was his usual pattern to jog home at least twice a week. His body was found just after at ten past five, by a local man, Bill Griffin, aged sixty three, who was walking his dog.

Mr Roger Dalton, the Head of St Steven's, the independent school where Nigel Fitzsimmons had taught for the past ten years, said, "His loss is a tremendous blow to our school. He was a well-respected teacher, a wonderful colleague and a thoroughly nice man. Our thoughts are with his wife and children at this sad time."

Police are baffled as to the reason behind the killing which they say has all the hallmarks of a hit man.

The very short time frame between his leaving school and entering the overgrown area where he was found indicate a well-planned execution. The assumption must be that his killer was lying in wait for him. An object found with his body has caused some interest and the police have said that it may help to establish a reason for his death. At this moment in time we are not at liberty to divulge what the item is, but we have been told that it has more to do with his footballing activities than his professional or personal life.

Anyone in the vicinity of Plower's Lane or Rutwell field yesterday, between four thirty and ten past five, or anyone who saw anything suspicious during yesterday afternoon in that locality, is asked to contact the police incident room, telephone number at 01772 378910.

I have absolutely no idea how much information the police received but they did not come knocking on my door. Eventually the fact that a football programme had been left on top of the body was given prominence in the newspapers and the link was made to the Play-Off Final. Several fans made contact with one of the many phone-in programmes on Radio 5 to say that they were at that match and believed that Mr Fitzsimmons had made serious mistakes, leading to Preston losing the game. Although (the ones who were broadcast) didn't go as far as agreeing with the murder it was pleasing to know that others understood my frustration and the need for him to be removed from any future participation in the "Beautiful Game". I was not alone.

Euphoria is an amazing sensation. It overwhelmed me all weekend. I was unable to function normally and continued to laugh, giggle, punch the air, cheer and dance with sheer joy. I didn't dare to go out as I was sure I would have been acting so strangely that I might have been sectioned by some well-meaning professional. I was in a state of total bliss, the kind sought by Buddhists trying to attain Nirvana, though I rather doubted whether my method for attaining such rapture would have been given their seal of approval. I almost wondered whether I had achieved my goal (yes, a pun) of committing the perfect murder.

My happiness was short-lived when I returned to work early on the Monday morning as my nemesis had returned. He really was like a bad penny.

'Your favourite man is back,' Marie joked as I walked in, 'I think he really must like you - can't think why else we keep having the pleasure of his company.'

'Philip not working his magic on this one?' I asked, knowing full well that Simon was beyond redemption, even the Salvation Army would have their work cut out with him.

'As you so love dealing with him I thought he could be in Court One with you. I started the rota on Friday afternoon and knew you'd want to deal with your favourite person.'

'You spoil me,' I replied bringing a sardonic smile to Sophie's face. I realised I must be more cautious in my reactions to Simon so that when I finally succeeded in removing him from this world no suspicion would fall on me. It would look bad if I had made my dislike of him too obvious.

The objectionable Mr Bell had broken his curfew on no fewer than six occasions and was his usual arrogant self, not appearing to care that this, in itself, meant, due to his parole restrictions, an immediate return to prison.

However there was an added charge of more serious proportions: "Assault occasioning actual bodily harm". This was a first for Mr Bell as I didn't remember him being violent before.

Simon's girlfriend (the latest in a long, ever changing retinue of empty-headed blondes) had found pornographic material on his lap-top, saved in his "favourites" section, when she had been looking for an Amazon Sales Special site. She would have let this pass but was horrified to discover numerous hard copies of the unpalatable photographs in his desk drawer. Her reward for challenging him about the material had been a hefty thump which had caused bruising to her face and the loss of a tooth.

Sally Wainwright was a pretty girl, but her looks were marred by the fear she was experiencing as she took the stand. I knew the witness protection lady, Andrea Brown, a retired social worker and a most capable and empathetic woman who had seen many a reluctant participant through the process, had spent hours with Sally reassuring her that she was doing the right thing bringing the case to court.

Simon pleaded not guilty and the trial began. Poor Sally walked in looking highly emotional. In all probability she had not been in a courtroom before and most people find their first time (whether as the accused or as a witness) a daunting experience. As a legal adviser it is part of my duty to put witnesses at their ease but it was an uphill task of Himalayan proportions as Miss Wainwright stood sobbing and shaking to such a degree that she could barely repeat the oath.

'I swear by Almighty God........ to..........tell....... the..........oh I can't do this. I want to go home.'

The case was stood down whilst Mrs Brown spent time with the distraught victim. Unfortunately, as is so often happens with domestic violence issues, Sally could not be persuaded to give evidence and so the case was dismissed.

'My client does not wish to pursue the matter Your Worships and so, with some reluctance, the CPS is withdrawing the case. Sally had crept quietly into the back of the room and as this was being announced she looked furtively at Simon who was giving a credible impression of a boxer who has just won his fight on points. He must have been aware that, had the trial continued, the verdict would have been guilty. I knew that the police and photographic evidence (from Sally's visit to casualty) would have determined the outcome. Simon was one very lucky boy.

What a disappointment that the trial was abandoned but what a new and enticing twist; the delightful Simon was interested in naughty pictures. I knew that there had been occasions when I had strayed, quite inadvertently, onto certain sites on the internet, and that I had found some of the images rather alluring. Perhaps though, some photos of my victims might be of long-term interest to me. Just a thought, but what a thought, my brain was working with a speed normally associated with an expensive Ferrari completing a Grand Prix.

Had the trial continued Simon's offence would most probably have come into Category Three: "lesser harm and lower culpability", no aggravating factors: premeditation, use of a weapon or intention to cause more serious harm, and even had he been found guilty the magistrates would almost certainly have fined him, merely adding to the irritating amount of money he already owed the court. In the event his curfew was resentenced, adding to the hours he was so reluctant to obey.

We all knew that Simon was due to appear in the Crown Court in the near future, where he would almost certainly be given a custodial sentence for his previous crimes: all fines and curfews would then be rescinded. There are times when the British justice system leaves me speechless and this was one of them.

He was indeed duly given a spell in prison and was incarcerated for many weeks.

The good news, as far as I was concerned, was that I now knew how I would deal with Mr Simon Bell. I also appreciated that my revenge must, inevitably, be some time in the future and would take the most detailed and careful planning I had ever undertaken. I was far more closely associated with him than was comfortable but my new plan was as delicious as any cake devised by the delectable Delia. It was all starting to fall into place, the pieces fitting like the children's toy where certain solid shapes pass through their respective openings. It was manna from heaven. The wandering tribes of Israel could not have been more grateful than I was. Yes I had the rudiments of a plan, only the finer details needed addressing.

Life resumed its normal pattern. My days spent at work are, for the most part, reasonably pleasant and the people I work with are good at their jobs. Below the court rooms are the offices staffed by the many people who do a sterling job keeping the daily court business organised. The general office is huge, a cavernous space. All the occupants are female and there are times when the room is dominated by an almost overwhelming smell of a variety of perfumes. Six large desks are placed around the walls and all the out of court business is undertaken here. It is always a hive of activity with, amongst other things, reports to give to the right people, the updating of the court lists for the magistrates each morning and afternoon, changing the sittings for magistrates who find they cannot fulfil one they have been allocated and the constant liaison with the various units such as the invaluable probation service. Considering the people working there are dealing with crimes all day every day they maintain a positive attitude, aided by a regular supply of biscuits and chocolates which are usually left open on the desk by the door.

'Here to sample our goodies?' is the usual rather risqué repost when I enter their domain. They all know I can't resist chocolate; it is one of my downfalls. What a good job they have no idea of the others. They treat me like a distant uncle and at times there is a lack of the respect that my position demands. But they make up for that with their willingness to complete all the tasks given to them and have never let me down professionally.

My office, yes I have my own as the chief legal adviser, is a much smaller affair. A locally made Waring and Gillow's desk dominates the room and it is a beautiful piece of mahogany. They say that Gillow has to be thanked for introducing such a splendid wood into England following his first visit to the West Indies. I like to keep the desk uncluttered so that as much of it as possible remains on show. The accompanying chair, a dark green leather-bound beauty, was purchased by the previous occupant, Mrs Mitchell, and was a state of the art design to aid her bad back.

'Can't believe your room, Benjamin, how do you keep it so tidy?' this was Sally who worked part time in the general office and who always tried (often unsuccessfully) to engage me in some lightweight conversation.

'Easy, I can't stand clutter it makes me feel ill. It's just a matter of organising and keeping on top of the paperwork.'

'You should have seen it when Mrs M. was here, papers strewn all over, but she could always find whatever she needed.' Thankfully that was the end of that brief exchange.

To amuse myself, and bring some originality to the room, I had hung several football posters on the walls. These were purchased when the Football Museum had its home at Deepdale. One shows the legendary PNE player Tom Finney with his right foot above the ball he is about to kick. Oh to have seen that in real life. The one near the door is a newspaper cutting with a photograph of Alan Kelly, the Preston goalie, jumping aloft and taking the ball from Jimmy Greaves, the great Spurs and England centre forward. One smaller poster is in an elevated position above my desk and is a team photo of the 1975-1976 squad - the first team I watched. It is the kind where all the players sit with the manager looking keen to start the new season, all full of hope, no points yet lost or disappointing matches endured.

My favourite however is the photo showing David Beckham during one of his five appearances for Preston when he was on loan, all too briefly, in 1995. Being David he managed two goals during those five outings.

Sally is an Everton fan and tells me, on a regular basis, that I should support the "Toffees". There was one rather embarrassing moment when she tried to get me there.

'If you came to Goodison you'd see a good game, I can get you a ticket any time you want to come. The seat next to mine isn't a season one.'

'Thanks for the offer Sally but you know how it is once you've pledged allegiance to a team there's no swapping.' The thought of going anywhere with Sally worried me for days.

The next few months passed with a speed that surprised me. I had no desire to murder again; not yet anyway. The last one had been particularly satisfying and I relived it each time I watched a match and saw one of the officials make a mistake. Never again would it be Mr Nigel Fitzsimmons.

Christmas was approaching. No sooner is one over than the next is looming, like an abhorrent science-fiction creature in a horror film meant to scare the living daylights out of you. To look at the shops one could be forgiven for thinking that Christmas was on its way from August, the tawdry decorations and tuneless carols appearing earlier and earlier each year.

'Shall I book at The Crooked Cockerel for our Christmas meal?' Josie, a most reliable secretary and our social organiser, asked in early September of the year in question.

'Stone the crows and crooked cockerels' I replied, 'surely we don't need to be thinking about this so early.'

'It does seem early but I've already received several fliers from various venues and if we don't book soon the best places will be gone,' was the calm reply.

'You'll be asking what we want to eat next. I may have turned vegetarian or have developed an allergy to turkey by then and it really is impossible to choose one's menu five months in advance.'

'You are a funny old stick, I won't require that info until nearer the time, but we did like it there when we went three years ago. None of the other restaurants have been as good.'

Others agreed that the venue under discussion had provided delicious meals and that the ambience had been great. And so our staff Christmas do was organised well in advance.

I loathe everything about the so called "Festive Season" with all its false jollity and excessive spending on presents that are ungratefully received. To make matters worse it has always been the one time of the year when I feel duty bound to see my family. We have never liked each other; we have never got on so why the charade of pretending it is a good idea to spend time in each-others' company?

Mother phoned at the beginning of December to say that we had all been invited to Talia's on Christmas Day. I agreed with a bad grace, thinking that if I really couldn't face it I would have to succumb to a sudden, but totally debilitating, bout of flu on Christmas Eve. No one would believe me but I suspected that they would, in all probability, feel greatly relieved. Talia's boys were by this time all teenagers so I had absolutely no idea what to buy and ended up with the usual "cop-out" of tokens. Mother and the girls were easier as they like things that are readily accessible and not too expensive: perfume, chocolate and scarves. Easy; shopping completed in under an hour.

Christmas: to celebrate a birth. Christmas in our house: to plan a death.

New Year: to make resolutions that this year life will be better. New Year in our house: to end a life.

Chapter 18

Daily Gazette

Defendant Takes the Stand

There were further dramatic scenes in Manchester Crown Court yesterday where the trial is taking place for the appalling murder of the toddler Jamie Richardson in Preston in May of this year. The case continued with the defendant taking the stand and being questioned by his lawyer, the eloquent Ms Hannigan. We are unable to print a photograph of the defendant but our artist's impression is an excellent likeness and shows him to be an exceptionally good looking man. He is the archetypal "tall, dark and handsome" though with piercing deep blue eyes which have been described as "cold". He was, as always, well dressed. Yesterday he wore a dark grey suit, pale blue shirt and dark navy tie. Throughout most the proceedings he has looked extremely confident and has even at times appeared aloof and to be taking little notice of what is being said. With the one exception that we reported recently it is almost as though he has distanced himself from the entire trial.

He delivered the oath in a loud, well-educated voice and his answers to the many question put to him were spoken with confidence. He refuted the allegation that he was involved in killing Jamie Richardson. When asked about the garage where the body was discovered he admitted to using it in the past but claimed to have been nowhere near it for the past two years.

A hushed courtroom heard him admit to having had an interest in pornography in the past but he was adamant that he had been able to curb this activity and that it had held no appeal for some time. He added that there was no way that he had either killed Jamie or taken the photos. He said that he found that kind of thing unacceptable and was never into young boys.

The defendant could not explain how his fingerprints came to be on the camera which he claimed was not his or the towels in which the child's tiny body was wrapped. He became angry when giving this part of his evidence and was asked to remain calm by the judge. He insisted that he had been in Wales at the time of the murder and said that he was many things but not a killer. Deidre Hannigan, asked him twice whether he was the man who had killed Jamie and both times he denied it.

The case continues.

Judge's Notes

He is sticking to his "it wasn't me 'guv" position. The man is almost over confident but speaks with such conviction that I suspect several members of the jury are being swayed by him. The lady in shocking pink (one of several lurid outfits) was nodding her head at some of his answers.

Perhaps some members of the jury are wondering whether "one of their own kind" could possibly have committed such a cold-blooded murder.

More from him after the weekend. Good for all concerned to have a couple of days away from such an awful case.

Snow arrived at ten o'clock making it the first "White Christmas" for many years. Needless to say it made Talia's boys more excited than usual and the day turned into an endurance test. Attempting to play my part as an enthusiastic uncle I took them down to the park to toboggan and throw snowballs. It was definitely preferable to be outside with them and was the only agreeable part of the day.

Christmas dinner was the usual, predictable turkey with all the trimmings. Talia was not a bad cook and the meal was edible. However it was as the bird was being carved that we became yoked on an out- of-control sledge. There was to be no getting off this ride.

'Billy has finally been diagnosed with Asperger's. It's only taken the school two years to say what's wrong.' Talia's timing has never been good but whilst the crackers were being pulled was not the best moment for such a pronouncement.

'You've suspected that for a while,' my mother replied adding, 'they wanted to test Benjamin at the same age but his father said no as nothing would have been done even if he was found to be Autistic.'

There was a moment when I wanted the floor to open up and swallow me. Was she talking about me? Who in the world had thought that I was on the Autistic spectrum? How dare she bring this up now and in front of the others?

My mother was not a quitter, neither, unfortunately, was she an intuitive person and she had no clue that her next statements were to ruin the already fragile relationship that had, up to that moment, managed to be maintained between us. Little did she realise that she was sealing her own fate.

'Yes Benjamin was very like Billy. He found it so hard to make friends and never understood that other people had feelings. In Year Three, Mrs Hallyard called your dad and me in to talk about Benjamin. She was worried about him. She said that he had laughed when the class hamster died and the rest of the children were upset. She said he wasn't being nasty just that she thought he didn't understand emotions. It was Mrs Hallyard who first pointed out that Benjamin never made eye contact and lacked the ability to interact with either the adults or the children in the school.'

As she drew breath I made the most dramatic eye contact that I could muster, but she was in full flow.

'At the end of Year Six Mr Jones told us that he was worried about Benjamin's obsessive interest in murder and he asked if we had reconsidered the test for Autism. We never followed that up either. It's good that Billy has been diagnosed. The school will be able to help him. What are they suggesting?'

'He'll get a teaching-assistant assigned to him as soon as the funding comes through and we've got an appointment with a paediatric psychiatrist in the middle of January. I don't know what they can do but at least I'm not alone with the problem now.'

'That's good dear. I always felt that your dad and I could have done with some help.'

It was as though Billy and I weren't there. They were talking about us and we were sitting right by them. At least Billy was rather too young to take in the seriousness of the conversation. I sat, unable to think, unable to respond. I needed time to consider what had been said, but at the table was neither the time nor the place. How I managed to eat the meal, which had lost all taste, I shall never know. As soon as possible I excused myself, claiming a headache, and returned home.

Mother's Dairy: Christmas Day

Oh dear! I think I've upset Benjamin. He went home in a huff, but nothing new there. Talia was talking about Billy and the good news that she has finally got somewhere with understanding his problems. His diagnosis has come through and they think he is on the Autistic spectrum or at least on the Asperger's side of it. It's good as she will get some help now. Ted and I always suspected that Benjamin had that problem, but Ted never wanted anything done. He would have found it hard to accept that a child of his had anything wrong. I started to talk about the times the teachers had wanted Benjamin tested and he just went quiet, the way he does when he opts out of anything that makes him uncomfortable. As soon as dinner was over he went home. I tried to phone him later on but there was no answer. Maybe I shouldn't have said as much but I was trying to help Talia. I had Ted but she is on her own with the boys.

The Christmas dinner was delicious and the boys loved their presents so the day was not a total disaster.

Yes I went quiet. Yes I "opted out". What was there to say? Yes I went home. Why stay? When I read this entry, a few months later, I knew I had done the right thing. Where in those lines was any understanding of my feelings? She was wrong: the day had been a "total disaster", a total disaster for her. The time had come for the next murder.

Matricide is probably not something that would come naturally to the average person, most appearing to get on quite well with their mothers. However it is a not an uncommon activity and has been practised over the centuries with an impressive regularity. I was fascinated by the incidents I discovered when I researched the topic. Here are some of the more interesting examples:

Amastris, queen of Heraclea, was drowned by her two sons in 284 BC.

Cleopatra III of Egypt was assassinated in 101 BC by order of her son, Ptolemy X, for her conspiring against him.

Ptolemy XI of Egypt had his wife, Berenice III, murdered shortly after their wedding in 80 BC. She was also his stepmother, or perhaps his mother.

In AD 59, the Roman Emperor Nero is said to have ordered the murder of his mother Agrippina the Younger, supposedly because she was conspiring against him.

Mary Ann Lamb, the mentally ill sister of essayist Charles Lamb, killed their invalid mother during an episode of mania in 1796.

Sidney Harry Fox, a British man, hanged in 1930 for killing his mother to gain from her insurance.

Antony Baekeland murdered his mother, Barbara Daly Baekeland on November 11, 1972, at their luxurious London apartment. She had allegedly forced him to have sex with her, in order to "cure" his homosexuality.

Brett Reider, a 15-year-old boy in Omaha, Nebraska, stabbed his mother to death during a dispute in 1993. He was convicted of second degree murder and sentenced as an adult to 11–20 years. In 1996, his older sister, Alissa Reider made an HBO documentary: "Brett Killed Mom: a sister's diary", claiming both of them suffered years of constant verbal and physical abuse from their mother. Brett was released in 1999.

Luke Woodham, Mississippi resident who killed his mother in June 1997 before killing two more and wounding seven others in the Pearl High School shooting. Currently serving a life sentence at the Mississippi State Penitentiary

Noura Jackson killed her mother by stabbing her more than 50 times on June 5, 2005.

Need I go on? Ten examples should suffice to illustrate the fact that killing one's mother is by no means a unique event (except to each mother!). I'd had the method ready for years: Temazepam. Having obtained my own regular supply I had encouraged mother to ask for her own tablets. Between us we had enough to kill an entire WI meeting of horrific mothers. It was just the timing I pondered over. I had waited for a good excuse and now felt I had one. She was the author of her own downfall. Would I have become the person I was if she had sought the requested help for me? The solution had been there but she had chosen not to take it and so the next event was inevitable.

Crushing packets of the small innocuous looking pills was easy. I had slipped into mother's house whilst she was out with her cronies for coffee (should the fatal concoction have been used in the café and seen off the rest, thus helping some other poor offspring who'd had enough of their parent?) and taken her packets of Temazepam. One was half full, but the other was unopened. Over the past few years I had already collected several almost empty packets from her bathroom cabinet. Thus all the containers left at the scene would bear her name on the prescription labels. The pills were to be crushed in a tumbler I had taken from her draining board and as I was careful to wear gloves, all the fingerprints on the glass would be hers.

'Hello. It's Benjamin. I've been thinking, maybe we could see the New Year in together.'

This must have been a huge surprise but I had to admire her, as, after the briefest of pauses, she took me up on the offer without surplus comment.

'That would be really good, Benjamin. We don't see enough of each other and we could have a little talk.'

'I've had a great idea, mother. We have always disagreed about which Chinese take-away is the best. Why don't you get your favourite sweet and sour chicken from the one at the end of your road and I'll bring one from my local and we can compare them. It will also save you cooking.'

'What a lovely idea. I'll get some wine and make a dessert. You have cheered me up, I usually see the New Year in alone. See you tomorrow at eight. I'm looking forward to it already.'

'Don't mention it to the girls or your friends as we can ring them at midnight and surprise them.'

Next I had to make sure the girls weren't planning on going round or at least not before midnight.

'Hello Talia. It's Benjamin.'

'Hello you, hope you've recovered from your migraine.'

'Yes thanks. I'm just ringing because I was thinking of going to mother's just after midnight tomorrow to be her "First-Foot". I'll stick to the rules: not in the house before midnight and I'll carry coal, bread, salt and some Whisky. Do you remember being told every year that they meant good luck for the next twelve months and represented prosperity, food, flavour and good cheer? As a tall, dark man I fit the human criteria and I'll even take a piece of coal to keep any Scottish ancestors happy. She used to love that old superstition when we were all young. I just wondered whether you were planning on being with her tomorrow evening?'

'No we're all at a party so we're taking her out for a meal on New Year's Day. You are very welcome to join us. I love your "First Foot" idea, mum will be so pleased. She made Dad go out every year, whatever the weather. Do you remember how he complained that year when there was the blizzard? '

'Yes, hope the weather is better tomorrow night. Thanks for the invite for New Year's Day but I've got other plans.'

'Well, Happy New Year when it comes and hope mum enjoys her surprise.'

I got a similar response from Helen, so my sisters were out of the picture.

At eight o'clock on the dot, so rude to be late, I arrived at mother's door. My parents had moved to the small detached house in Broughton when our family home, Oaklands, in the Trough of Bowland, was deemed to be too large after the girls left home. I suspect bad memories also played a part in the decision to down size and move closer to Preston. The wonderful garden at Oaklands, so beloved by me and Pops, was never the same after he died. My father tried to keep it under control but he lacked the vision to retain its originality and the beauty it had displayed in all seasons. I never enjoyed living in the new house which was devoid of any character, being one of many identical ones on a most ordinary road. The old song "Little Boxes" always came to mind when I thought of it. My parents were happy enough there and whilst he was still working it had the advantage of being much nearer my father's school.

Mother must have been looking out for me as the door was opened before I had time to ring the bell.

'Come in it is good to see you. I have been looking forward to this. Come and get warm, the fire is on, it's freezing out there. My version of the sweet and sour is keeping warm in the oven. This is going to be fun.'

This was mother at her most sociable and I suffered a momentary lapse of conviction that I was about to do the wrong thing. Only momentary you understand. She smelt, as always, of carbolic soap believing that germs must be kept at bay at all times, even the thirty-first of December and I suspected that the various bottles of perfume I had given her over the years were kept at the back of a cupboard only to be used on some extra special occasion. What a shame that this evening did not merit such a title. It had to be admitted that she had dressed for the occasion in a rather becoming silky looking purple dress that I had not seen before. She had added the pearls that Father had given her one birthday. Her hair was in its "I've just been to the hairdressers and not a hair will dare to move" mode. She had a good head of dark blonde hair, the kind that never seems to turn grey, though it had faded from the photos, showing it in all its ash blond glory, taken when she was young.

'Sorry to be a kill joy, but I've not brought my Chinese. I've had a funny tummy all day and think I'd be better without anything. You sit down and I'll bring yours through.'

'Oh Benjamin that is a shame, I was so looking forward to our little contest. We'll have to keep it in mind for another time. Never mind I splashed out and got a good bottle of wine. Maybe you'll feel well enough to enjoy a small glass. It's in the fridge so bring that through as well. I feel like celebrating tonight. I'm certain next year is going to be a great one.' Yes, I thought, it will be for me.

Once in the kitchen it took me a matter of seconds to take the tumbler from my pocket, remove the cling-film and empty the contents into her sweet and sour and combine the two. I hoped that the strength of the food would disguise any taste from the pills. I also added the remaining crushed pills to the wine. This was not as successful but I reasoned that if I poured the drink she wouldn't notice the slight sediment that had been created.

Mother was in a good mood which I thought at the time was a satisfactory way to end one's time on this earth. I am not a cruel man and made sure that her final moments passed as pleasantly as possible. We chatted about Talia and Helen and I even pretended to take an interest in the grandchildren. She enjoyed the food and wolfed it down with an amazing amount of wine which was of a far better quality than the bottles she usually bought. I pleaded my upset tummy as an excuse to stick to water. It was as she started on the gateau she had made that the first signs of drowsiness began. Her speech became slurred and she drooped over the table.

'I do feel tired. What a funny feeling. It's come over me all of a sudden. I think I'll have to lie down. Sorry Benjamin.' By the end of this little speech she had become almost incoherent. They were to be her last words. And the final two were so appropriate - she had a lot to be sorry about. I helped her to her chair, a winged-back one recently re-covered by her in a deep blue fabric. She slumped down without a sound.

It didn't take long. She was asleep within seconds. Eventually her breathing stopped. It is hard to say with any accuracy how long the final part of the procedure lasted. I sat and watched, fascinated, as always, by the frailty of the human body. A few dozen pills and that was it. The end. Life extinguished. No more mother.

Whilst I didn't experience any sorrow I was amazed to realise that I was not enjoying my usual euphoria. Both my parents were now dead and so I was, I supposed, technically an orphan. When both have gone one realises that it is one's turn next; no buffer zone remains.

Would her death look like suicide? I had planned meticulously and went through my check-list.

I washed the tumbler and my glass and put them away. The empty pill packets, the ones with her name on, were in the kitchen. Remnants of the Temazepam would be present in the Chinese food containers. Her plate, the half empty bottle of wine and her glass were on the dining room table, all with tiny particles of the pills. I had been careful to wear gloves when touching any of this evidence, no point wiping things clean afterwards as spotless surfaces with no fingerprints would look most suspicious.

The cause of death would be obvious. The only problem would be that she had not appeared to be suicidal and there was no note. It is estimated that only twelve to twenty per cent of suicides are accompanied by a letter so perhaps the lack of one would not appear too unusual. The experts say that there are many explanations why an individual has not written a farewell or tried to give an explanation for their untimely demise. One reason given is that it was an impulsive, spur of the moment decision. Not in mother's case as she had to have spent some time buying the meal and crushing the pills. Another idea is that the person wants it to look like an accident, to save her family extra pain. Hardly believable in mother's demise with the many pills crushed into the meal, no room for error there! The only reason that I thought might satisfy, not only the girls but also the coroner, was that she simply couldn't put her final feelings into words.

It was not yet nine o'clock, three hours before I was due to "First Foot" and discover her body, so I decided to have a good look around the house. Most rooms hadn't changed in the years since father's death, the exception being their bedroom. It had been transformed and the overall effect was mesmerising and horrifically feminine. Helen had done her daughterly duty and had redecorated the room during one of her recent holidays. Various shades of purple assaulted my eyes: flowery curtains, carpet, paint work and the frilly duvet cover. It has never been my favourite colour and the sight before me did little to improve the situation. I was horrified to think that it reminded me of Amanda's boudoir. What is it about the female psyche that desires such tomfoolery?

Although I have never visited such an establishment I thought the room would not have been out of place in a brothel though not for one minute did I think that this was the desired effect.

I stood at the door with roles reversed, I became the victim (of such overwhelmingly poor taste) and what remained of her the assassin. For what seemed like an age I was unable to enter. It was as though she was still there, like Banquo's ghost she had returned to haunt the murderer. Fear coursed through my veins and it took all my self-control to pull myself together. She was dead and couldn't harm me.

The room was full of the furniture they had lived with for decades: two large built-in wardrobes, a queen size bed, a dressing table with a flouncy surround (in a muted lilac) and an antique chest of drawers which I recalled my parents buying on their Silver wedding anniversary; a beautiful piece of furniture with intricately carved wood. It looked continental and I remembered them saying it was from the late nineteenth century.

The room was rather cluttered with the cast-off clothes she had probably been wearing earlier, make up, books and magazines occupying every available surface. I was tempted to tidy up but knew that would be highly inappropriate and the girls would be surprised if they saw a neat room, definitely not mother's style, as she had never been the most organised person in the world.

It was strange to realise that the woman who had slept in this room for so many years was lying down-stairs enjoying her final slumber. A book was open on her bed-side table and I was interested to learn what she had been reading. It was the only book she had once told me that she could read and re-read: Moon Tiger by Penelope Lively, a one-time winner of the Booker prize. At least she knew the ending so it didn't really matter that she wouldn't have the opportunity to finish it.

'No!' it took a few seconds for me to realise that the word had been uttered by me. Next to the novel there was another book, lying open but face down. To start with it looked innocuous if rather attractive: small, dark green and leather bound. I picked it up and turned it over. A diary. Mother's diary! She had already written an entry for that day and as I read it I felt like a poor swimmer doing doggy paddle against a tidal wave.

Almost the end of the year. They fly past and it's true what they say that they seem to go faster the older one gets. Not the best year ever with Muriel dying and Pat next door being told she's got terminal cancer but I feel happy tonight as Benjamin rang yesterday. He sounded very well and, for him, amazingly cheerful. The good news is that he is coming to bring in the NEW Year with me! Typical Benjamin, he wants to include a test……… which is the better sweet and sour?!!! We have, rather sadly, discussed this in the past and he says this will decide who is right. He's buying one version and wants me to buy another at my local Chinese. Sampling and judging will then begin. It will be so good to see him. Maybe it's the start of better times. I'm not to tell the girls as he wants to surprise them with a call at midnight. Fancy, Benjamin thinking of that. I am really excited, can't wait to see him. I rang the girls but kept his secret.

For a few seconds my usual decorum was sorely tested. Sweaty palms and an inability to swallow were quickly followed by palpitations, similar to those I had experienced in the past. Jeepers Creepers what would have happened if the girls or the police had found this? A most ridiculous question as the answer was obvious.

That entry would have dammed me. I would have been rumbled. As I sat, immobilised by a panic attack, I was only too aware that this was the closest I had ever come to being found out. In future I must be more careful, far more careful. Everyone who has ever committed a murder and been found out has made some basic mistake. I must rise above that. With what sorrow I realised that this was not to be my perfect murder.

If this was the current diary, were there others? The hounds of hell were after me as I searched the room. I was in such a state that there was no logic to my increasingly frantic rummaging.

'Thank God, yes, thank you God,' the words exploded from my mouth. They were hidden at the back of the larger of the two wardrobes. There were scores of them going back almost sixty years. They were in plastic bags, each holding a decade's worth. She had never given any hint that she kept a diary and, during our time at home, must have written them when we were in bed at night. The early ones were penned in a large childish hand and at first glance looked utterly banal full of details about the lessons at school that day, teachers both strict and kind and details of what she had eaten for dinner.

There was little of interest during her teenage years when she appeared to have led a blameless existence, no under-age drinking or taking of illegal substances for her. Her one boyfriend, Chas, only led to furtive kisses at the end of an evening at the local youth club. My mother had kept strictly to the rules of her middle-class upbringing and never gave her parents cause for concern. Did she ever regret not having pushed the boundaries more or was she happy to have led a fairly blameless, if plebeian, early life?

What could I do with them? There were too many to hide and I didn't have time to take them home and would in any case have risked being seen. Obviously the one by her bed had to disappear. I knew that would fit easily in my coat pocket and could then be removed from the scene. However when the others were discovered the question would be where was this year's? Then an idea struck: take the ones since father's death and it would look as though she had been unable to keep recording her life after such a sad event. The rest, of little consequence to today's happening, could remain in the wardrobe to be collected at a later date. My rucksack could easily accommodate the recent ones and I didn't suppose anyone would be likely to be remotely interested in its contents once there was the more pressing issue of her body.

The remainder of the time passed in a blur. One can be left with no idea of what has happened or of any thoughts, logical or otherwise. One can almost believe in a parallel universe where a different you enacts events none of which can be recalled. After all the excitement (both planned and totally unexpected) of the previous few hours the year was limping to its close.

It may surprise you to know that I cared sufficiently for the girls not to want either of them to be the one who found her. Just before midnight I left the house by the back door and climbed over the low fence into the alley that runs behind the property. A deluge of rain was descending from the heavens and I was glad I was wearing my anorak, though as I wanted to be noticed I did not use my umbrella. I moved round to the front and made sure that I was seen walking up the front path just as midnight was striking on the bells of the old church nearby. I let myself in through the front door, calling out a loud greeting as I did so. It was most fortuitous as at that moment a small group of revelers were joining the party next door. They were already rather the worse for wear but I hoped were sufficiently aware to remember me arriving.

'Hi mum, surprise. Happy New Year,' I yelled loudly enough for any passer-by to hear.

What happened next reinstated my usual post-killing happiness. As soon as I "discovered" the body I phoned the police who arrived with admirable haste considering it is traditionally one of their busiest nights. They were most efficient and called the pathologist, an attractive young woman who looked totally out of place in that gruesome job. She seemed to spend what felt like an eternity (a time scale mother had believed in having spoken regularly of some future existence; had I done her a massive favour propelling her into it sooner rather than later?) inspecting mother. Everyone agreed that she was dead. I did my best to appear rather upset and confused saying that she had sounded so upbeat when I had phoned her yesterday.

'I didn't tell her I was coming. I wanted it to be a surprise. When we were young she wanted my father to be the first in the house after midnight to bring good luck for the next year. I was going to do that. I have all the things with me: coal, bread......' I broke down, covering my face and produced tears of which I was so proud, thinking to myself that shortlisting for another Oscar was in order.

'Is there anyone you want us to contact? Family liaison can be with you if that would help.' I knew the police constable by sight. He had given evidence in court recently and was an earnest young man, keen to do his job well.

'My sisters,' I moaned through loud sobs,' Talia and Helen, their numbers are in mother's phone book, but I think they're both out tonight.'

'It will wait until morning,' he replied. Yes everything would wait; no hurry now the deed was completed.

Chapter 19

Daily Gazette

Defendant Continues to Give his Evidence

The defendant, this time wearing a pin-striped black suit and silver tie, returned to the witness box to continue giving his evidence to a packed courtroom in the appalling case of the murder of an innocent child. Once again he spoke confidently and appeared to be unperturbed by his hours in the dock. He stood throughout, declining the opportunity to be seated and almost looked as though he was enjoying the interrogation.

In an attempt to break the defendant's alibi Sir Anthony Pinkerton, the eminent barrister leading the prosecution, questioned him at length about his whereabouts at the time of the murder of the tiny toddler, Jamie Richardson. The defendant, speaking loudly and clearly, claimed to be on holiday at the time the child was killed. The little boy was snatched on May 3rd and his body discovered on May 11th. You will recall that this paper was one of the few quality papers to provide daily in-depth coverage in the days following his disappearance.

Sir Anthony said that forensic evidence proved that the boy was murdered soon after his abduction.

By the time his body was discovered Jamie had been dead for over a week. The garages, where the little boy's body was found, had been searched several times so the prosecution said that the body must have been kept somewhere else before being dumped at the back of the unit once used by the defendant to house his car.

He repeated his claim that during most of that period under discussion he was on holiday in North Wales. He swore under oath that he was away from the 2nd to the 8th of May. He added that he camped in an empty field near Llandudno, not on an official site. Despite the best efforts of our wonderful police force, there has been no corroboration of this trip. No witnesses have been found. The defendant's explanation was that he did not go out much preferring his own company. He stated that he had taken some food and a lot of books to read so had no need to venture far. He said that he had visited a grocery shop and a pub but that those had been his only outings. When cross examined he was unable to give the names of either establishment.

The eminent prosecutor called this version of events "a flight of fancy."

The case continues.

Judge's Notes

No alibi
Not looking good for him.
The man must realise this.

But he is obviously well educated and sounds so self-assured. In addition he is invariably smartly dressed in a selection of top quality suits.

All are things that influence a jury. Time will tell.

Diary Entry of Mrs Samantha Turner, member of the jury.

I have sat for two long days listening to the defendant being questioned by that top lawyer. Sir Anthony is obviously a very clever man and is doing a good job but I think the defendant is getting the better of him.

He has an answer for every question and gives them all with such confidence. Could someone who is guilty appear that self-assured and unafraid?

It is horrible not being able to discuss the case with Jim, he can give me such good advice, but then he's not in the court room and hasn't heard all the evidence and the papers and television are only allowed to report some of it.

I quake each day when I have to go and sit in the jury box. I know we haven't heard all there is and hopefully that will help me, and the others, to make up our minds, but at the moment I don't know what to think.

I am changing my mind about certain members of the jury. "Mrs Professional", whom I had assumed would be chosen as the chairperson, has been superseded in my estimation by a gentleman who appears to be riveted by every moment of the trial. He sits writing copious notes (though he may perhaps be mirroring me and writing his memoires) and he will certainly have a fund of detailed information when the jury retire to consider their verdict. I have dubbed him "Mr Army" as he has the demeanour of an ex-soldier and probably one of fairly high rank. He looks to be in his mid-sixties, has a good head of grey hair and a rather impressive moustache. He dresses each day in a selection of tweed jackets and I suspect that his ties are mostly military. Despite the gruesome nature of some of the evidence he has remained impassive and has shown absolutely no emotion. Because of this it is impossible to gauge his thoughts. If he is chosen he will probably make a strong leader, able to organise the rest.

Back to the matricide. My sisters were distraught. Both were, by this juncture, in their mid-forties and must have known that mother would die at some point. It was the idea of suicide that they found so difficult to accept. We were told that grief after a suicide is different from other types of bereavement, and can cause many unwarranted feelings on top of the heartache usually felt after a death. The Family Liaison Officer came to talk to us.

'The grief you are and will continue to experience is heart-wrenching. Any death is traumatic and difficult to come to terms with but when a loved one commits suicide, reactions are more complicated. Overwhelming emotions will leave you reeling - and you may be consumed by guilt, wondering if you could have done something to prevent your mother's death. You will ask yourselves all the "What ifs". However in the vast majority of cases nothing anyone might have done or said would have prevented the person taking their life. As you face the future after a loved one's suicide remember that you don't have to go through it alone.'

Ye gods, I thought, not another offer of counselling. Talia and Helen lapped it up and went for regular "talking sessions" for at least a year. If they thought me strange for not partaking of such gobbledegook they never said, though to be honest not many words passed between us immediately after mother's demise. We did however all meet up at the inquest.

The day was overcast, a shame after a few weeks of unseasonably warm weather with clear skies and sunshine. Having arrived early I went for a walk through the gardens that surrounded the newly erected building, on the outskirts of town, where all inquests were scheduled to take place. Being in the garden was so calming and the gardeners in charge of this one knew how to make it look good. It was a riot of very early spring flowers which had been encouraged by the unexpected days of warmth. As I walked I found myself thinking of mother. I was not sorry about my part in her demise but very sorry that things had not been better between us. She had given birth to me but that was probably the extent of any positive influence she had had on my life.

Sufficient time had elapsed for most negative thought to disappear, no point dwelling on the past - nothing can change that. The only thing that remained to do was to revise the statements I would give at the inquest. Easy: stick to the truth where possible and as for the rest, tell them what they wanted to hear.

As Talia and Helen arrived outside the court the thought crossed my mind that they looked as though they had come to audition for the parts of two of the three witches in Macbeth. Both looked utterly dishevelled: faces blotchy from crying, clothes un-ironed and hair that needed some attention. They held onto each other like people caught up in a hurricane. Having seen little of them since the morning mother died I was surprised that the episode had had quite such a profound effect on them. I walked over to them and we shook hands. No "new-age" hugs for us.

'I can't face this,' wailed Talia, ever the drama queen, 'it's too much, just too much.'

'It will soon be over,' I replied, 'these things seldom take more than an hour.' For some reason this brought little comfort and both women were once again making enough noise to raise the dead let alone decide what had killed them.

I led them as quickly as possible into Court Number Four, the one set aside for the coroner. Admitting I was nervous (albeit for a very different reason) would have been a mistake and I continued to appear calm and in control. Well one of us had to remain so. I had dressed sombrely, as befitted the occasion, and was attired in my new pin-striped navy suit with white shirt and black tie. At least I looked the part.

I explained what was about to happen, remembering it verbatim from my recent research and if my sisters thought my delivery rather pedantic they didn't show it, though I rather suspected they weren't really listening.

'Coroners are either lawyers or doctors. They hold their office under the crown and are not local government officials even though they are appointed and paid for by local councils. There are over a hundred and twenty of them in England. Their unenviable job is to establish the medical cause of death. The cases that come before them are of sudden or unexplained deaths. An inquest is ordered when more evidence needs to be examined. An inquest is not a trial but witnesses may be called,' (by this point both were staring at me open-mouthed, but I had learnt my lines and was determined to complete my soliloquy).

'The possible verdicts are: natural causes, accident, suicide, unlawful or lawful killing, industrial disease or the rather unpopular open verdicts where there is insufficient evidence for any other verdict.' As I completed this well-rehearsed explanation I realised that they were shuffling awkwardly and looking at their watches. So much for attempting to be helpful.

As we walked in through the modern glass doors, decorated with Her Majesty's insignia, it struck me that the coroner for mother's case had the choice of one out of three of the options that I had highlighted so carefully: suicide, unlawful killing or open verdict. He was a pleasant looking man in his late fifties. He must have seen, heard and dealt with every variation of death but gave no indication that ours was merely one of the many cases that he was due to hear that week. He gave the appearance of being interested in mother's sudden demise and was certainly thorough. I was called as the first witness and gave my rather edited version of the events surrounding the New Year.

'When I phoned her the day before she did seem a little subdued and I almost told her about my plan to "first-foot". I wish I had as it might have given her something else to look forward to, though she was happy about the prospect of going out with my sisters on New Year's Day for lunch.'

'No I didn't think she was suicidal but as I said just a little subdued, a tad down.'

'I had the shock of my life when I entered the house and found her sitting in her chair. I knew at once she was dead, she looked so different. It is a moment that will be with me for the rest of my life. I called for an ambulance even though I knew it was too late (how good it was to keep to the truth).' The coroner was looking at me in a sympathetic way so I assumed my little story was being believed.

'I expect she bought the Chinese as a final treat, she did love it. It's comforting to know that she enjoyed her last meal and perhaps she knew that any taste from the pills would be well hidden in the spicy food.' Was I laying it on too thickly?

'My sisters and I are still coming to terms with the fact that mother took her life. We were all so pleased that she had become more positive in recent years, after suffering years of debilitating depression. Although she'd been a bit lonely since dad died she often said that the grandchildren gave her a purpose in life. She doted on them. It was totally out of character.'

The coroner reminded me, in a kindly voice, that the verdict of suicide had not yet been reached and that it must be noted that those were my words, at this point in the proceedings, and not his.

Talia and Helen stumbled through their evidence which added very little to the proceedings. They confirmed that they were due to take mother out on New Year's Day and had thought that she was looking forward to it.

'She was in such good spirits the day before when I spoke to her and she almost sounded excited by something but she wouldn't tell me what. She said it was a secret and that I would soon know all about it. Surely she can't have meant that she was going to end it all,' this was what I think Talia said though there were so many pauses and loud sobs that it was almost impossible to decipher every word.

Helen was more composed and reiterated Talia's sentiments adding, 'There were times in the past when I would not have been surprised if my mother had committed suicide but over the last few years she seemed to have come to terms with her demons and hadn't suffered from her periods of awful depression.'

Both said that her death had devastated them.

The medical evidence was disturbingly detailed and Talia and Helen were reduced to sobbing wrecks. I maintained the dignity due in a Coroner's Courtroom. Residue from the sleeping tablets had been found in the appropriate places and the presence of the beaker with some of the crushed pills was also given as evidence. The empty packets of sleeping pills had been discovered beside the container that had held the sweet and sour chicken.

Paul Cartwright, mother's doctor and a young looking sixty, gave evidence that could have been scripted by me. 'Mrs Doyle had been my patient for many years. She appeared to have overcome her long term psychosis and the only reason I have seen her in recent years was to issue her with the sleeping pills she requested. She said that she had trouble sleeping and I assumed that she was taking all the tablets in each packet and had absolutely no idea that she appears to have been stock-piling them. When I last saw her in September she was in good spirits. All I wrote on her record that day was: "Temazepam prescribed. Twenty-eight tablets. Mrs Doyle appears to be in good health." It's a tragic situation and I am aware that I have played a part in her demise but she never presented as being suicidal.'

Mother had been seen purchasing her meal at just before eight o'clock and the receipt for the wine was in the waste bin in the kitchen. The fact that she had mixed Temazepam with alcohol was duly noted as a contributory factor to her death. Each detail of my plan was being introduced as evidence. I loved every moment of it.

Coroner's Verdict on the death of Mrs Jennifer Doyle

A sudden death is always a shock for the family and my sincere condolence are extended to Benjamin, Talia and Helen. Their mother, Mrs Jennifer Doyle, appeared to be in good health and had not visited her doctor for several months prior to her untimely death. The one problem she had complained of was trouble sleeping and for this she had been prescribed Temazepam over a period of several years. At the time of her death she appears to have accumulated many packets of the sleeping pills and several empty containers were discovered in her kitchen.

Before the evening in question Jennifer gave no indication that she was unduly unhappy or that she was depressed. She left no note, though this is not unusual. However, all the evidence points to a carefully planned suicide. The meal was purchased by her, the crushed pills were mixed in with the Chinese take-away, the wine had tablets added and then all were consumed.

She was unaware that her son, Benjamin, was planning a surprise visit though she must have realised that one of her children would find her body the next day. It is to be hoped that her family will not think too badly of her for this seemingly cruel act as when a person is contemplating suicide the effect that this will have on others does not feature in their thinking.

It does not appear that any other person was involved and so I declare the verdict to be suicide. May I extend my sincere condolences to her family.

I did my brotherly duty and led my deranged siblings from the building. They declined my offer of lunch and asked that I accompany them to mother's house.

'Are you sure you want to go there today?' I asked, thinking that they were emotional enough without visiting the scene of her final moments.

'I want to begin sorting her things and if we all go now we can make a start,' Helen declared, in a voice she must have employed regularly when organising the nurses on her ward. There was to be no argument; she had decided.

'I know it's not that long since she died but it's never going to be an easy thing to do and the longer we leave it the harder it will get,' she added, a sentiment that I did not agree with entirely, but my opinion has never counted for much with my sisters. We went in Talia's car, though I wasn't convinced that she was safe to drive.

The house was surprisingly warm and I discovered that Helen had been in several times and had set the central heating to come on for lengthy periods twice a day. No burst pipes would add to her anguish. Despite wanting to remove the diaries I had been unable to visit the place since that night. Was I developing a conscience? It was very strange to enter the house that had been our family home for so many years and to realise that the three of us were all that remained of the family unit. However it was no longer of any consequence in our lives and simply required clearing so that it could be sold to some other unsuspecting people who thought they might, unlike me, be happy there.

Talia resumed her pathetic tears and exclaimed that she couldn't possibly have anything to do with mother's personal possessions. She and Helen were to make a start on the kitchen and I was dispatched to the bedroom. They little knew that was exactly where I needed to be.

'Put her clothes into two piles: those to bin and any that could go to a charity shop,' Helen instructed me. How they imagined that I would be able to distinguish between the two was beyond me, but I wasn't in a mood to argue and did as I was bidden.

I had no intention of spending longer than necessary on the unsavoury task set for me. Mother had not been particularly fashion conscious and kept things for a very long time so most of her clothes fell into the first of Helen's categories. Her dressing table was more difficult, with numerous items of jewellery, and as I had absolutely no idea which if any were valuable, I ended up creating a third batch which I labelled not sure. My sisters could sort that out.

'We're just off to collect Kyle and give the boys their tea,' Talia informed me.

'How long will you be?' I asked trying not to sound too interested in the answer.

'About a couple of hours, maybe less, then we'll be back to carry on. See you later.'

The diaries had obviously been disturbed, the police doing a thorough search in the immediate aftermath of the death, but I was confident that they were all there. How fortuitous that the girls were unaware of their existence. Once they had all been placed in one of the black bin liners we were using I phoned for a taxi.

It arrived promptly and I flung the bags full of diaries in the back.

'Weather back to normal,' the taxi driver announced as soon as we set off.

'Yes, rather disappointing,' I managed as a rather feeble reply. I was determined not to give him any reason to remember me.

'Don't bother me,' he smirked, 'off to the sun at the weekend, two weeks of guaranteed good weather. Decided to make sure this year so we've booked for the Caribbean. Ever been there?'

I told him that I had not been that fortunate but hoped he had a good time.

'Bound to with temperatures in the eighties and a five star hotel right on the beach.' There was to be no stopping him and all that was required of me were a selection of appropriate noises.

On arriving at my house I took the diaries upstairs and hid them under my bed. They would be safe there as in the rare event of having visitors it would be extremely unlikely that they would peek under it. I returned to mother's house, running most of the way. I needn't have hurried as it took ages for my sisters to return. Once Talia and Helen were there auto-pilot kicked in and they were fooled into thinking that I was coping better than they were. I have to admit that I have little recollection of the remainder of our time spent clearing the house.

It was late when I arrived home for the second time. I knew I should leave the diaries, with their intimate revelations, until the morning, but I became Pandora, lured by an irresistible temptation. Would I have the luck of the Greeks and retain hope once they were opened and read?

Where to start? It had been hard at times but I hadn't looked at any of the ones that I had taken at New Year. Now I had them all the fun could begin. I chose the day I was born, that day seemed most apposite. How did she feel on the day I arrived in the world?

Mother's Diary June 18th 1970

I have a son! Benjamin Doyle! I was so sure he was another girl that it was a complete surprise when the midwife told me I had a boy. He is gorgeous, 8lbs 6ozs, far heavier than the girls were. He has a shock of black hair and deep blue eyes. The nurses all say how handsome he is.

It was an easy birth, just over four hours. Edward came with the girls to see him about an hour after he was born and he thinks he looks like his dad. Pops will be pleased to have a grandson and said last week that if it's a boy he will take him to watch Preston North End. Poor child! I am exhausted but so happy. He is feeding well and latches on easily and drinks me dry (that made me feel slightly nauseous but I persevered). We are staying in hospital for a few days which will be a lovely rest for me. He seems a very contented baby........so far. I have a son, the Doyle name continues.

So, it all started well enough. What about a few years later? I flipped through the years until I came upon an interesting entry.

Mother's Diary September 4th 1976

Not the best day ever! Edward and I were called into school. Mrs Hallyard, Benjamin's teacher, wanted "a word." You know it's not going to be good news when you are summonsed to school. Apparently there had been a meeting about Benjamin last week. The Special Needs co-ordinator was involved and is keen to have Benjamin assessed. They say that he is displaying antisocial tendencies, ignores all the adults in the school and has very little to do with the other children. He doesn't hurt or bully them, just shows an inability to interact and has no interest in them, either in the classroom or the playground.

Although this is the second time we've been asked to a meeting Edward said that it was far too early to test a child and that many children grow out of unusual behaviour patterns given time. I am not so sure and have felt for many years that Benjamin is "different" to others of his age. The one person he really relates to is Pops. They get on like the proverbial house on fire.

Life seems so fraught with difficulties at the moment. We have said that we will monitor Benjamin's behaviour. Certainly the girls were never like this at that age but then they hadn't had the trauma that Benjamin experienced last year. They have dealt with that better than Benjamin.

What a strange euphemism "trauma". The event I will not discuss. As a matter of interest I looked the word up:

1. *A serious injury or shock to the body, as from violence or an accident.*
2. *An emotional wound or shock that creates substantial, lasting damage to the psychological development of a person, often leading to neurosis.*
3. *An event or situation that causes great distress and disruption.*

All might be apposite to mother, thinking of the happening that had been "experienced last year" but my mother was always given to exaggeration. Trauma indeed.

I was never tested. What would they have learnt? What would they have done if they had discovered something? My father was right. With maturity I learnt to interact with people: though not always to their advantage!

Back to the present. The trial has now lasted for three weeks and I am growing weary of it. Endless day follows endless day of unbelievably repetitive evidence. The lawyers cannot take anyone's answer at face value and probe all the details ad nauseam. That having been said there was some excitement for the jury today.

Chapter 20

Defendant's Evidence: Day Three

Conversation that evening between Colin Heaton, a member of the jury, and his wife, Alice.

'Hello, you're back early.'

'We were sent home, the defendant needed to see a doctor.'

'See a doctor? What happened?'

'I probably shouldn't say anything but I might as well tell you, it will be all over the papers tomorrow. You know how "together" he's been so far, only displaying any emotion once before.'

'Yes, you've called him "Mr Cool Calm and Collected".'

'Well he was anything but today, totally lost it: couldn't take the cross-examination and went to pieces - began sobbing, then shouting and finally began to scream blue murder. Far worse than last time.'

'Goodness what started that reaction?'

'Sir Anthony returned to the photos and asked him about the ones that were found with the little boy's body. He kept saying that they were vital evidence in the case against him and proved that he was guilty.

'Were those the ones that upset some of the women jurors?'

'Yes, they were horrific: pornographic, cruel, sadistic, oh words fail, they were so disgusting. I'm glad you'll never see them. He has already admitted that he had some pornography on his computer but shouted very loudly that he wasn't into kiddy stuff so why did they think he had taken those found with the body. He claimed that no one was listening to him and that he was telling the truth. Then he really started to lose it and he began ranting and raving about not even owning a camera. He yelled the place down when Sir Anthony repeated that that was very strange as his fingerprints were on it.

Mr Cool was definitely Mr Uncool and he seemed to have some sort of breakdown. He collapsed in a heap and suddenly went quiet. The court officers were called and helped him out of the dock and a doctor was sent for. We were asked to leave and as it was well into the afternoon we were told to go home but be back as normal tomorrow. We were warned not to talk about the day's events but as I said it will be in the papers tomorrow.'

Telephone call from Nigel Simpson, reporter for the Daily Gazette, to his editor, Philip Monroe.

'Hi Phil. We've got a problem. What a story but it's been blocked. The defendant lost it, completely and utterly, went totally ballistic. He was swearing and shouting then crying like a baby and the proceedings were stopped and a doctor called. The judge has warned us not to print the story, says it would be "prejudicial to the outcome of the case". Can't see why but maybe there's a way around it. We could say the trial was stopped whilst the defendant needed medical assistance without saying why. What do you think?*

Daily Gazette

Breaking News: The trial for the sadistic murder of toddler, Jamie Richardson, came to a dramatic halt when the defendant needed urgent medical assistance. No details are available at this time but it is believed that the trial is set to resume this morning.

Judge's Notes

I must speak to the jury about yesterday's "meltdown". The man became quite unwell but the doctor has assured me that he will be able to return to court today.

The person before us each day is a man of extremes. Most of the time he maintains a detached demeanour, it is almost as though he is not involved in the proceedings and appears to be unaware of all that is happening. At such times one is left wondering whether he realises just how serious the situation is and how near he may be to spending untold years in prison. However, we have now seen his other side twice, where he loses all control and acts like a man possessed. I was amused to hear one juror speak of a "split personality".

Are the jury affected by such extremes of behaviour? Is this influencing them towards a guilty verdict? Are they asking themselves whether someone who can indulge in such Jekyll and Hyde antics is indeed capable of the inhumane crime they are being asked to determine?

After more than seven weeks the coroner was able to release mother's body for burial. Almost two months should be ample time to come to terms with a death and face the funeral, but my sisters were not of that persuasion. Perhaps they had had too long to plan it: readings, hymns, flowers, and heaven help us the eulogies; all caused endless debate and futile introspection. They kept asking each other what mother would have wanted, a ridiculous question to which none of us had the answer. No one had thought to ask her whilst she was alive so, as far as I was concerned, none of it mattered now she was dead. The one thing we were sure of was that she wanted to be cremated and for her ashes to be interred beside father's in the Garden of Remembrance.

The funeral took place at the beginning of March. I don't know whether mother was bound for hell but that day I thought I was already there. It was appalling. Grief unbounded; sorrow unrestrained; no emotion left untrammelled. There were enough tears to stock the local reservoir and so many tons of paper hankies were used that their disposal would require a new land-fill site.

It was a beautiful spring day and the daffodils were a superb sight in the crematorium garden. Despite loathing the entire fiasco I was on my best behaviour.

'Mother always loved daffodils,' I said, trying to say something positive.

'She won't see them this year,' was Talia's wailed response.

'I expect she will, in heaven,' Helen added, inducing a fresh deluge from both of them. If Noah had been there he would have been planning another ark.

The service was blessedly short. All the planning had resulted in two hymns, a reading from Matthew's

Gospel about "the sheep and the goats," a follow up eulogy from Helen (Talia giving up at the last moment at any attempt to speak) about mother being a sheep which I found so funny that I had to splutter into my hanky and pretend I was overcome with grief. It was the one light moment in an otherwise dark day.

The curtains closing on the coffin, for which I had paid an excessive amount, considering its brief appearance and final destination, was the instant for all decorum to vanish, faster than the cards up a magician's sleeve. Hindu widows immolating themselves on their husband's funeral pyres could never have created a more dramatic scene than the one which followed mother's final disappearance. Helen fainted and Talia slumped beside her. What a way to behave. Acting the part of the considerate brother I helped them up and out into the sunshine to acknowledge the other mourners.

'She had a good turn out,' Hilda, one of her oldest friends said at the buffet organised in a local café, 'she was such a lovely woman, always so kind and helpful. She'd do anything for anybody.' Was this the same woman I had called "mother"?

'I shall miss her,' this was uttered in a maudlin whisper by great aunt Lucy who we only saw at weddings and funerals. Quite why she would miss mother, when to the best of my knowledge she never contacted her, was beyond me. Talia and Helen managed to pull themselves together during the remainder of the afternoon and I felt able to leave early saying that I would be in touch. It may not surprise you to learn that I have had very little contact with either of them since that horrendous day.

Chapter 21

Instructions from Sir Cecil Montgomery to Members of the Jury.

Ladies and gentlemen of the jury, this is proving to be a most unsavoury, and for many of you, a distressing and depressing case. You are listening to some exceedingly disturbing evidence, but evidence that it is necessary for you to hear. Many of you are taking detailed notes which will prove useful when the time comes for you to deliberate, as a group, on the matter of the defendant's innocence or guilt. That will, when all the evidence has been presented, be your decision. However I am going to ask you now to forget the events of yesterday. The defendant became extremely upset but this must, under no circumstances, be allowed to colour your judgement or sway your opinion. You must not think that his behaviour was an indication of either his innocence or his guilt.

The scenes in this court room yesterday afternoon were unfortunate and some of you will find it hard to erase them from your memory but I will repeat that they must play no part in your thinking or be allowed to sway your judgement: either now or when the time comes to retire and discuss the case.

When the court resumes in a few moments, the proceedings will continue from the point at which the defendant became unwell. Thank you for your attention and your dedication to this onerous duty.

Back to normal. No further histrionics.

The case is being presented as though it comes straight from the Marquis de Sade's book of torture. Nothing could be further from the truth. The child did not suffer whilst alive and all injuries were sustained post-mortem (with the obvious exception of the one that stopped his heart beating).

Why kill a two year old? Why extinguish such a young life? The simple answer was that the little lad was better off dead. He had no future. He had the misfortune to be born into deprivation: financial, emotional and spiritual. He was a spoke in a wheel of adversity from which there would have been no escape. He would merely have continued the ride.

The Richardson tribe were, and will probably remain, notorious in their neighbourhood, a run-down area of Preston, where my father was head teacher of the local primary for so many years. Even he, dedicated as he was to helping both the children in his care and their families, became disillusioned and of the opinion that little could be done to help those who refused to help themselves.

As far as I know none of the Richardsons have ever done a day's work in their miserable lives, unless it was the unpaid Community Service variety ordered by the J.P.'s. The entire family has always lived off the benefit system, which they manage to compose so that it plays their tune. Fines, Community sentences, periods in prison are all hall-marks of the sorry tribe. Not one of them seems able to avoid the familial traits. Their disregard for the law usually starts early, the average age being eight years old, giving them two years to practise their misdemeanours before appearing in the Youth Court. By the time they reach the dizzy heights of the Adult Court they almost invariably have a catalogue of appearances and convictions that would have made Al Capone proud.

Sharon Richardson, Jamie's mother, was a well-known and particularly unpleasant member of the clan. Petty thieving whilst still at Primary school was soon followed by arrests for distributing drugs, being drunk and disorderly and soliciting. God alone knew who Jamie's father was. I rather doubt whether she had any idea and to the best of my knowledge he was no longer on the scene. She was a registered heroin addict and had been prescribed methadone which she declined to accept, preferring the short term hits afforded by her addiction, though how she paid for this was a matter of conjecture.

Could Jamie possibly be left to her not so tender ministrations? Aged two I reckoned he had about another five or six years before he would be lured into anti-social then criminal behaviour. Let's face it the lad was better off out of it. No hope for him this time around. Not with that background.

On the days when I walked the long way home I passed the flats where Sharon lived. As the Richardsons appear to have no difficulty adding to their numbers I was not surprised to see her pushing a buggy. The next morning I mentioned to Julie, the person in the office who knows everything about everyone, that I had seen them.

'That poor little mite. He was born two months prematurely and addicted to heroin. What a start in life. He had to be de-toxed in the hospital and put on Metha-done soon after he was born. I watched a programme about the effects of drugs on new-borns and it was horrendous. They shake and scream and have to go through withdrawal just like any adult would and once they're off it they're not out of the woods. Most will need on-going medical and social service input and as their brains haven't been properly developed in the womb they are usually behind at school. It makes me so mad.'

Having made the appropriate noises I left to get on with the day's work. Jamie's situation stayed at the back of my mind. He did not have much of a future ahead of him: Special Needs' group at school, no qualifications, little prospect of a job (should he be the first and only Richardson to want one) and a lifetime of Court appearances leading, almost inevitably, to weeks then months and even years in prison. The Good Fairies had not put in much of an appearance at his birth.

As Sharon had been in court for possession of drugs on several occasions it was rather surprising that she had been allowed to keep Jamie. Social Services were heavily involved, a somewhat dubious use of our hard earned taxes. Perhaps had Jamie lived he would eventually have found himself taken into care like his older sister and would have then spent his time in either a children's home or with some frazzled foster parents who would try their best to reverse the harm already done to him. Neither prospect looked particularly appealing and he was, I surmised, once again, almost certainly better off dead.

Over the next few months I saw the pair quite regularly. Sharon was looking haggard and I imagined that her son was unusually demanding. Even in the best of circumstances she would not have featured in nominations for "Mother of the Year" but it appeared that the whole experience was taking its toll. She had never been exactly what might be deemed attractive but each time I saw her she looked worse: hair unwashed, clothes un-ironed, bags the size of Tesco's weekly food carriers beneath her eyes. She looked permanently jittery and I never saw her without a cigarette in her mouth.

It was on a cold Thursday evening that the master plan zoomed into my mind, like an Exocet missile finding its target. That evening Jamie must have been cold, sitting in his push chair and wearing the most inadequate outfit of T shirt and thin trousers. He was complaining in the only way he knew, by crying.

Sharon responded, without thinking that there might be a reason for his distress and yelled, 'Shut the fuck up, for God's sake stop that bleeding noise; it's doing me head in.' She had bent over him and was so near his face that spittle was landing on his already sodden cheeks. Two hefty slaps followed in quick succession, each making his little head wobble. His screaming reached rock concert pitch at which she resumed her verbal abuse, 'Why I had to have a little fucker like you I don't know. You're a bloody nuisance. I hate you. I wish you'd never been born.'

Had the little lad been capable of speech I rather think he would have agreed with that last comment. It was obviously my duty to assist him. There would have been no advantage in berating her there and then as that would merely have resulted in me being on the receiving end of her foul tongue. A far greater intervention was required, but at a time and place of my choosing. This world, with Sharon as a mother and the future that lay ahead for Jamie was too horrendous to contemplate so I would be his saviour. Whatever his existence in the next world you must surely agree that it had to be better than the present one.

This would be my most audacious murder to date. It would require a master plan. The added dimension I had in mind was delicious in its simplicity but would require the utmost attention to detail. This time it just might be "perfect".

During the evenings when I wasn't working on my plan I read mother's diaries. They illuminated aspects of her to which I had not been privy when she was alive. Her worries (about the family); her disappointments (never going for promotion at work) and her tragedy (the event with which she never came to terms). The "trauma"; the incident that still wrecks my nights, haunts my dreams and the one that it is time to reveal.

Chapter 22

Mother's Diary October 14th 1975

I am writing this many weeks on. I have been unable to do anything since Billy's death. Life is torture. Each day is black and so unbearably sad. No one should outlive their children. It is against the laws of nature. Why was Billy taken from us? He was such an adorable little chap. At the funeral the vicar said that we cannot know why such terrible things happen. We cannot know the mind of God. I felt like yelling that there cannot be a God if he can allow such awful, awful tragedies. I don't think I will ever get over this. Every day is a day spent in hell.

Edward is so strong I think he is putting on a brave face for my sake as I know he is as unhappy as I am. The girls are being kind and making me cups of tea and helping to cook and clean. Henry and Amy are feeling guilty that they didn't watch the boys more carefully and they are doing everything they can to help us.

That day is etched into my brain, a daily torture. Benjamin was the one who found him but he seems quite calm about it all. Perhaps he is too young to understand. I have tried talking to him but he just looks away and never says a word. They were so close, such good pals and Billy adored him but for Benjamin it is as though Billy never existed.

Why oh why did we not watch them more carefully? Why did we leave them alone in the garden? We thought it was safe but it wasn't. Benjamin was too young to look after Billy but they were only alone for a few minutes, such a very short time but that was all it took to devastate my world, to tear it apart for ever. How I long to turn back the clock to earlier that afternoon but time only travels one way. How I wish it could move on without me but as Ted says I've got the rest of the family to think about.

Enough, the writing has exhausted me.

Oh well, here goes, the episode that has tortured my life. The one deed I would undo should I be given Dr Who's time travelling powers. Where to start? How to explain?

Two and a half years after I was born Billy came along. My parents thought that a sibling, close in age to me, would be a play-mate, a companion and that a friendship would form such as that enjoyed by my sisters. Billy was as different to me as it is possible for two boys to be. In appearance he was blond to my black, small to my large and gentle to my rough. He was a gorgeous child: bright, smiley and almost endlessly happy. He enchanted all who met him.

Strange to report I enjoyed his company and the two of us were friends, just as my parents had planned. I was the big brother and I remember feeling important as he followed me everywhere. I was the one in charge, the one who made up the games and decided what we would do. There must have been fallings out and arguments but I can honestly say that I have no recollection of them.

That autumn, the one of the "trauma", I had started school and my grandparents told me how much Billy missed me when I wasn't at home. Mother had returned to work and Pops and Nana looked after Billy every afternoon and the two days he didn't attend nursery. Each afternoon Pops and Nana met me at the school gates and Billy would race across the playground and throw himself into my arms.

'Ben-Ben,' (the closest he could get to my name) would be yelled as soon as he saw me.

So what went wrong?

Nana was still alive at the time and so Pops was not yet living with us. They lived in a large detached house a short walk away. It was an amazing place, numerous rooms, cupboards and hidey-holes, perfect for games of "Hide- and- Seek" that we all played over and over. Billy and I loved going there each afternoon before mother returned from work to collect us.

The huge garden was a children's wonder world of slides, swings and the three thick ropes that were attached to the ancient oak tree which we were encouraged to climb when supervised. Nana loved baking and my memory is of the most delicious cakes, tarts and biscuits waiting for us in the old-fashioned kitchen each afternoon. In winter there was a roaring fire in the corner of the room with a cushion-strewn settle beside it, just big enough to accommodate all four of us.

In the summer we loved opening both halves of the wooden door and eating on the patio. The door amazed us as it was the only one we knew that came with an upper and a lower part. As I grew older I adored hoisting myself over the lower portion and descending, albeit rather ungracefully, down the other side. Billy never grew tall enough to attempt this athletic feat. On many occasions we begged to be allowed to stay for our tea and Nana would then take us back home in time for bed.

Those were idyllic times, and along with my years at Oxford were the best I have ever experienced. My early years have left me with many happy memories. Would I have turned out differently had Nana and then my beloved Pops not been taken from me quite so soon? I have often found myself asking in a similar fashion to Topol when he demands of his God, "Would it spoil some vast eternal plan?" not in my case to be a wealthy man, but one who continued to be loved.

Most Sundays my grandparents would walk along after church and join us for a traditional roast dinner. Pops would then spend the afternoon gardening. We were living in the Trough of Bowland and our house had a huge area of land, well over an acre. Father, whilst enjoying gardening in theory, never found enough time to keep it totally under control. That was where Pops came in, with me as his chief assistant.

Until that fateful day, Billy had been in the habit of having an afternoon nap and so it was always Pops and me "Bill and Ben the Flowerpot Men" dead-heading the flowers, cleaning the pots and pulling up the weeds. That was "our" time. From the very beginning Pops and I had a special relationship, a bond that, as far as I was concerned, could not survive an interloper. No "ménage a trios" for us.

'Me help, me help, me do it,' Billy implored, toddling out on his rather thin, unsteady legs. Pops and I were just beginning that afternoon's task of tidying up the borders ready for their winter's rest. My grandfather was a kind, accommodating soul and laughed, 'Another gardener, I'll be getting the sack.' He sat Billy beside the soil and gave him the plastic trowel from the sand pit.

Can words describe how I felt? I have never, before or since, experienced the blinding fury that coursed through me. I was incoherent with rage. Pops was mine during those afternoons and no one, not even Billy, could be allowed to interfere. Young as I was I realised that this was the end of my unique relationship with Pops. Nothing would be the same with a third person around.

Mother chose that moment to call Pops in to join Amy for a cup of tea. He left Billy and me sitting digging in the soil. Our garden was perfectly safe. The large wooden gate was kept shut and had we ventured out onto the lane that ran past the house we would still have been alright as it was rarely used by traffic. However I was forbidden from leaving the garden and had been warned, time and again, about the dangers of the ford a short distance away. There was no time to plan, no conscious malice aforethought, the next few minutes were purely instinctive. I had to remain Pop's number one.

It was all too easy. As I said Billy followed me everywhere. He was too young to think about safety and in any case I was the source of his amusements; I was the one with whom he had adventures.

'Let's go down to the ford,' I whispered as though I had invented a new game. I grabbed his hand and led him down the gravel path to the gate. I could just reach the catch and it opened easily. Within a few seconds we were standing by the water. There had been days of autumnal gales and torrential rain, the results of hurricane Teresa which had fought its way across the Atlantic to continue wreaking havoc this side of the "pond". In those conditions the water, which was normally a shallow trickle easily crossed by vehicles, became a fast moving onslaught; a dark brown torrent.

Billy looked up at me, waiting for the game to start. That look of complete trust is the image that plagues me. What I did next felt inevitable. He was so small, so easy to hold under the water. Such a simple killing. Yes he struggled, the desire for life affording him strength beyond his years, but I was so much larger and more powerful. And so determined.

'Help! Billy's fallen in the water,' I exploded back into the garden and ran as fast as my five year old legs would carry me, finally reaching the back door. 'It's Billy, he's gone in the water,' was my childish, and to some extent truthful, explanation.

Never had my family moved with such speed. They were by the ford in seconds. Billy had been carried a short distance down-stream where his body had become lodged against the mesh fencing that allowed water but no debris through. What a dreadful thought - Billy had become "debris", though at the time I didn't know that particular word, or its disturbing connotations. Father rushed into the muddy deluge and lifted Billy out. He laid him on the bank and Pops started to give him the kiss of life. Mother and Nana were screaming in utter panic, both beyond logical thought or the giving of practical help. Father rushed back to the house to call for an ambulance.

'What happened? What in God's name happened? How did Billy get out of the garden? The gate was shut. It's always shut when the boys are in the garden. How did Billy get in the water?' my mother's voice strident with fear. She didn't appear to be expecting any answers and it wasn't the right moment to begin any explanations. Time enough for that.

We didn't live near any of the emergency services and so it was an age before we heard the ambulance coming, its sirens wailing. The paramedics were wonderful. They worked on Billy for over an hour then decided that it would be better to take him back to Preston General. Mother and father went with him and Nana, my sisters and I followed with Pops in his car. The only thing I recall from the journey was the silence. No one uttered a word or even made a sound. My grandparents, being staunch Christians, were no doubt offering silent prayers to their deity; perhaps offering their lives in return for Billy's.

Accident and Emergency was fairly quiet when we arrived. We sat and waited for news. Drinks were suggested and refused though I would dearly have loved some lemonade. It was unusual for my sisters to be so still, to have nothing to say, but then my five year old self knew that these were unusual circumstances.

'Oh my dears, my poor, poor dears,' Pops muttered when he saw my parents walking towards us. There was no need for them to say a word. It was obvious from their faces and their look of complete defeat that Billy was dead. 'Let's get you all home. You both come with us and the girls can take a taxi with Benjamin.'

Until that day I had never seen adults cry, that was something other children did, but not an affliction from which I had, or indeed have, ever suffered. Once back in the kitchen, where so much tea was drunk that it must have necessitated a new assignment from India, the questioning began, or should I say the interrogation.

'Benjamin, you're not in trouble, just tell us what happened,' this was Pops, the only one who was retaining a modicum of self-control. 'You see son, we're all sure the gate was shut and Billy (loud sobs from Mother and Nana at the mention of his name) wasn't tall enough to open it himself. Do you know what happened?'

I sat mesmerised. Would they believe my version of events? It was then, for the first time that I learnt how to be an actor, to play a part that might have been written for me. My thespian talent emerged. I was Macbeth, King Lear and Hamlet all rolled into one. A Shakespearean triumvirate! Let the tragedy unfold.

'It's my fault (that much was true) we were bored and I said to Billy that it would be fun to go and look at the water as it was really exciting.'

'How many times have you been told not to go near the water?' my mother was yelling and had gone puce with anger.

'I know, but I thought if we were together it would be safe.'

'Well it very obviously wasn't was it?'

'No, I'm sorry I thought it would be O.K.'

'What happened next son, when you got to the ford?' Pops was still calm.

'Billy slipped and fell in. I tried to get him out but the water pulled him away from me, so I ran back to the house.' Looking at everyone else crying had no effect on me but I managed a few theatrical sobs and moans which seemed to work as Nana put her arms around me saying that I had had a terrible experience and should be asked about it later.

Supper was a miserable affair though I was allowed a larger than normal helping of ice cream (chocolate-chip, my favourite).

'He was here this morning, I can't believe he's gone, it's not possible,' this was mother at her most inane. Her first two sentiments were correct but definitely not the last. Anything is possible. It was at that exact instant that, young as I was, I understood that I was the one who had created the impossible. The supremacy that such power affords overwhelmed me. There have been countless times since when I have regretted Billy's death but that was not one of them. At bedtime (later than usual which I found most pleasing) I climbed the stairs to dreamland an extremely happy little boy. Looking back I suspect that I was the only one to enjoy an unbroken night's sleep.

The next morning the house was like the morgue where Billy's remains were lying in a freezer awaiting the post mortem. I asked about that but no one wanted to talk about it. The police arrived and to my surprise they wanted to ask me "a few questions". I wanted to tell them that I had answered all the questions I'd been asked the previous evening and that Pops could give them all the details, but as they were wearing uniforms and we had been told at school to do what the police said I kept quiet.

'Hello Ben, I'm Sandy, and I'm a policewoman. This is my friend Johnny, he's a policeman (did they think I was stupid?) and we'd like to talk to you about what happened yesterday afternoon. Is that O.K.?' Well let's face it I could hardly say no.

'Do you remember being in the garden with Billy?' cue sobs from mother.

'Yes,' I wasn't going to make it easy for her.

'Your granddad says he went into the house and you and Billy were digging in the soil. Can you tell me what you did then?'

'It was a game; we were going to look at the water cos it's been dead fast since the big storm.'

'Did you open the gate all by yourself?' Did she think I was a baby? Of course I could reach the catch.

'Yes then me and Billy walked down to the water.'

'What happened when you got to the water?'

'I got some stones to throw in but Billy fell over when he was throwing his.'

The session became tedious as Sandy (who I remember thinking was far too pretty to be a policewoman and should have been a pop singer) asked the same questions over and over, using slightly different words each time. I stuck to my story and eventually the pair left.

The post mortem showed that death was due to drowning; an unfortunate accident. The following weeks were a miasma of despair. Mother was inconsolable and though she never said that she blamed me our relationship was never quite the same again. There were times, especially in the years immediately following Billy's accident, when I would find her looking at me as though she was trying to understand something. She never asked me directly if I had deliberately hurt him but I suspect the thought wasn't too far from her mind.

It was the following summer that we all suffered from her first bout of debilitating depression. She alternated between prolonged episodes of weeping and even longer periods of silence and total, surreal stillness when she would sit for days on end like one of the human statues one sees in town centres acting out their strange mimes. Hers was bereavement. Totally withdrawing into her own hell she endured weeks of self-inflicted isolation. Our grandparents maintained some sense of normality for the rest of us. They took over the day to day running of the house: shopping, cleaning, washing and making sure we all got to school on time. Without them our family would have fallen apart as it was all father could do to stumble to work and once home try to provide his distant wife with some comfort. It is to his credit that he did this for hours on end. To this day I am not sure whether that was out of love or duty - probably both.

Dr Evans attended on a regular basis and gave mother prescriptions for a variety of pills, none of which appeared to make any difference. Each time in the years that followed when mother succumbed to her "blues", on average every twelve months around the anniversary of Billy's death, the misery lasted longer until she was admitted eventually to the local psychiatric unit where she endured weeks of treatment. No visits were allowed for the first fortnight and were quickly curtailed as seeing the family (especially me) undid any progress she had made.

Was I culpable? Did I feel any remorse? At the time I was too young to marry my part in Billy's death with her illness and as the years passed I thought that one small death should not have had such an incapacitating effect on any normal person. She could have done more to help herself to cope; after all she had three other children to bring up.

Nana died the following winter, her cancer no longer responding to treatment and her demise probably accelerated by the death of her beloved grandson, and soon after that Pops moved in with us. As time went on Billy's name was seldom mentioned, the episode being deemed too tragic for words.

Mother's Diary December 12th 1975

The days are not getting easier. Each morning I wake up to an all too brief moment of forgetfulness when I feel happy; then it hits me and my fragile edifice is bulldozed by the truth: Billy is dead. Then follows a day of despair when the whole world, or definitely my world, is shades of black, like an old fashioned television but without the contrasting white.

Edward is still trying to be stoical but he isn't really coping much better than me. He sits and cries at night when the children are in bed. We are not much comfort to each other. The girls vary between being O.K. and extremely upset.

Benjamin is the strange one. I keep thinking about the dreadful fact that he was there when it happened. You would expect him to talk about it but he never says a word or seems bothered. For him it is as though Billy was never here, though he has started to have nightmares and wakes up screaming. I can't tell what he is saying but when I wake him he looks terrified. Being Benjamin he will not say what the dreams are about. They were such good friends that it seems unusual, to say the very least. God forgive me but I sometimes wonder what really happened, was there more to it than Billy falling in and Benjamin not being able to help him? Edward gets so cross if I mention anything along those lines. But I still wonder.

Well there you have it: my ultimate confession. Guilty as charged. Was I fated to start with Billy? Would the subsequent killings have occurred if he had not drowned that day? Might I have enjoyed a very different life without that first murder? Questions to which there are no answers. The two I can answer: Am I sorry I killed him? Yes. Am I sorry about the others? No.

Chapter 23

Court Evidence in the Trial for the Murder of Jamie Richardson

Eye Witness Accounts: Alibis for the Defendant?

Testimony of Mr George Jones, Proprietor of "The Little Shop on the Corner", Llandudno.

My wife and I have had our shop, which is about a mile from the centre of Llandudno, for ten years. It's near a caravan park and a lot of the houses around us are holiday cottages so we are usually busy, especially in the summer months. We are also near a housing estate and we are packed at the beginning and end of the school day when the mums come in for a few bits and pieces.

Lizzie and I have come forward as witnesses after seeing the defendant's picture in the papers. It was only an artist's likeness but we were sure it was him. It was Liz who recognised him to start with and she got all excited and said that she was sure that he was the good looking man who had been in our shop earlier in the year. She had commented at the time that he was gorgeous enough to be in the movies and that we don't often get film stars in our shop.

I remember the day very well. It was the 4th of May. I know that because it was Liz's brother's birthday.

Liz and I run the shop together. It was Taffy's, that's her brother's, "big one" life beginning and all that so we had planned a bit of a do for the evening. Yes it was definitely the 4th of May.

Well to tell you the truth, and as I've just sworn on the Bible that's what I'm doing anyway, I have to admit that I wouldn't have noticed him particularly. I'm usually too busy to pay much attention to what customers look like. But when I saw his picture in the paper I did think I might have seen him before.

Yes I am talking about the defendant, the man sitting over there in the dock.

As I say I wouldn't have noticed him, he was just another holiday maker as far as I was concerned. It was Liz. I was putting his items through the check-out on the counter, and she was standing behind me, filling up the cigarettes. As he was leaving she said that he was a bit of alright.

Sorry I didn't mean to make everyone laugh, but that was what she said. Being a bloke I hadn't noticed anything special but when she made that remark I had another look.

Well, yes, I suppose he did have his back turned by that stage, but I realised how tall he was, much taller than the average man and he had very dark hair.

I think it was him, the defendant sitting over there.

I suppose I can't be a hundred per cent sure but maybe ninety. Yes I think it was him.

No we never saw him again but the man I'm thinking of had bought quite a lot that day so had probably got enough for the week.

Testimony of Mrs Elizabeth Jones, wife of George Jones.

I work with my husband and we run a shop on the outskirts of Llandudno. We've been there for about seven years and enjoy working together though we do have the odd words. Any couple would, being together twenty four seven as the saying goes.

May 4th was my brother, Taffy's, 40th birthday so it's a day that sticks in my mind. The time you're asking about was early afternoon so we were not too busy. We tend to get really busy when the schools come out and the mums come in, also the teenagers from the local secondary. You've got to keep your eyes on them.

Sorry, I will stick to answering the questions.

A man came in and filled his basket, almost to overflowing, so it took George a few minutes to put it all through the till. I was behind my husband, sorting the cigarette shelves which had become rather empty, though why anyone smokes these days with all the health warnings..............sorry off I go again........... and I noticed him, the man in the dock, because he was so good looking. We don't get too many like that in Llandudno.

Well it was several months ago but I'm certain it was the man sitting over there.

Pretty certain, but we see so many customers and a lot of them are holiday makers who only shop with us for a week or a fortnight at the most but he was not like the normal run of the mill shoppers, he stood out from the crowd as the saying goes.

I am sure that it was him. As I said it was his looks that struck me. Could have been a film star I said to George afterwards. I was sorry he never came back.

I agree that other men must be similar to him but it would be strange if it wasn't him as he mentioned us and we both remember him in our shop on the day in question. If it wasn't the man sitting over there it was someone incredibly like him.

Judge's Notes

Interesting that witnesses who claim to provide the man with an alibi have come forward - albeit rather late in the proceedings. They appear to corroborate the defendant's story.

Reasonably strong accounts but both rather wilted under the prosecution cross examination. Sir Anthony pressing until Mrs Jones was almost in tears.

The defendant looked pleased and took an interest in today's proceedings. He smiled for the first time.

I would dearly love to know what the jury made of today.

To tell you the truth most of the jurors looked somewhat confused by the testimonies of both Mr and Mrs Jones. I know from long years of experience that it is a dangerous practice for lawyers, whether for the prosecution or the defence, to rely on the testimony of eye witnesses. Statistics show that eyewitness identifications are wrong about fifty per cent of the time. It has been said that such evidence is the greatest cause of wrongful convictions. However a seemingly reliable eyewitness account can prove overwhelmingly persuasive, making a deep impression on both Magistrates and juries. The problem is that the mind of the average human being is not like a photograph that can produce a dependable picture as people don't tend to record events exactly as they occur. Seldom is the witness trying to deliberately mislead but they can, unwittingly manage to change the appearance of the person they are trying to identify to an alarming degree. Because of such evidence the police are often sent down "blind alleys" focusing on the wrong person whilst the perpetrator can get away.

When I was first appointed as a Legal Adviser I became very interested in the role of eyewitness, being particularly unimpressed by the majority of them in my trials, and I did some research. It was fascinating to read that psychiatrists speak of "original memory" and state that interpretation of events and people occurs at the very moment the memory is formulated and so distortion is introduced from the very beginning and false memories are put in place. Once witnesses identify a perpetrator, they become unwilling or even unable to "re-think" their initial understanding. As I have a photographic memory I like to think that I would prove a superb eyewitness, but few are blessed with such an attribute.

All in all, despite their best efforts, the Jones duo did little to aid the case for the defence. It is impossible to read the minds of the twelve worthy citizens sitting there preparing to pass judgement. Their faces are for the most part passive, the exception being when the details of Jamie's murder are highlighted. On occasion some even appear bored. How I would love to know their innermost thoughts. Are they being swayed one way or the other? Will the verdict be guilty or innocent?

The old English word for guilty was "nocent", the opposite of innocent. This jury will, almost certainly, attempt to reach the verdict that they consider to be the correct one. Following a notorious trial in 1670 the judge informed the jury that "I will have a positive (guilty) verdict or you'll starve for it" and followed up his threat by locking them up for two days without food, water, heat or light. Since then juries have had to be independent with no interference allowed. An interesting foot note to the seventeenth century tale is that the jury, though strong enough to acquit the defendants, were themselves heavily fined and jailed until released by Sir John Vaughan the chief justice at the time.

Deidre Hannigan drove home in a confident mood. The day's evidence had given her some hope: two people substantiating her client's story that he was on holiday at the time of the murder. To give him his due she realised that he had never altered his story by one syllable.

'I'm home,' she announced in a voice that sounded more cheerful than it had since the trial began.

'You seem happy, must have had a good day,' Walter smiled, glad that at last there had been something positive.

'It was the eye-witnesses I was telling you about, the Jones' from Llandudno.'

'They came up trumps did they?'

'Well they rather crumbled under the cross examination, you know what Sir Anthony is like, and both were forced to admit that they couldn't be totally sure he was the man in their shop...do know what they call it "The Little Shop on the Corner!".........but I think, well I hope, that the jury will have had the idea put in their minds that he has an alibi. It will at the very least make them think that he might be telling the truth. And if he was in Wales then he can't have committed the murder.'

'How did our friend take it?'

'He thinks that's it; that his version of events will now be believed and he will be acquitted. I did tell him that their evidence did not provide him with cast-iron alibis, but by that time he had stopped listening. Nothing new there then!'

The press are, as always, well represented and I am amused to see the parts of the trial that they find the most noteworthy. During the testimonies delivered by Mr and Mrs Jones the reporters were scribbling furiously. No doubt George and Elizabeth will feature prominently in tomorrow's headlines. They will have their fifteen minutes of fame. It is to be hoped they will not be castigated too severely for their rather inept statements. They were only doing their civic duty.

Chapter 24

Daily Gazette

Eyewitnesses Found! Statements Prove Unreliable.

The case for the defence in the trial for the shocking murder of toddler Jamie Richardson took a strange turn yesterday when George and Elizabeth Jones were called as eyewitnesses. The defendant had claimed to be in the Llandudno area at the time when Jamie was murdered but no one had been found to corroborate his story.

Mr and Mrs Jones came forward to give evidence after reading about the case in this newspaper. They claimed that they had served him in their shop, the prosaically named, "Little Shop on the Corner" which is situated a mile out of Llandudno, at the time the defendant says he was on holiday in the area.

However after lengthy questioning neither was able to be one hundred per cent certain that the defendant was the man they had seen in their shop on the 4th of May the day after Jamie went missing. Forensic evidence shows that this was roughly the date on which Jamie was killed.

Elizabeth Jones was distraught after giving evidence and told our reporter, through loud sobs, "I am still sure it was him but the lawyer got me so confused and I wasn't able to swear on the Bible that is was definitely him. But I know it was."

Is the defendant left without an alibi for the period in question? The vital week is the one starting the 3rd of May when Jamie disappeared, to the 11th, the day his body was discovered.

The case continues.

Can I assure you Jamie did not suffer at my hands whilst he was alive. I reckoned he'd had more than enough of that already.

Planning his demise seemed to take forever as I was able only to observe the two of them on my days off, but eventually I was ready. This was, without doubt, my most auspicious murder and had to be without blemish. Following the months I spent watching the delightful Sharon I knew that each time she went into Sam's Store she invariably left Jamie sitting outside, whatever the weather. I had timed her absenteeism and it averaged five and half minutes. Ample time to take Jamie.

On the day in question I was careful in my mode of attire, no point drawing attention to myself. Blend in with the crowd, look like one of the local dads (though in truth in that area there weren't many of those around) and walk off with the pushchair. I knew that Jamie faced away from the person pushing so would not know it wasn't his mother. I surmised that, in all probability, he would not find the absence of any form of communication with him unusual.

My old jeans and a dark hoody, purchased for the occasion, seemed suitable. The weather was atrocious and an anorak would have been more appropriate but few men who live in that area wear them. I followed the pair from their block of flats and as soon as Sharon entered the shop, leaving Jamie sitting in his push-chair its hood hardly sheltering him from the downpour, I walked up and calmly collected my next victim. No one gave me a second glance and Jamie was silent through-out our walk along the street and into the park. The eye witnesses who, early in the trial, gave most unusual accounts of a man carrying a heavy bundle and one approaching the pelican crossing were fantasising. In neither case was I the person they saw.

I knew what I had to do but I had no intention of making Jamie suffer unnecessarily or even experience more fear than was absolutely essential. Once through the park we walked for several miles down a canal path which at that time of day, and in such appalling weather, was only populated by the homeless who having drunk rather too much were unlikely to notice us or to remember a dad and child having an afternoon stroll by the water. I surmised that I had little to fear from them should they be called as witnesses. None of them, in their inebriated state, would question the fact that others were out walking on a day such as that.

Only one, a certain Jimmy McGovern, bothered me. He was what is euphemistically called a gentleman of the road and looked and smelt as if he hadn't seen a square meal or enjoyed a bath for months. Like others I have often wondered what brings an individual to such a low ebb. Many make regular appearances in court and have sad tales to tell: loss of employment, the break-up of a marriage, illness, both physical and mental and of course the downward descent into alcohol or drug abuse. Jimmy lurched drunkenly towards us.

'I had a bairn once, a wee laddie. That's a great wee one you've got there.' His speech was so slurred that he was hard to understand and I was confident that he would have no recollection of our meeting.

A good hour later Jamie and I arrived at our destination: an abandoned yard just off the tow-path. Fortunately for both of us he had slept most of the way. The yard was surrounded by a wall which had seen better days making entry to it easily accessible. Once, long ago, there had been a factory there but the owners had become bankrupt and once the factory closed vandals soon made it unsafe and it had been demolished. All that remained of its previous incarnation was a dilapidated outbuilding used occasionally by the down and outs. I had been to visit the site on two previous occasions and had purchased and fitted a strong lock and key to prevent any such person from entering the shed during its planned, but brief, occupation. Litter was strewn throughout the yard including many empty plastic cider bottles, the cheap route to oblivion employed by the vagrants.

The gods were smiling on me that day. No one else was there as the usual occupants must have sought shelter elsewhere. Even they would need some respite from the incessant rain. It was to go down on record as one of the wettest Mays since statistics began, quite an achievement in the North of England.

I undid the lock and took the unsuspecting Jamie inside. He gazed at me with a blank expression, the sort employed, even at such a tender age, by those who expect little from life. There was no fear. He had probably been left, on numerous occasions, with a variety of what Sharon would euphemistically call baby-sitters.

It all proved too easy and so enjoyable. I smothered him with the towel I had brought, as he sat in the push-chair that must have been used by many children before him. It took such a short time. Strange that it takes nine months for a baby to grow in the womb, the Biblical three score and ten years for those fortunate enough to live that long but less than a minute to end it, to snuff out an existence like dampened fingers extinguishing a candle flame. He was a poor little mite and hardly struggled. Perhaps he agreed with me that he was better off out of it; a life with few redeeming features.

The first part of the plan had been accomplished. Jamie was dead. You may be wondering why that was only the beginning. I have to tell you that there was so much more to this murder than the suffocation, pleasurable as that had been. It was the next part that would prove tricky, the climax that would require the most audacious and careful completion.

Days at work can become so repetitive that it is hard to distinguish one from the other. I enjoy that and am not inclined to suffer from boredom. However the day after Jamie's demise a thunderbolt descended, shattering my post annihilation state of euphoria. Perhaps the Olympian gods were teasing me or proving that they were, after all, in total command.

'Philip says that Simon Bell (the name that I really didn't want to hear in the middle of this murder) has gone off on his hols again, left the day after his "freebie", must be getting the taste for it. Honestly, we know who paid for the last one, you and me, the good old British tax payer. It's a joke.' My ears pricked up at the mention of his name. Marie was almost as perturbed by the dreadful Mr Bell as I was and gave regular updates about his latest activities to anyone who happened to be in the staff room. A few weeks ago she had told us, in no uncertain terms and using some choice language, about the trip at the end of April intended to "develop self-belief". Several of our regular clients had been invited on this almost unbelievably ridiculous initiative. Her husband, Philip, had the pleasure of planning a "time away to reflect on their behaviour" for each of them. Unbelievable! What a crazy waste of time and money. As if he was going to sit considering the error of his ways then come back having had a "Road to Damascus" moment.

'Ye gods and little fishes,' I exploded - a phrase often used by Pops, 'what a load of arrant nonsense. When is this holiday due to end?'

'Yes, an interesting question,' Marie laughed, 'you want to know so you can arrange his next court appearance.'

'Something like that,' I replied, savouring her proximity to the fate I had arranged for him.

'No doubt we'll "see him" again when he returns though Philip is really hopeful this time and says that he's seen a real change in him. We're off to visit Simon tonight. Phil's in court this afternoon then we're setting off straight after work, dashing down the motorway, not the best way to spend Friday evening but Phil is determined to see him. At least we're then having the rest of the weekend away in a posh hotel, can't wait for that, we've not been away for ages.'

Marie was staring at me as she finished saying this and asked if I was alright. No, I was anything but. I stood, fear freezing me to the core and setting me adrift like an iceberg sheared off the security of its glacier. All my careful planning was being destroyed;

totally annihilated and as my legs gave way I slumped onto my chair. My mind, normally so reliable, had stopped working, all logical thought disappearing.

Marie brought me a cup of tea (milk and two sugars, not my normal tipple but ideal in the circumstances) and suggested that I go home as I wasn't looking too well. I agreed and said that I would after I had finished some paperwork. Then it came to me the only solution possible – the visit to Simon must be stopped – permanently.

B.B.C. Ceefax

Tragic Accident on the M6

Several cars were involved in an accident on the south bound carriage way of the M6 motorway just south of Preston on Friday evening. Three people were air-lifted to Preston General but are said to be in a stable condition. Unfortunately the occupants of a silver Mondeo were declared dead at the scene. They have been named as Philip and Marie Coulston, aged forty two and thirty nine respectively, who lived in Barton. Eye witnesses reported that their car seemed to be driving well in excess of the speed limit and appeared to make no attempt to slow down as it approached traffic that was moving slowly as three lanes became two due to the long-term road works.

Oh dear, amazing what a lack of brake fluid can do. Such a lovely couple. So sad. So necessary.

After three murders in an inexcusably short time, a first for me, I wondered whether I should treat myself and go away. A holiday might be just what I needed. Switzerland was tempting but maybe somewhere nearer home would be easier. Scotland, Wales or the Lake District all appealed. Somewhere I could get away from people and enjoy my own company for a short time. I could go for a few days and be back in time to complete the next and the most glorious part of the whole plan. A weekend should suffice and allow me the space to enjoy what had been completed and know that the best was yet to come. I left early on the Saturday morning but kept to the A roads and went nowhere near the M6.

Jamie's body remained in the shed for five days, not as long as I had scheduled but on the fifth night I went to survey my handiwork.

'We've had a call, Bob, incident in Manor Road. We'll have to come back here in the morning.' I almost fainted. The police had got this far in their search for Jamie. On opening the door just a fraction I could see there were two of them with the most intelligent looking dog, an enormous German Shepherd, I had ever seen and one that would surely have found the body given another few minutes. He was a truly magnificent animal, but for my purposes would have proved far too efficient.

This was not in the plan. Was I getting careless? Should I not have realised that the police would search an ever expanding area in their hunt for the missing child? I had got away with it, but only just. Was I being careful enough? Most convictions happen due to a mistake on the part of the criminal and I realised I was not immune to such errors. I comforted myself with the knowledge that none of my previous murders had led to appearances in court.

Despite having worn gloves I used the towel to remove any traces of fingerprints from the push-chair and deposited it in the canal. Fortunately the water was deep at that point and with the aid of a couple of bricks on the seat it disappeared from view.

Plan B was now a necessity; move the body to its final resting place sooner than intended. Jamie had been small in life but had become even smaller in death. He was so easy to wrap in the towel I had stored in the shed and once packaged up, like a miniature pass the parcel, he fitted into the hold-all also left waiting for its raison d'etre.

Sitting, waiting for the small hours, when fewer people would be around, was an extremely unnerving experience. If my meticulous planning could be undone so easily what else might go awry? I realised that acting with undue haste might lead to mistakes and that I must be extra careful. As I sat ready to move him I reconsidered the next part. Should I continue with the master-plan or be satisfied with having committed yet more murders? No, no, no. Too much effort had been expended to stop now. The second and most delicious course was about to be served. It would be "sweet" in both meanings of the word. Surely the fact that it was slightly ahead of schedule shouldn't make too much difference?

The walk from the shed to the garage where I needed to leave Jamie's body took far longer than I had anticipated. The lad might have been small but he made the hold-all feel surprisingly heavy.

It is hard not to look suspicious in such circumstances and I was relieved that I passed only a few people en route. None of them gave me a second glance. They probably assumed that I was, like them, on my way to an early shift at work.

On entering the garage I laid the body on the towel and took the camera out. Everything was back on track, the plan was being realised.

Mutilating the body gave me a new and strange frisson of excitement. His private parts were so incredibly tiny and no longer of any consequence. As I cut the various bits off (amazingly easy with a sharp kitchen knife) I allowed myself a few moments to gloat that no more Richardsons would emerge from his pathetic loins. I wondered whether I was due an MBE for services to the local community. His rotten branch of the repulsive family tree was lopped off - the end of that lineage. I placed the small penis and undeveloped balls by his side. His body was all there but just not quite as it had been.

Taking the photos was such fun that I wondered why I had never done it before. I amused myself imagining I was a member of the paparazzi who love to have their work published and admired by millions. I knew, in all probability, that my works of art would not be published in the press, but I gained inordinate satisfaction from the knowledge that they would be seen and studied by the many officials investigating the murder. Life should contain new experiences and this one was delightful. I was pleased with the photos which were automatically printed at the touch of a button. They were hardly the sort of image normally reproduced at Boots the Chemist!

No sounds were heard from outside though more early morning workers would soon be about. There was so little time to admire my handiwork and I was forced to leave in more of a hurry than was ideal. I hoped I had not made any further mistakes.

Every one of my previous corpses had been found. This one would, I knew, be no different. It was just a matter of time, time I could spend awaiting its discovery and the ensuing press extravaganza. They would, as the saying goes "have a field day" and so it proved. Certainly, at least for the moment, it is my most reported and high profile killing. Prior to the trial I revelled in the daily items which took up pages of each and every daily and weekend paper. Months later the frenzy continues, with hourly updates on the television and daily reports in all the papers. I have started a scrap book with a variety of cuttings which are so entertaining. Nothing in the news lasts for very long but whilst it is of such interest I rejoice in the publicity. Will I ever better this for notoriety? The case is even headline news abroad. I have become world famous.

Chapter 25

Daily Gazette

Prosecution Sums Up in the Jamie Richardson Murder Trial

Yesterday the jury in the trial for the brutal murder of innocent toddler, Jamie Richardson, sat and listened to a lengthy and highly detailed final review of the evidence that has been presented by the prosecution in this most nauseating case. They were told that the forensic findings leave absolutely no doubt that the defendant was the person who committed this horrendous and callous crime which is the murder of the truly innocent.

They were reminded of the "damming" fact that his fingerprints were found on the camera that had taken the pornographic photos of the mutilations perpetrated on the boy post mortem and which were then left by Jamie's tiny body. Disgusting images of a similar nature were also on the defendant's computer at home showing his interest in such depravity. His claim that he no longer had any interest in such wickedness does not therefore "hold water". Further DNA evidence on the towels in which Jamie's body was wrapped links the defendant to this dastardly crime.

The jury were asked to disregard the so called eye witnesses who say they saw the defendant on holiday, in Wales, at the time of the murder. He called Mr and Mrs Jones "unreliable and inconsistent" and said that they could not be considered to have added anything to the case. The jury were advised that they should assume that the defendant has no alibis for the period in question and his assertion that he was holidaying alone was pure fabrication.

Sir Anthony admitted that the defendant made an extremely confident and erudite witness with an answer to every question. Many juries might be swayed by such a bravura performance but he felt confident that the present jury would not be influenced by the man's eloquence and self-belief. It was, he added, all a sham: a charade intended to mislead, a trick to delude his audi-ence. His frequent protestations regarding his innocence were the posturing of a self-delusional man.

His complete loss of self-control on at least two memorable occasions during the trial display a deeply disturbed personality – one more than capable of committing the crime for which he is charged.

After speaking for over three hours this most impressive of lawyers concluded by saying there was absolutely no doubt in his mind that the defendant was guilty and that he had every confidence that the jury would return this verdict.

Conversation between Mr John Alderton, a member of the jury, and his wife, Jenny

'I know we shouldn't talk about the events in court but we listened to the closing remarks for the prosecution today.'

'Did it help? I know you've said there has been so much evidence to take in that it is hard to sort it out.'

'Sir Anthony was very persuasive and went over all the prosecution evidence again which put it in some sort of sequence. He is so convincing and made it seem as though there was absolutely no doubt that the defendant is guilty but we haven't heard the defence lawyer yet and that might make me feel differently. At the moment I just don't know what to think.'

'Well it only has to be beyond reasonable doubt, doesn't it?'

'Yes, but if we get it wrong we take away an innocent man's liberty. One thing that really troubles me is that he doesn't look or act like a man would who could commit such a crime. And he sounds so believable when he says he is innocent.'

'Probably a lot of murderers look and sound just like you or me and he is fighting for his liberty.'

'Maybe; but the trouble is I'm not sure I'm thinking straight. I feel as though I'm beginning to eat, breathe and sleep this case. We were advised to look at the "Jury Handbook" again. I think I'll read the relevant bit.'

'Good idea, dinner in half an hour.'

Jury Handbook

Closing Arguments or Summations

After all the evidence has been formally presented, the lawyers for each side will make their closing arguments for the benefit of the jury. This will form a summation of their case and they will give the reasons why they think their side should be believed. If the *testimony of witnesses is conflicting, the lawyers will tell the jury why the witnesses on their side have more credibility than those on the other side.*

What the lawyers say in closing arguments or summations is not evidence and should not be considered as such, it is an overview of the proceedings. Jurors should, however, pay careful attention to the arguments because lawyers have experience and training in analysing and interpreting evidence, and these arguments are permitted so that you may have the benefit of that experience and training. Nevertheless, it will be for the jury to determine, through judgment and common sense, which of the arguments is the most reasonable analysis of the facts.

'Listen to this, Jenny, "it will be for the jury to determine, through judgement and common sense", not sure I have either or those at the moment.'

Sir Anthony was a practised and highly effective orator. He had me mesmerised and I was as au fait with the evidence as it is possible to be. Indeed, if asked, I could have written his closing speech. As he spoke, at great length, hardly seeming to pause for breath or further thought, I watched the people chosen to decide the outcome of the case with great interest. They hung on his every word, sometimes nodding in agreement or looking at each other with knowing smiles. Had that been the last thing they heard the verdict would undoubtedly have been a resounding "guilty".

Very little of the trial remains: the defence summation, the judge's advice and then the wait as the jury reach their verdict. Hopefully it will give me more than enough time to consider the discovery of my handiwork.

Jamie's body was found less than twenty four hours after I placed it in the garage. Was it the same police dog which discovered it? Once again I realised how incredibly close I had come to failing in my audacious planning. Serendipity plays such a huge part in life but this time she had been on my side.

I was at work when Jenny burst into my room. 'They've found him, little Jamie, they've found him.' She was in such a state I asked her to sit down and tell me what she had heard.

'It's just been on the news. Mum texted me, so I rang her to find out what they've said.'

'Is he alright?' I asked trying to sound as though I was interested in the answer.

'No he's dead the poor little soul. His poor mother, I don't know how I'd cope if anyone hurt either of my two. I think I'd want to kill them.' Jenny has always been on the emotional side and in an attempt to calm her down I pretended to take some interest in the discovery.

'Have the police given any more details?' I asked, hoping that the answer would be no and we could both return to our duties. Her sentimentality was beginning to irritate me though I was careful not to display this, knowing that it would make me appear to be unfeeling, but it was an indisputable fact that she had more than enough feelings for both of us.

'All that the police have said is that his body was discovered this morning, not far from where he was taken. Oh! The poor child, he's dead, I was so hoping that he would be found safe and well.' I had heard enough and leading her to the door assured her that there would be a lot more information on the evening news.

However the news that evening was disappointing. The authorities were being extremely cautious and were not disclosing any details. Despite the paucity of information it appeared to be everyone's main topic of conversation. I was famous, or I suppose to the vast majority of humanity, infamous. Terrible things were written about me: the "monster", "depraved lunatic", "fiend from hell" and "the amoral being" who could have committed such a crime. There were times when I was tempted to add morsels to the mix but common sense prevailed and I maintained a distant interest in the many, of necessity, ignorant exchanges on the topic. Articles filled the papers on the decline in standards of behaviour. Schools which lacked discipline, dysfunctional families and youth unemployment were all blamed. The vital question seemed to be "How could society produce someone who could kill a child for pleasure"? The idea of enjoying such an act was present in the media from the earliest days and I suspected that the papers had some insider knowledge of the pornographic aspect of the murder.

The trial did not begin for several months. Being of a patient nature this did not bother me. I knew the evidence had to be collected: visual aids, video footage, still photographs, catalogued pieces of evidence (the exhibits), audio recordings and several transcripts of conversations that had taken place. As it was a murder trial I also thought it highly likely that the jury would, at some stage, visit the scene of the crime to gain more of an understanding into the nature of the killing and that this would need to be organised for them. Expert witnesses would be needed for the forensic evidence. They would be called upon by the prosecution in order to give informative and easily digestible (and most unsavoury) testimony to the jury. All necessary. All time-consuming. Tomorrow it's the turn of the defence to draw all their evidence together. Now that should prove interesting.

Chapter 26

Diary Entry of Mrs Samantha Turner, member of the jury

Confusion, oh confusion! Having listened to Sir Anthony summing up for the prosecution at the end of last week I was ready to convict, thought the man who has sat, for the most part so impassively in the dock all these weeks was as guilty as hell and wanted to send him there. The couple of outbursts about his innocence did not impress most of us though one or two of the others thought he sounded as though he genuinely believed what he was saying which gave rise to doubts. Adam, who has sat next to me throughout the trial, wondered if he had blocked the incident from his mind and had convinced himself that he had played no part in the event. Others thought he was so convincing that he must be innocent.

All weekend I was convinced that the decision we would reach would be guilty. Now I am not sure. Mrs Deidre Hannigan, his lawyer, was so erudite that she cast doubt on everything we had heard. She seems such a clever lady with a wonderful turn of phrase entreating us "not to be like Euridice, returning with Orpheus from Hades afraid to turn round when crossing the River Styx in case all was lost. We must be bold and turn again and reconsider the evidence!!" Was the defendant in fact in Wales as he claimed? Mr and Mrs Jones were confident eye witnesses, far more so than had been acknowledged by the prosecution. They gave strong accounts that he was the customer they served in Wales during the time he was allegedly committing the murder in Preston.

She attacked the forensic evidence and the alleged allegation that his fingerprints were found at the scene of the crime. She said that although there are advantages to digital fingerprint technology, we must be aware of its limitations. There was always room for either human or computer error. She pointed out something I hadn't realised before (maybe it had been said and I missed it, rather worrying!) that there were other fingerprints on the camera and none of them had been followed up.

Mrs Hannigan made one point that set us all thinking (not that we have discussed it yet but I could tell from the reaction of the others) that both the police and the expert witness said that this was the type of murder usually committed by someone who has murdered before, even by a serial killer, and the defendant has no record of that sort. I know it's a pathetic thing to say but he doesn't look like a killer, though I know I shouldn't be swayed by his good looks.

I hope the judge will provide some enlightenment tomorrow. I need it as I suspect do the others. None of us are looking forward to the time when we have to make a decision.

Mrs Hannigan is my kind of lawyer. Organised to a fault: all evidence re-visited, a confident manner and impressively erudite. She did however keep the summing up fairly brief and never used a dozen words when one would do. Although of slim build and mature years she is a pugilist

confronting any evidence she can dismantle with the ferocity of a heavy weight boxer and is certainly prepared to
go all ten rounds. I had thought Sir Anthony was good but
she was ahead on points. I could see that the jury were
impressed and not one of them took their eyes off her,
during her most scholarly compilation of the evidence for
the defence. She definitely made an impact with her assertion that the eyewitness accounts had validity. Ending by
stating that the expert testimony on the fingerprints found
on the camera was to some degree dubious was her piece
de resistance and may well have swung at least some of the
jurors towards an acquittal. Time will tell. I wonder how
the judge will perform his penultimate duty?

Jury Handbook

*After the closing arguments are made, the
judge will give instructions to the jury on which
questions it is there to decide and what specific
law applies to that particular case. The kind and
amount of proof required will be pointed out.
The juror should listen to these instructions very
carefully. If, in considering the case in the jury
room, there is any disagreement as to what the
judge instructed, or its meaning, the jury may
seek further instructions. Such a request should be
made in writing and given to the court bailiff
who will pass the request on to the judge.*

Are you ready for this? Sir Cecil Montgomery, Q.C. is
about to sum up with his esteemed guidance to the jury.

'Ladies and gentlemen of the jury, this has been a long
and most upsetting case. The death of a young child is

always a cause for sorrow. Jamie Richardson had his entire life before him and was denied it in a callous and heartless manner. You have heard evidence both for and against the man in the dock who stands accused of that most heinous of crimes: the murder of a child. Much of the evidence has seemed compelling and yet much has sounded contradictory. You must, as a group, spend time deciding which evidence you find credible and which you think may not be true. Your task is to decide which witnesses were reliable and therefore to be believed and which were not. This may prove a good starting point in your deliberations.

Many of you have been taking notes each day and I would ask you to study and discuss these carefully. Should you so wish I will be available to aid you with any misunderstandings though I can in no way influence your thinking: the final decision is yours to make. Reaching a verdict is your civic task as a jury and at the end of this particular trial it is not an easy one.

The law states that any defendant is innocent until proven guilty. To find him guilty you must be certain beyond reasonable doubt. Please keep that phrase in your minds at all times. Your first task will be to appoint a foreperson, in other words a spokesperson for the group. This man or woman must see that the discussion is carried out in a sensible and orderly fashion, that the issues submitted for a decision are fully and fairly addressed, and that every juror has a chance to say what he or she thinks about every aspect of the case. The spokesperson will organise any voting and will also sign any written verdicts required and any written requests made of the judge. Whilst the spokesperson should express his or her opinions during the deliberations, these opinions are entitled to no more or no less weight than those of the other jurors.

Differences of opinion often arise between jurors during deliberations. Should this happen, each juror should say what he or she thinks and give explanations referring to their notes as necessary. By reasoning the matter out, it should be possible for you, the jurors, to agree. Each one of you should be prepared to change your mind if you decide your first opinion was not correct, but you should not change your decision unless your reason and judgment is truly changed. You should vote according to your own honest judging of the evidence. Only the evidence that has been presented in court can be discussed and used to determine your verdict. Should you not be able to agree, within a reasonable time, it may be necessary for a new trial to be organised.

You will not find this an easy case to discuss but take as much time as you need and make sure you allow yourselves breaks to recharge your batteries. I must remind you that everything that is said in the retiring room must stay within those four walls. For the duration of your deliberations you will be sleeping at the Preston Marriott Hotel which I trust you will find comfortable. I wish you well in the task that faces you.'

Judge Montgomery cuts an impressive figure. I had always viewed the regalia of red gown and cream wig as archaic but he suits them and this long established dress code adds a certain sobriety to the proceedings. He reminds me of my headmaster at Preston Grammar who wore his academic gown to every assembly and his Cambridge hood on special occasions such as Speech Day. How I loathed that man with an adolescent vehemence

I now realise was inappropriate. Dr Ellerton was the man for the job, completely in charge and willing to put his proverbial boot up the backside of any pupil who failed to toe the line or think of underachieving.

Time is passing so slowly. The jury has been out for a week. The waiting is beginning to worry me. They are obviously unable to reach a verdict. I have no idea whether a prolonged discussion is more or less likely to lead to a guilty verdict. How I wish I could be the Invisible Man sitting listening to them. I know there is no set procedure which jurors have to follow to reach their decision and I wonder how they have gone about their deliberations. Who was chosen as the spokesperson? Is he or she able to ensure that the discussion is all relevant? Are they keeping to the facts? Is each juror being given a chance to participate? Is the one elected able to respect each and every opinion? Are they being fair? These and other questions are like a sandstorm raging in my head.

Once the jury has decided on a verdict, I know that the spokesperson will send a note with the court officer advising the judge they are ready, a decision has been reached. At this point there will be no disclosure, no result will be declared. The waiting for this moment is agony. The hounds of hell have me surrounded - indeed I would gladly face Cerberus at the gates of Hades rather than endure another day of this fearful waiting. The not knowing is excruciating. Until the verdict is announced my writing has become laboured, the words not flowing as they did. My one and only logical thought is "Was this my perfect murder"?

Finally there is movement. We have been summoned back to the court room. In extremis it is strange to experience parts of one's body becoming alien, uncontrollable entities: legs that move like a marionettes, hands that shake and sweat, butterflies that invade one's stomach. One's mind, normally so reliable, turns to an imbecilic mush.

The jury looks exhausted as well they might after almost ten days of deliberation. The spokesperson is indeed the lady I had, from the start, dubbed "Mrs Organised", alias Mrs Cooper. She stands looking assured and utterly professional and has obviously taken her duties seriously.

'Have you reached a verdict on which you all agree?' Judge Montgomery's voice echoes in the expectant quiet of the packed courtroom. My heart is playing a drum roll that must surely be heard by others.

'We have Your Honour,' from her tone of voice it is impossible to tell how they have decided. Then comes the moment that all involved have been anticipating for days, 'We find the defendant guilty.'

Pandemonium greets this statement and the Richardson tribe yell and shriek, calling for the death penalty to be reinstated. Members of the press rush out to send their copy as soon as humanly possible. I sit mesmerized. It is over. The verdict is in. I compose myself and drink in the atmosphere like an alcoholic imbibing his first liquor of the day. Never again will I experience this scene. I must commit it to memory to re-live whenever I please.

The judge looks more impressive than ever and at least six inches taller as he sits bolt upright and turns to face the dock. He utters the words I have dreamt about.

'Simon Bell you have been found guilty of this most abhorrent of murders by a jury of your peers. There is no doubt in my mind that the members of the jury have reached the correct decision.'

Epilogue

The shriek that emanated from Simon's mouth will live with me for ever; no words, just an animal howl of pure agony. He followed this with proclamations of his innocence; assertions shrieked with a truth that I alone acknowledged as true.

'I never killed anybody, you've bloody well got the wrong bloke, it wasn't me, it just wasn't me.'(I have omitted some of the more colourful language that accompanied these declarations).

The judge, perhaps used to such outbursts, allowed Simon a few moments to compose himself and then continued, 'Sentencing is a contentious issue and as you have heard there are those present today who would welcome the return of hanging. This is no longer an option. Judges are unfortunately not allowed to act in accordance with their own unfettered viewpoint but must remain within the law as it stands.

It is my duty to inform you that, in cases such as this, judges are obliged to follow Section 21 of the Sentencing Guidelines which sets out the four basic starting points for adults aged twenty one and over who are found guilty of committing a murder. They are: a whole life order; 30 years; 25 years and 15 years.

The murder you committed involved the abduction of an innocent child and in addition there was a sexually sadistic motivation behind the deed. These factors determine that it is the first and most serious sentence that must be passed: a whole life order. This means that you will spend the rest of your life in prison having committed a murder so grave that the early release provisions in Section 28 of the Crime Sentences Act will not apply.

You will therefore have many years to consider your abominable act and the public will be able to rest more easily in their beds knowing that you will never be free to repeat your callous exploits. Take him down.'

Handcuffs were applied and Simon was led down to the cells, still proclaiming his innocence, his shrieks and protestations falling on deaf ears. I could only imagine what torment he was experiencing. Was his punishment too extreme? Had I overdone it? I comforted myself with the knowledge that he was at least still alive - the original plan for him didn't make that provision! It was good to think that, at this moment, he might have preferred that outcome.

I had done it! All my careful planning had worked. I had framed the odious Simon Bell. I felt nothing for him as he descended, the howls seeming strangely to rise in volume. I felt confident that should he appeal the same verdict would be reached.

It was the camera, left so carelessly in the exhibits box, with his fingerprints all over it that gave me the initial idea. To start with I assumed that I would merely take pictures of my future victims to gloat over in private and I knew that such an activity would be most rewarding. Then it came to me, the Eureka moment: commit a murder, take some photos, leave the photos beside the body and the camera with Simon's fingerprints nearby and goodbye Mr Bell: guilty as charged.

Having heard that he had a liking for pornography gave me the idea of spicing the photos with some sexual extras. As his defence advocate said there may indeed have been other fingerprints on the camera but not mine as I was careful to wear gloves, but in any case no one had any reason to think that I had anything at all to do with such an abhorrent murder. The mix-up over ruck-sacks following our arrests at Deepdale was also serendipitous, for I knew that more of the man's DNA would be on his towels. I found out, from conversations with the garage owner (the garrulous sort who love a good gossip) about the termination of Simon's use of a garage so it was the ideal place to leave the body.

The one event that might have scuppered my plans was the fact that Simon was on his "holidays", self-funded this time, when I committed the murder. At that point I almost gave up and thought I should be satisfied with another murder, but I was so close to removing him from society that it seemed better to continue with the plan. Fortunately the couple who could have provided him with an alibi (such a shame about Marie and Philip but they would have provided him with a caste–iron one) for the period under investigation proved to be weak witnesses. No one apart from Mr Bell and I knew that he had indeed been many miles from Preston when Jamie met his end. All so incredibly easy.

What a satisfactory state of affairs. I feel inordinately pleased with myself. A murder and a miscreant locked up, probably for life. As you know I spent a great deal of time thinking about ending Simon's miserable existence but this state of affairs is far superior as he will have many years incarcerated in jail, no doubt proclaiming his innocence ad infinitum. What a shame that no one will believe him.

As you know I am not the greatest fan of holidays so I had a lot of leave due. Vague comments to my colleagues led them to believe that I would be "somewhere in the middle of England, possibly touring around" and thus enjoying the weeks I had accrued. In fact I booked into a large, impersonal hotel near the middle of Manchester, the kind where one can remain totally unnoticed. The many days I have spent at the back of the Crown Court have been amongst the most enjoyable of my life.

Tomorrow I will buy every newspaper and make a scrap book of the various, entertaining reports. As the years go by I will love reading them for I will remain free: to go to work, to run, to go on holiday and to watch my beloved Preston North End................ unlike Simon Bell who will do none of these.

Was this perfect? Have I achieved my life-long aim? Not quite. The mix up over the extra holiday was too annoying and caused me some sleepless nights. So far I have carried out many, most satisfactory and utterly enjoyable, murders but the perfect one is still in the future. It will come. I will reach my objective. Should we meet please do not give me any reason to think that you should be my next victim and be the one I deem my "Perfect Murder".

Lightning Source UK Ltd.
Milton Keynes UK
UKOW03f2000110314

227952UK00001B/2/P